PLAGUE

BRET JORDAN

Purple Sword Publications
www.PurpleSword.com

This is a work of fiction. Names, places, characters, and events are fictitious in every regard. Any similarities to actual events and persons, living or dead, is purely coincidental. Any trademarks, service marks, product names, or named features are assumed to be the property of their respective owners, and are used only for reference. There is no implied endorsement if any of these terms are used.

PLAGUE
Copyright © 2011 BRET JORDAN
ISBN: 978-1-61292-018-4
ISBN 10: 1612920187
Cover Art Designed by Anastasia Rabiyah
Photographs Copyright © 3Dclipartsde (Ralf Kraft) and Satori12, Dreamstime.com

Interior Art Copyright © by the following artists:
Brandon Layng, www.brandonlayng.wordpress.com
Art on Page 51 and 276
Alex McVey, www.alexmcvey.com
Art on Page 2 and 164
Tom Moran, www.grimamericana.com
Art on Page 230
Bret Jordan, www.bretjordan.com
Art on Pages 21, 81, 117, and 312.

Edited by Brieanna Robertson and Traci Markou
Published by Purple Sword Publications, LLC
Tucson, Arizona, USA
www.PurpleSword.com

Prologue

In the last days of the reign of men, when their sins have over-come them and they are choked on their own pride, she will come to put them back in their place and remind them that gods do reign on high in both Heaven and Hell.

~Prophecy of Dokkien the Wise

Shadows danced against the stone like convulsing phantoms. Dozens of candles sat sporadically around the room, haphazardly placed without rhyme or reason. They created havens of light in a sea of midnight. Cracked columns with the girth of ancient oaks climbed from the floor and disappeared into the ceiling. The pillars appeared to breathe in the stuttering candlelight, each carved with runes from a world long dead and gone. The age-faded etchings shone like whispers in the stone. The runes spelled out an evil that could twist minds, dark words that existed nowhere else, words long hidden from the eyes of mortal men.

Silence dominated the room. Stagnant air laden with sulfur and the smell of death choked out any aroma the candles might have had. A chill radiated from the columns, bringing winter to a room that had never experienced the cycle of seasons. Condensation clung to the walls, and moisture dripped from the ceiling.

A rune-scratched pedestal sat in the center of the room. Though only waist high, the pedestal dominated the area as though the chamber had been constructed around it. A smooth obsidian bowl lay on its flat surface. The bowl's silhouette stood out from the shadows, a void cut from the

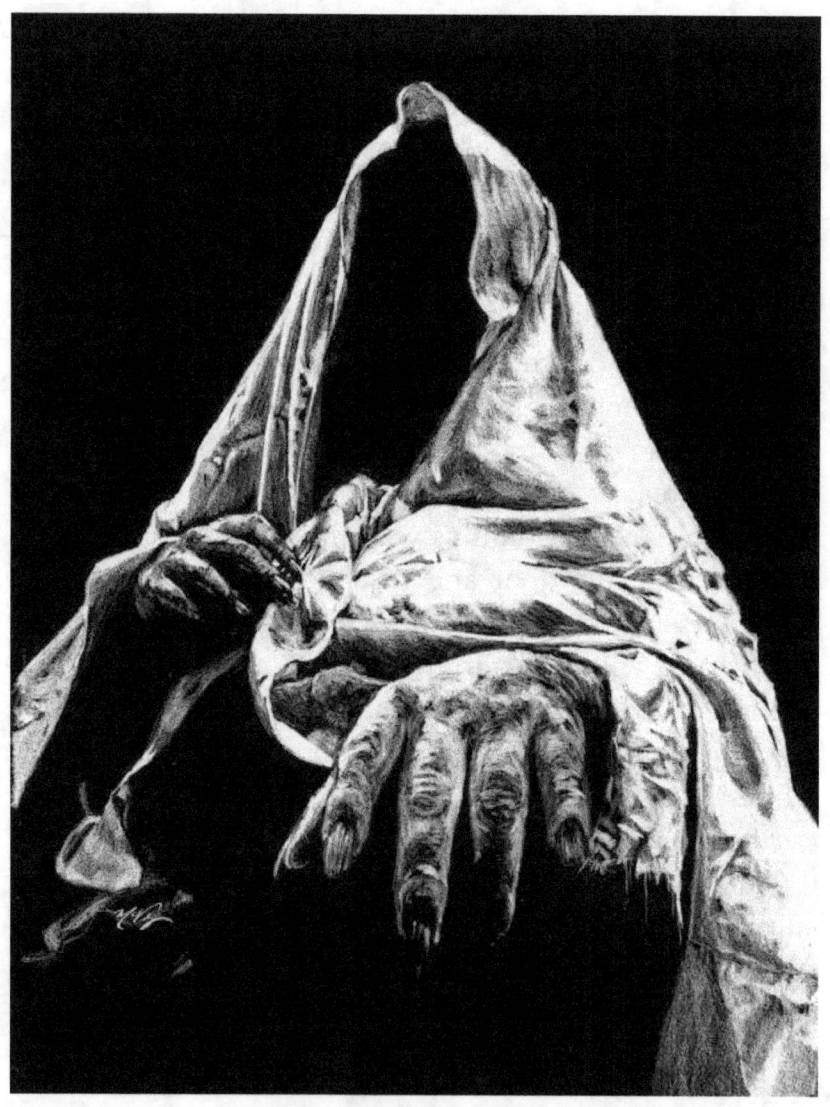

fabric of reality. It absorbed the candles' flickering glow, drawing in the light, but reflecting nothing.

A hulking figure leaned over the bowl. Its tattered gray robes shifted as it lifted its arms and gazed into the dish.

Black, syrup-thick liquid filled the bowl. Ripples moved across the surface. Claws slid from the being's threadbare sleeves. Knotted fingers waved over the bowl, and fresh ripples formed. They pushed toward the rim, meeting the old ones that lapped in from the edge.

The figure watched, observing the spaces between ripples. It noted the way the energy shifted as the rings collided. It studied the new patterns formed by the collisions. The figure twitched its fingers, creating new ripples, new observations. It soon saw more than circular patterns on the black surface. The movement hypnotized the cloaked figure. Within moments, the oily syrup shone with a faint light, the light of dusk minutes before the sun sets. A touch of air wafted up from the bowl. The air smelled of salt, fish, and sea. Dozens of voices spoke within the bowl, a chattering of sound blended into a static of noise.

Yellow fangs gleamed within the being's dark cowl, like a wolf baring its teeth at a sheep that would soon be eaten.

The figure's eyes darted over the scene, black pits in blood-veined orbs. Its nostrils flared as it inhaled the sea's odor. Words hissed from between cracked lips. Fingers danced over the water, forming new patterns, sending new commands.

It drew breath through clenched teeth, tasting air from a distant land. Its left hand clenched into a fist. Particles of the ancient shroud drifted to the ground like dust.

"I'm sorry, my lord. We are just passing through," the thing within the robes whispered. The odor of rotting meat and festering wounds overwhelmed the smell of the sea.

Static from distant voices underscored the silence. A gruff voice burst from the bowl, bellowing in anger. The figure stood transfixed, its eyes narrowed to thin slits, lips twisted, displaying yellowed fangs. The bellowing ended. The quiet lasted only seconds before the figure hissed again, the whisper made by hundreds of spider legs clicking on a hard surface. "My lord, we merely wish to pass through your..."

"Maaassster..." An emaciated man stepped from the shadows. He stared at his master with dull, doltish eyes. His jaw hung loose. Drool formed a puddle that dripped from the edge of his mouth. The man beckoned with his arms and spoke in a slow, raspy manner, oblivious of his master's fury. "Eeeat. Food. Reeeeady."

The cloaked figure raised a claw, palm-out, fingers extended—a knobby-jointed spider in the candlelight. The servant crumpled to the floor in a boneless heap, the idiot expression still on his face.

Rage consumed the figure. Its hand pulled in tight to its chest, claws clenched into fists. With a roar, the figure slung the claw forward, fingers extended. The servant's limp body lifted from the floor and sailed across the room. It disappeared into the darkness with the force of a cannon-ball. The silent room filled with the thunder of flesh striking stone, the shattering of bones.

The robed figure turned to the bowl, waving its arms over the rippling liquid. It whispered, "... pass through your city."

A wolf-like snarl reverberated inside the dark cowl, a low growl that dripped with hatred. The figure burst into movement. Bony claws swept over the liquid, from one side of the bowl to the other. The room remained silent except for the rustle of cloth, the shifting of feet, and the roar of hatred.

With a sudden, furious hiss, the figure reeled from the bowl. Its fangs gleamed ivory as cold eyes blazed into the dark corner of the chamber. The figure stood for several moments, teeth clenched together, before marching into the darkness. As the creature passed the ruined body of its servant, the man's one good eye opened and gazed without comprehension. His mouth moved, but no sound passed his lips. His hand waved as if to tell his master that dinner was ready. The figure extended its claws and closed them into a tight fist. The servant's skull exploded in a spray of coagulated blood, bone, and quivering gray chunks.

The figure released a satisfied growl then stormed across the chamber, up a flight of stone steps, and disappeared into a corridor.

PART I
INFECTION

Chapter 1

The hearts and souls of men are linked to the waters of life. Should the waters run dry, whence then will men drink? Shall they die of thirst, praying to their gods for something that is no more?
~Secret Holy Scriptures of the Waken Book

Drummen's brow throbbed with each heartbeat, an annoying drum that only he could hear. His stomach grumbled. Bitter acid percolated to the back of his throat. He grew nauseous with every turn of his head. In case that wasn't bad enough, his bowels were loose, liquefied, and ready to give way. He didn't bother to run into the can again; it wasn't worth it. He would just sit at his desk until he got the situation under control. He took a deep breath and thought of anything but vomiting.

Drummen wore the dreary uniform of captain of the dock area watch. If he really wanted to split hairs, he would add night division. *Gods blasted night division!* Drummen was a single man. His nights should be spent drinking and having a good time. Instead, he spent them arresting folks who drank and had a good time. It just didn't seem right.

He blamed his situation on his disregard of authority, hot temper, and love of strong drink. He could also begrudgingly add gambling, fighting, or his frequent visits to the hired ladies. His superiors complained that his personality conflicted with the friendly authority image they strove to maintain. *Stupid pansies, boy lovers all. What do they know about respect?*

Drummen's old man had taught him respect. With knuckles and foot, he had taught his son respect. As a city guard, he should have the authority to do the same as long as it didn't get out of hand...again. Nope, if he beat one more drunk half to death, he would be cleaning chicken coops for Uncle Olsten. He hated chickens. For what it was worth, he hated Uncle Olsten, too.

He groaned and belched as another burst of acid burned his throat. His bowels gurgled.

Gotta keep my hands to myself. Drummen knew what he was. He could hold one of two positions in life. Either he would be the law, or the law could lock him up. He was too uncivilized to be anything in between, a man with the mentality of an earlier era, somewhere between mountain barbarian and apish Neanderthal. Nobody in this pansy-loving city knew how to be a real man. They all ran crying to the law when someone hit them or took their stuff. A bunch of stinking babies that didn't understand that *might made right.*

Hell, the law would have arrested him twelve hours ago if he hadn't been captain of the city watch. *Stupid night division.* The other guards knew the hell they would pay if they tried to arrest him. Not only would he beat them to a bloody pulp, but he would also make sure that they got assigned to the dock area. Nobody wanted to work the docks. It reeked of fish, and most of the folks in that district had less regard for the law than Drummen. Sometimes he wished one of them would try to bust him. Yeah, that would make for an interesting evening. Not one of those sissy boys could take him down. Hell, there weren't three of them together that could do it.

Drummen smiled to himself as he remembered the previous night. It had been one hell of an evening and a good portion of the morning too. The fun started as a bit of roughhousing with some blokes at old Jon Geary's Tavern. A seedy dockside pub where they watered down the ale, but for the price of a couple of pints, he could get himself a woman. The whores weren't the prettiest of Renier's women, but with a bit of ale and a dark alley, it didn't make any difference. Women were pretty much all the same for his intents and purposes, something to be used and discarded afterward. The roughhousing had progressed to singing, then wenching, then...well, after that he wasn't sure, but he must have had a great time to feel so bad.

He reached across the wooden desk and wrapped his hairy fist around a mug of water. It tasted tepid, metallic. The stale whiskey coated the back of his tongue and made his thirst almost unquenchable. Normally, he would dump the water out and get something fresher, but he didn't have the energy to bother with it. He emptied the mug in three gulps. Liquid trickled down his wiry bearded chin and dripped onto his leather armor. The warm water only made him want more. He needed something better.

He looked around the station, making sure no one lingered about. Empty chairs lined the far wall; a couple of desks sat across from him. Stiles had some sort of stupid hat sitting atop his desk. The ignorant kid was always trying to keep up with the latest fashions. Maybe it helped him get girls, but Drummen wouldn't be caught dead in the stupid, wide-billed thing. There wasn't another soul in the station. The place was empty except for some loser the day watch had arrested, and he restlessly slept in a cot perched against a cell wall.

Drummen reached into the shoulder section of his armor where a small pouch had been discretely added. He extracted a clay flask and uncorked the worn neck. Taking one last look around the station, he tipped the bottle to his lips and took a deep, throat-burning gulp. The amber liquid met his molten stomach acids. He belched to relieve the biting fumes that rose up his throat. The whiskey burned, but he knew his system would settle out as soon as his stomach had absorbed the alcohol. *Give the gut what it's beggin' for* was Drummen's motto when it came to hang over recovery.

The station doors burst open with a crash. Drummen winced as the sound blasted into the center of his forehead with throbbing force. Stiles rushed through and came to a sudden stop. In a *you aren't going to believe this* tone, the grinning guard said, "Hey Drummen...Sir."

Drummen coughed and spun away, stashing his flask back into his armor. Glancing over his shoulder he growled, "Doesn't anybody stinkin' knock anymore!" Running a large hand over his red beard, Drummen asked, "What's so bloody important that you gotta come bargin' in here like that?" He spun around in his chair to face the guard.

Drummen glared at Stiles. The fumes of old whiskey leaked from his pores and tainted his breath. The guard's smile disappeared. Drummen liked making smiles vanish.

The boy was a good soldier, but Drummen was in no mood to listen to the guard's cheerful yapping.

"Lepers, sir. Stinkin' rotters are inside the city gates."

Oh yeah, what a way to start his shift. Drummen sighed, "Who let them in?"

"Don't know, sir." Stiles grinned. "Wasn't me."

Drummen would have to work on cowing this one down. The guy just couldn't take a hint. Maybe he would start by making fun of his stupid hat. Yeah, telling him that the hat made him look like a man-loving pansy would knock a bit of that spunk from his step. Maybe even make him quit wearing the ridiculous thing altogether.

Shaking his head, Drummen replied, "Let's get this crap over with. Show me where the bastards are so we can give them an escort out of town."

With a smile and eager stride, the guard strolled out the door.

Drummen grabbed his helmet and raised it to his head. A burst of acid boiled up his throat, and he lowered the helmet. He belched and decided he didn't want to stick his head in that bucket. With another rumbling belch, he tucked the helmet under his arm and followed Stiles through the door.

∞ ∞ ∞ ∞

Renier was the largest city on the Gulf Coast, a gateway of trade and commerce. The city itself didn't manufacture a product, raise livestock, or farm the land. Instead, Renier acted as a trading hub for other communities that had products and services to sell; a portal to a larger world.

The ever-growing city meant streets full of shoppers, vendors, hawkers, and gawkers. People continuously bustled back and forth, running errands, delivering products and shopping. The vendors stood out from the rest of the crowd, easily spotted in their colorful clothing and outlandish booths. Each seller hoped to be a beacon to the needy shoppers. The buyers dressed more conservatively in grays and earth tones. To Drummen, they looked like fools who catered to the foolish.

Most people enjoyed the growth and commerce, but it only made Drummen's job harder.

As he and Stiles navigated through the city's fading light, the crowds of people parted before them. Most were fortunate enough to get out of the way, but many didn't. Drummen shoved those to the side, sometimes all the way to the ground. Most knew of the burly man's temper so no one protested the occasional push. Normally, pushing folks around made him feel good, in control. With bowels that threatened to give way at any moment and a stomach that felt like he had been drinking lantern oil, he just wanted to throw the lepers from the city and get back to the station.

Stiles glanced back as he squeezed between two burly merchants. "Just a little farther, sir. They came through the port gate. They must have a boat moored out there somewhere."

Drummen shook his head as he watched Stiles politely squeeze between the two overweight merchants. He replied with a grunt and bulled his way between the merchants and through the crowded street.

They only traveled a few blocks before Stiles pointed at five figures in filthy gray robes shuffling against the flow of the crowd, toward the open market. "There they are, sir!"

Oh great. With dusk approaching, the merchants and shoppers moved in one direction, away from the booths and vendors. As Stiles and Drummen headed toward the shops, the crowd grew thicker and fewer people managed to move out of their way. Drummen felt like a salmon battling his way upstream as he shoved his way along. His head throbbed harder with every step, and his bowels threatened to let loose with every push until he was close enough to bellow, "You. You there in the robes. I order you to stop!" The five gray shapes continued on.

Drummen growled and pushed his way past Stiles.

He sped up, slinging people aside, barreling through the crowd with Stiles in close pursuit. When he caught up to the little group, he stood in their path, lifted his broad hand and roared, "Stop!"

The five lepers stopped and stared at him with pale pus-clouded eyes. Their stench drifted forward and filled Drummen's nostrils with the smell of rotten meat. Filth stained bandages covered every inch of them that wasn't cloaked in robes. Bands of cloth wrapped their heads from necks to eyes. A slimy yellow stain tarnished the bandages around the nose-shaped hump.

He had heard stories about lepers, how they lived while their flesh festered and rotted away a little more every day. The odor confirmed the stories. The scent wasn't strong, but it carried a foul odor, decay, and the smell of death.

"Didn't you rotters hear me?" Drummen roared.

Five pairs of clouded eyes stared straight ahead without fear or concern. The lepers stood a foot shorter than the burly captain. Instead of looking into his eyes, their heads remained straight ahead, and they stared at the top of his breastplate.

Their lack of fear sent a spear of hatred through him. His fists shook with anger and he callously raged, "Have your blasted ears rotted off too? Maybe your tongues?" They didn't respond, didn't seem to care that Drummen had begun to scream, or notice the heated flush that warmed his cheeks.

People stared and whispered as they passed, but continued to go about their business. He glared at the crowd before turning back to the five lepers.

Drummen opened his mouth to start a cursing that would make a sailor cringe when the lead rotter croaked, "I'm sorry, my lord. We are just passing through." The bandages hardly moved as the leper spoke in a coarse, passionless hiss, his tone devoid of emotion and as blank as his eyes. Stiles stepped back, behind Drummen. The leper's gaze never left the base of Drummen's neck, and the raspy voice sent a chill down his spine.

The chill made Drummen raise his voice, partly to make himself feel in control again, and partly to let Stiles and the crowd know that he wasn't afraid of a few pathetic rotters. "You're sorry? No, you just think you're sorry." He pointed back at the port gate where the lepers had come from. "You're going to march your rotting, stinking carcass back through that gate, get on whatever ungodly transport that brought you here, and paddle your stinkin' asses back to whatever gods-awful hell you came from!"

The lepers stared straight ahead. He didn't see the terror in their eyes that such a ranting should have created.

Their lack of fear fed his anger and tempted to drive him to violence. He began to take a step forward, but stopped as their full stench wafted to him. His stomach gurgled in protest. The hoarse voice of the leader whispered again, "My Lord, we merely wish to pass through your..."

The monotone words stopped in mid sentence. His eyes still locked on Drummen's neck with an eerie detachment. The bandage squirmed between the leper's parted lips as its tongue worked through the gauze, making a wet circle around the rotter's mouth, reminding Drummen of an eel he had once netted.

He had seen enough. He reached for the speaker, but stopped himself.

Weren't lepers contagious?

He pulled his hand back and roared, "I said to turn around and get the hell out of here! You won't get another warning!"

The lepers ignored the command. They stared through Drummen with blank eyes. Again, a chill of fear shivered down his back and stuck between his shoulders. Fear was an alien emotion for him. Its presence enraged him and drove him to action.

He grabbed the speaker by the shoulder, fingers sinking deep into the fabric. Soft meat rolled on top of bone beneath the material. A wet stain formed below his hand, and an unholy stench filled the air. "What the..."

".....pass through your city," finished the rotter. Drummen's viselike grip went unnoticed. The leper spoke as though nothing had taken place since he'd started his sentence almost a minute ago.

Drummen yanked his hand away, holding it in the air so the yellow slime coating his palm and fingers wouldn't touch his clothing or armor. His anger died like a campfire in a hard rain. His eyes widened. Fear replaced the rage, a fear of the unknown, a fear of something he couldn't comprehend.

Before he could pull himself together, the lepers burst into action. They bolted in different directions, their gray robes bobbing through the crowded streets.

Drummen watched them go, too overwhelmed by the encounter to grasp what had happened. He held his ichor-stained hand to his face. A shiny yellow film glossed his palm and fingers. The smell of wet pus filled his nostrils and made the stale whiskey rise in his already upset stomach.

Stiles' voice quivered as he asked, "Sir, should we go after them?"

Drummen continued to stare at the foul stain on his palm, collecting his thoughts and getting himself under control. Finally, he wiped his hand on his britches. In an unsteady voice, he replied, "Yeah, Stiles. Blow the whistle and get us some assistance. We can't chase five rotters down by ourselves." Without further comment, he ran after the lead leper, the shrill sound of Stiles' whistle shrieking in the background.

Before he got out of calling distance, Stiles yelled, "Sir, why did they run? Why did they run away like that?"

Without slowing or turning, Drummen mumbled back, "I don't know, but I'm damned sure going to find out."

∞ ∞ ∞ ∞

He glared into the wave of bodies, looking for the leper. The celebration of the Day of the Gods was fast approaching. It filled the busy streets with even more people than usual as vendors and buyers traveled home after a day of selling and buying religious items.

A block over, the crowd parted like streamwater flowing past an old stump as the leper raced through the street, making him easy to spot. Within seconds, the other lepers had disappeared around corners and behind buildings, but he kept his eyes on the leader. That rotter was his.

The man moved faster than Drummen had given him credit for, weaving in and out of the crowded road, but he wasn't fast enough to get away. Drummen closed the distance between them, shoving his way through the crowd until he ran just behind the leper. He gave the rotter a push. The man overbalanced and fell forward. He didn't raise his arms to break the fall and crashed face first into the rough cobblestone street, skidding several feet before stopping. Around him, people gasped at the leper and glared at Drummen. Their outrage didn't bother him. He received the same glares every day for his acts of brutality. *If they have a complaint, they can get in the back of the line behind everyone else who hates me.*

Drummen towered over the rotter. Air billowed in and out of his lungs, and sweat dripped from his nose. Blood pulsed in his ears with the impact of a drum. The acid in his stomach pushed against the back of his throat with more force than ever. He had reached the end of his already limited patience. "Get up."

On his hands and knees, the leper turned to Drummen and let out a hissing gasp of foul air.

The rotter's fall had shredded the bandages on his face, allowing Drummen to see the horror lying behind the mask. Two mucus clogged holes gaped where a nose had once rested. A bubble of snot burst as the leper let out another fetid hiss. Part of the bandages had fallen away from his mouth, displaying crooked, rot-pitted teeth and gums peppered with black fungus and decay. The lips were a thick, jagged line, chewed off at the base of the blackened teeth, giving the rotter a ghoulish grimace.

The crowd's gasps and glares over his abuse of the leper became screams as they turned away from the disturbing sight.

Drummen stepped back with a gasp as the leper stood on wobbly legs and extended his gauze wrapped hand. He walked toward Drummen, arms stretched out before him. Fingers grasped open and closed as if expecting a hug. Drummen stood frozen in place by loathing and disgust. His eyes rolled down, tracking the man as the leper grasped his leather chest plate with bony fingers. The gauze had torn at the end of his middle digit, allowing Drummen to see pus oozing from the crescent shape indention where a fingernail should have been. The rotter's mouth rose to Drummen's neck. The smell of decay wafted from the leper's mouth and filled his nostrils.

The vile odor pulled him from his sudden paralysis. The fear melted like ice in the flame of his rage. He pushed the rotter back and drew his sword. The leper stumbled, but didn't flinch. With suicidal determination, the man resumed his advance toward Drummen.

Without a second thought, he shoved the sword through the rotter's stomach, meeting little resistance as the blade passed through the disease-infested body. The leper didn't miss a step, pushing himself along the gore-coated steel. Thick, black ichor marbled with yellowed pus oozed from the wound and flowed down the blade. The air filled with the stench of a vulture-covered battlefield. Enraged and disgusted, Drummen screamed and jerked the sword sideways. The pull of the weapon made the rotter stumble to the right as the blade ripped through organs and muscle, erupting from the man's waist. Putrid gore and gray intestines burst from the rotter's side.

The few gawkers that remained rushed from the scene, but some paused long enough to vomit their dinner onto the cobbled street. Drummen hardly noticed.

The gaping wound didn't bother the leper; with a desperate limp, he stumbled toward Drummen, arms outstretched.

His heart pounded and threatened to burst through his chest as he swung the sword, severing the leper's hands at mid forearm. Little of the black and yellow substance dripped from the ragged stumps, but tiny white maggots fell to the cobblestone road, squirming on the hard surface.

Sanity slipped away from Drummen. His mind couldn't make sense of what he saw. It simply wasn't possible. The leper shouldn't still be coming for him. A voice within him screamed, *Get the hell out of here.* He took a step back.

The rotter took two steps forward. Two putrid stumps faced Drummen.

Drummen howled with desperation and did the only thing his confused mind could think of, letting instinct take over where logic couldn't. He swung the sword. Steel connected with the man's neck. The head tumbled away, landing with a hollow thump a short distance from the body. The corpse swayed for a second before collapsing to the ground.

Gasping for breath, Drummen gazed at the lifeless mound. His dazed stare moved from the body to his ichor-covered sword. A bead of black, thinned with yellow, dripped from the tip of the blade. He slung it away. The weapon clattered as it struck the road. Bending over with his hands on his knees, he retched. Bile and a thick stream of water dribbled down to mix with the dirty street.

No more gawkers stood about to see Drummen empty his stomach. Only the sound of their presence several streets over gave any indication that he wasn't alone. Out of the corner of his eye, he saw movement. Not wanting to look, but unable to turn aside, he shifted his eyes to see. The rotter's decapitated head wobbled back and forth. Drummen gasped. The head continued to warble, the jaw working up and down, until it rolled itself onto its cheek, facing Drummen. The mouth continued to bite, gnawing at what it could no longer reach. The sound of teeth clacking together echoed like horse hooves.

"Oh…Oh gods no!" Drummen cried.

The decapitated head and clacking teeth forced his consciousness to seek sanctuary deep in the recesses of his mind. Seconds later, fear and the desire to survive brought his thoughts back, but the fight or flight instinct of a wild beast had taken over. Rational thought had been left behind. With a maniacal howl, he ran to the severed head and stomped on it with the heel of his boot, cursing and screaming. A satisfying crack resounded with the first stomp. He slammed his foot down, and the crack became louder, wet. He continued to stomp, and stomp, and stomp until the night watch arrived to pull him off. It took a half dozen men and as many tries before they could pull him away. *Pansies.*

∞ ∞ ∞ ∞

One leper didn't run far before scurrying into an alleyway. The Voice compelled him to hide in the narrow shadows and wait for further instructions.

He hungered, but he couldn't feed. The Voice wouldn't release him to feed. He could sense food everywhere. It walked in the streets all around him, ignorant of his desires. Oh, how he wanted it, tender flesh, warm blood and pulpy organs. He craved the elastic texture of the flesh as it parted between his clenched teeth. He needed to taste that coppery tang on the remains of his decaying tongue. He desired to feel warm skin stretch to its limits then rip as he bit down. It filled his cold chest with a quiver and made his mouth water with excitement. He wanted these things more than anything, but he wasn't free yet.

Voices tormented him as more meat strolled by his hiding spot. His tongue pushed against the bandages with a will of its own, hoping to get a taste of the flesh he craved. The bandages parted. His gray and black-splotched tongue protruded past the gauze, swiping back and forth. It acted without any instruction from him, a creature following his suppressed will.

A dozen tormenting minutes passed before the Voice spoke. The time had come to continue his mission. He crept from the alleyway and slunk through a maze of streets. His gaze pointed to the ground, his head hidden deep within the hood of his robes. He stayed on the side streets and walked within the lengthening shadows; the Voice instructed his every move. The Voice gave him no choice in the matter. Choices had been given up long ago. He didn't miss them. He didn't remember them. The Voice and his hunger defined his world. Sometimes, the Voice left him and only his hunger remained to guide his actions.

Within minutes, he arrived at his destination. "Wait!" The Voice commanded. He stayed in the shadows, just another dark form in a pattern of silhouettes. More meat moved nearby. He could see them, could sense their presence. Two women stood with buckets next to a well. The sound of their laughter drew him like a leech to blood. His tongue frantically darted out through the gauze, a snake tasting the air for prey.

He stumbled forward, overcome with hunger. "Wait!" He stopped; the hunger almost overrode the Voice. The desire for flesh buffeted him in painful waves, but he stopped. He could taste it. He could feel it. The smell of skin and meat drifted through the air tantalizing him, calling him forward. His jaws worked up and down. His mouth chewed what remained of his lips, biting on his decayed and rotting tongue. Black blood filled his mouth and soaked the bandages. It spilled over the ragged slit where his tongue protruded through the gauze. He didn't notice. He didn't feel it. His own blood didn't help, an hors d'oeuvre held before a starving man. The chewing was neither a conscious nor unconscious reaction to his hunger; it simply happened.

If he could have let out a gasp of frustration, he would have, but his lungs had given up on the same day that he gave up having a choice about matters. They only worked for The Voice now.

The women collected their buckets and walked away, their chatter fading into the darkness. They became like wisps of smoke in his mind, diminishing in proportion with their chatter until he forgot about them all together.

"Now!"

As commanded, he walked to the well, pulling a narrow, black dagger from his robes. He placed his boil-riddled hand over the lip of the well. Without hesitation, he brought the edge of the dagger down on the last two fingers, pinching them between the blade and the hard stone of the well. He pushed down on the knife. He didn't stop when tendons separated or when black blood puddled under his hand and ran down the side of the well. He didn't quit until bones snapped and his fingers separated from his hand to tumble down the narrow shaft. They hardly made a splash as they fell into the water far below.

"Good. Good. Now, on to the next one."

Chapter 2

Soulless, he stands before you.
His whispered words appear true.
You think he is the danger you fear,
but the true danger isn't that near.
~A Parable

his is the leper that the night watch captured this morning," Captain Patrell, commander of the day watch, announced, cocking his head in the prisoner's direction, his voice hoarse with exhaustion.

The dungeon stank of hay, feces, and a new aroma, the sickly sweet smell of dead flesh. The odor of death was mild and nothing new for the dungeon, but the stench of rot cut through all other smells like oil on water. Wellan couldn't have described the difference to Patrell, but it clung to him long after it should have dissipated.

Shortly after apprehending the leper, the soldiers began talking amongst themselves of the rotters' will to fight, of how nothing short of dismemberment would stop them. The stories had spread like a wildfire across the ranks.

Wellan would never have guessed that soldiers could gossip like old biddies. The rumors didn't take long to reach the highest ranks and, finally, the duke himself. After hearing the bizarre stories, Duke Renier had sent Wellan to investigate.

The stench took Wellan back half a century to the construction of Rory's dungeon. He remembered how the prisoners had carved corridors and chambers into the side of the mountain. Many of the men spent years in the claustrophobic tunnels, chiseling rock by lamplight. Once they completed the dungeon, it became their new home. The prisoners hadn't been a bad lot; most were simply petty thieves. Tears still threatened when he thought back to that tragedy, the day the roof caved in. Tons of stone had killed dozens of prisoners and mangled more.

The duke's grandfather, Rory Renier, had commissioned the dungeon with the grand idea of saving money by engineering it himself and having the prisoners build it. The old duke thought it ironic that the prisoners would be making their own cage. The real irony came when the duke had to pay reparations to the mothers, wives, and children of the dead and injured prisoners. After the tragedy, Wellan suggested that he hire dwarves who, at that time, lived on the other side of the Barclave Mountains. The hearty folk were a strange lot, but damned fine stoneworkers. The duke had grudgingly conceded.

The old wizard had visited the dungeon only once since the dwarves left. It happened during the reign of Duke Renier's father. A sadistic murderer had claimed to commit his atrocities in the name of sorcery. Like most of the seaside community, the guards were a superstitious lot and when the prisoner threatened to place a curse on them, they began bowing to his wishes. The duke feared the guards would release the prisoner to avoid a curse, so Wellan had been brought in to question him. After several interviews and tests of magic, Wellan confirmed the man to be a bloodthirsty lunatic with no magic at all.

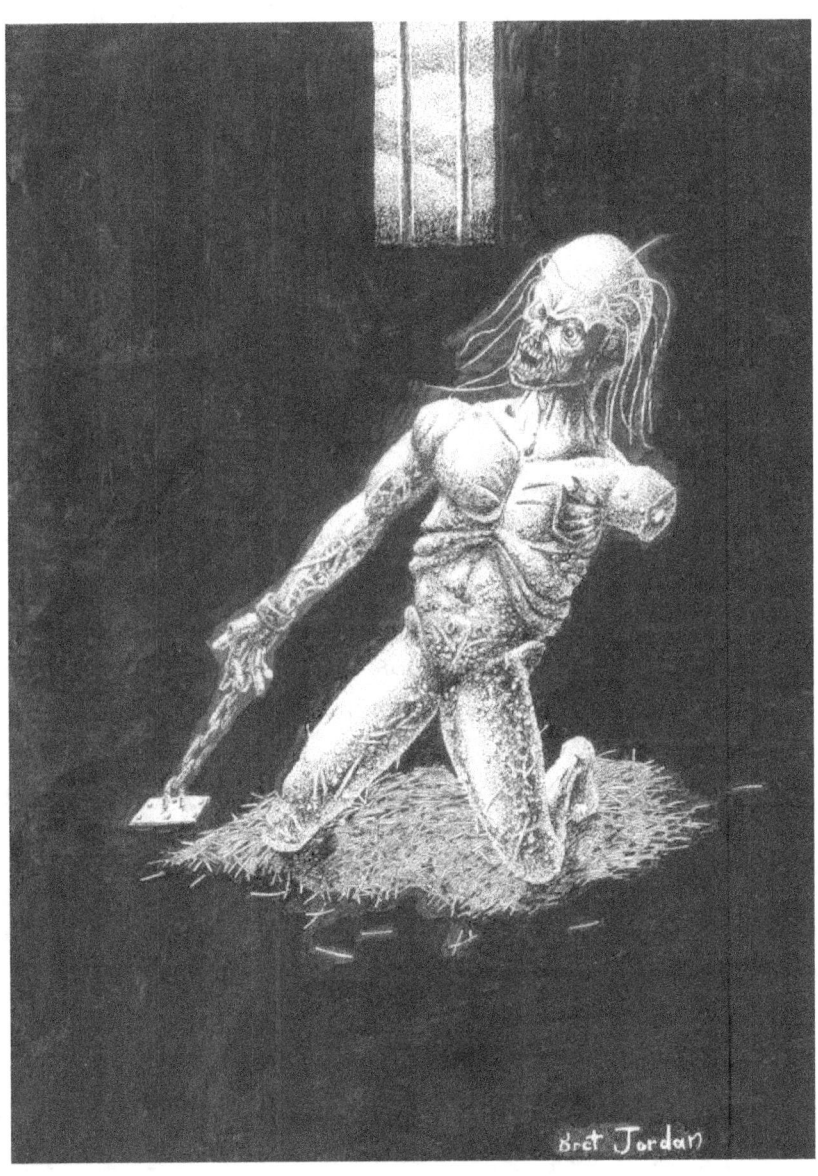

It looked like each generation of Reniers would require his presence in the dungeon. Hopefully, this would be his only visit during the present duke's reign.

Wellan rubbed the bird's nest of hair on his chin and squinted as he observed the leper. Chains rattled as the solitary prisoner rolled and thrashed on the cell floor. Grime and straw stuck to his naked body. Wellan turned to Patrell and said, "I heard there were five of them. What happened to the others?"

Patrell sighed. "The night watch did a hell of a job on them. Their captain, *Drummen*, beat one so badly that you wouldn't recognize him as a person no more."

Patrell spat Drummen's name like a curse. Wellan had heard rumors of the brutish guard. A drunkard, gambler, womanizer, bully…the list went on and on. How he had advanced to captain was anyone's guess. Time served perhaps. Maybe he knew a dirty secret and blackmailed his way into the career. Why Patrell hated the captain so vehemently was a mystery to Wellan. Perhaps Drummen owed him money, maybe the man lost a fight or was bullied by the barbarian. Though curious, the spite Patrell felt for Drummen was none of Wellan's business. He didn't pry.

Patrell scratched the back of his head, a nervous habit. "The other lepers didn't come out much better."

Wellan kept his eyes on the prisoner as he asked, "I see. Yet this one was able to be captured?"

Patrell shuffled his feet and rubbed the nape of his neck. He reminded Wellan of a flea-infested street urchin. Patrell rarely looked him in the eyes. If he did happen to catch the wizard's glance, he quickly looked away.

Though it was rarely his intention, Wellan made people nervous; it came with the title. The common folk knew him as the Duke's Wizard, the man who had served the duke since birth and served his father before that and his father before that. Only the most diligent of historians knew anything about him. Most folks only knew that he had been around for a very long time.

"Yeah, this one was seriously maimed when they found him. His left arm was severed, and most of his toes were gone. Heck, there was a good chunk of his chest missing, too. Never seen nothin' like that." Patrell switched from rubbing the back of his neck to scratching the top of his head. "We don't know how he got that way. Stiles, one o' the young men on the night watch, reported that all o' them looked relatively whole when they entered the city. O'course they was wearin' cloaks, but still... All that aside, the guards used a net, didn't lay a finger on him."

"And he was found just beyond the walls of the duke's palace?"

Patrell swallowed. He glanced at Wellan then turned back to the leper. "Uh...well...he hadn't made it up there yet. He was captured two blocks from the Palace's main gate, near the Tristall estate."

Heavy footsteps and the clinking of gold links and expensive jewelry announced the approach of Piet Lithor, High Priest of Vaspar the Just.

Wellan turned to see an overweight peacock of a man strut toward the cell, nose upturned and condescending frown in place. A purple robe adorned with gold-embroidered holy symbols stitched into the cuffs and shoulders covered his heavy frame. His bald head, tattooed in black and red with those same holy symbols, shone in the torch-

light like glossed pottery. Gold jewelry glittered with diamonds. Sapphires and rubies adorned his fingers and neck.

A thin boy followed the priest into the chamber, a street
urchin clothed in tattered rags. The child sported a fresh
bruise under one eye and sniffled as he carried the back of
Piet Lithor's robes, preventing the cloth from becoming
soiled by the floor.

The piet looked over Wellan's shoulder, at the leper,
and gasped. "Oh my!"

Wellan stepped back from the cell to give the priest a
better look at the prisoner. He acknowledged the piet in a
neutral tone. "Piet." Then, he smiled at the boy and nodded.
"Toby."

The boy never looked up from the cloth bunched in his
hands, but Wellan didn't miss the boy's smile. Neither did
the piet, who glared down at him. The boy's smile vanished.

Patrell's nervous itch grew to all out scratching as he
said, "Evenin', Piet Lithor."

The priest turned to Patrell, ignoring Wellan for the
moment. "Good evening…Patrell, isn't it?"

Patrell grinned. "Yes, Piet Lithor."

Wellan had to give the man credit for his ability to
remember names. The fellow had the uncanny talent to see
a face and hear a name once then mentally bind the two
together. Remembering faces and names was an invaluable
asset for a man climbing the social ladder of success.

Piet Lithor turned to Wellan. His smile vanished, and
his tone became dry and uncordial. He acknowledged
Wellan with a nod, "Wizard."

Wellan stepped around the priest and continued studying the prisoner. Patrell told the piet how the leper had
been captured.

As Patrell finished, Piet Lithor turned to the prisoner with a quizzical look. His thick lips puckered in thought. "I wonder why he isn't dead. Any one of the wounds appears fatal."

Wellan continued watching the leper as he replied. "He's as dead as any of the men you have said rites over as you consecrated them to your god, Lithor."

Anger flashed across Piet Lithor's face. Patrell cringed. No one referenced the high priest without including the honorific, no one but the Duke's Wizard. Piet Lithor hissed, "Well, *wizard*. He looks amazingly lively for a dead man."

Wellan smiled at the priest, knowing his lack of anger would only infuriate him more. "Yes. To the casual observer, he does, doesn't he?"

Piet Lithor's face flushed; his nostrils flared. Wellan ignored him and turned to Patrell. "When Lithor has finished examining the prisoner, have him taken outside and burned. Burn him to..."

Piet Lithor gasped. "Wizard, have you gone mad? We don't burn men here. If they must be executed, then they are hanged...in a respectable manner."

"If you wish to hang him, you are more than welcome to. Just don't touch him. Make sure and burn the body to ash when you realize that hanging doesn't seem to bother him a great deal." Dismissing the priest, Wellan turned once again to Patrell. "As I was saying, when Lithor is done with the abomination, whether he chooses to examine him, preach to him, or hang him, burn the body to ash. Don't touch it in any way. Use a rope around its trunk. Tying a rope around what's left of his limbs will just pull them off. Most importantly, remember not to touch the thing."

Wellan knew he should be more respectful of Lithor, but after years of tolerating the condescending priest, he had grown tired of coddling the self-righteous fool. Wellan had eons of experience to draw from, experience that told him what sort of creature thrashed behind the bars. He knew the abomination's abilities and danger, but he didn't know the how and why of it yet. With a little research, he should soon know.

Piet Lithor's jowls quivered. He sputtered, "You have no authority here, wizard! I will file a complaint with…"

The priest's whining earned Wellan's disdain. "I am going now to give a report to Duke Renier. If you don't agree with me, then I suggest you do the same."

With that, he walked up the stairs and out of the dungeon.

∞ ∞ ∞ ∞

Drummen sat at a table with his head in his hands. Slashes of moonlight shone through slits in the wall, creating vertical bars of light across the room. He lifted a bottle of whiskey to his lips. The liquor gurgled from the bottle and burned his throat. A roach skittered across the table. Its antennae grazed his hand, probing for food, sex, or whatever a roach might want. He didn't care. His thoughts drifted elsewhere.

Once the night watch had calmed Drummen down, he had sat on the street curb and yanked off his boots. A red paste covered the heel and soaked into the leather. He had thrown them as far as he could. He didn't want any part of that *thing* on him. Drummen wanted to forget that last hour. He regretted showing up for duty and wished he had stayed home drinking. Drowning his mind in alcohol until he forgot about the rotter appealed to him more than any coddling the guards had done. A bottle of spirits wouldn't make the nightmare go away, but it would drown his troubles for a little while. Without saying a word, he had lumbered down the street on bare feet. His men had called to him, asked him to come back, but he had ignored them. He couldn't help them, and they sure as hell could do nothing for him.

Two hours later, Drummen sat staring at the food stains on his dining room table through a half empty bottle of whiskey. To call it a dining room was stretching the truth since it also served as his bedroom and kitchen.

The booze didn't help. The images and sounds still flashed through his mind with unbidden regularity. The leper's face as he pushed himself off the ground. The meat sack's guts as they spilled from his side. The bastard's severed hand flying through the air. The way he kept coming at Drummen. His dead eyes devoid of emotion or pain. The severed head gnawing empty air. That was the worst. He couldn't release that image.

He lifted the bottle to his lips and took a generous swig. Bubbles floated up as the liquor gurgled down his throat. The spirits burned, but not enough to sear away the memories.

Drummen slammed the bottle down. His hand shook. He locked his fingers over his head, elbows out. Anguish contorted his face. A groan escaped his clenched teeth.

The godsdamned thing was dead! DEAD! DEAD! DEAD! It had to be dead! He was sure of it. Yet it had moved. The severed head had rocked itself around until it faced Drummen. Glazed eyes gazed at him with pupils no bigger than a pinhead. Its teeth gnashed together. Click... Click...

Click... Click... Click... Click. *Stop! Stop moving! Stop looking at me! Gods, please STOP!* What he saw wasn't possible. It couldn't have happened, but it had. All of it had!

Drummen's fingers quivered as they ran through sweat soaked hair. He reached for the bottle. He grasped the neck. A chill coursed through his body. He shuddered. The room tilted. He pinched his eyes closed. A tear squeezed out and ran down his cheek. He put a hand to his forehead. The chill dissipated, warmth replaced it, the heat of a freshly turned compost pile, humid and foul. His dizziness became nausea.

"Cheap rotgut," he mumbled. With both hands on the table, he tried to stand. He fell back in the chair instead. It groaned under his weight. The room tilted and warbled. He couldn't get his bearings. *I haven't drunk enough to feel this damned bad. Even if it's cheap rotgut, it still don't account fer this.*

His stomach clenched. He vomited. The liquor in his gut splashed across the table. His sinuses burned with whiskey and stomach acid. He grabbed the edge of the furniture and retched another pint of spirits onto the table. The liquid ran between the boards and over the edge. It pooled onto the floor and into his lap. He let go with one hand, but before he could gather his bearings, he turned and heaved again. His stomach clenched with a will of its own, a beast trying to break away from its chain. Little spewed out of his empty stomach, but what did come was thick. Strings of slime textured with chunks of meat stretched from his lips to the floor. It clung to his beard as he lifted his head.

"What the hell?" He let go of the table and slammed his fist down on its edge. The bottle bounced, tipped over, and crashed to the table. The liquor gurgled out the open neck to mix with the filth already soaking into the table.

"Awe great. That's just bloody gr—" He retched. His stomach knotted, and he gasped for breath. His face burned red; veins pulsed at his temples like earthworms contracting beneath his skin. A groan rumbled in his throat. His stomach clenched tighter and his jaw opened wide, gasping for air that wouldn't come. His stomach unclenched. Copper filled his mouth. Blood hung from his beard and glistened on his lips like red spider-webs.

He gasped for breath like a freshly caught fish and wiped the back of his hand across his mouth. His fingers trembled as he gazed at the red film coating the back of his hand. Spidery legs of fear crawled up his back. Drummen had done his share of vomiting, but he had never puked blood before. He retched again. The blood flowed freely. It painted the front of his armor red and soaked his britches.

He leaped up. The chair crashed to the floor. The room tilted out of control. He couldn't tell up from down as he took a wobbly step forward. The world shifted beneath his feet. Everything warped out of focus and became a collage of moonlit stripes and shapes. He stumbled sideways and reached for the edge of the table. He missed and crashed to the ground. Drummen lay on the floor and twitched. His hand raised and lowered several times then remained still.

∞ ∞ ∞ ∞

"Would you please use the honorific when talking to Piet Lithor? At least do it when you address him directly."

"I am sorry, my friend. I didn't realize that it meant so much to him," Wellan replied. A smile twisted his lips.

His research into the prisoner's condition had taken more time than he anticipated, allowing Lithor to reach Duke Renier before Wellan had a chance to meet with him. It couldn't be helped. Wellan was thorough, as all wizards were, at least all who wanted to excel beyond the level of street magicians.

"Oh, you damned well know what it means to him. You do it just to get under his skin without appearing to do so." The duke winked and grinned at Wellan as he added, "I find it rather amusing, but unfortunately, I have to listen to his whining when you get his feathers ruffled, and that is nothing to laugh at. Sometimes I think he will make my ears bleed. So, if he asks, you have been officially scolded."

Wellan looked at the duke and nodded with a feigned innocence.

The duke met with Wellan in a small room not far from the main audience chamber. He picked it not only for comfort, but because it sat in a remote corner of the castle, away from prying ears.

After pouring another cup of coffee, the duke leaned back in his chair. The leather was thin and faded with wear. He held the cup with both hands, sipped, and propped his boots on a table next to the coffee decanter. He gave Wellan a grin, relaxed and carefree. The duke's charming smile had closed many lucrative business deals for the city of Renier. It was the same grin his father had, and his father before him, as the city expanded through three generations of Reniers. A knowing smile threatened to sneak past Wellan's lips. *He reminds me of his father.* He had seen three sets of grins through three generations. Little did the duke know, the smile was a trademark of his hereditary line. It made him loved by the rich and poor alike throughout the city and even most of the neighboring kingdoms.

The duke took another sip of coffee, dropped both boots to the floor, and leaned forward. His smile vanished. In a tone full of conspiracy, he asked, "So...what did you find out about that unfortunate man? Piet Lithor said you want him burned to ash, though he hasn't committed any real crime, other than running from the city guard. Piet Lithor also said the man is quite lively, considering his condition."

"Yes, considering its condition, it is amazingly lively." Wellan's brow furrowed. He set his cup down and leaned forward on the couch. "I didn't order it burned because of any crime it had committed; I ordered it burned because it is a dangerous abomination."

"Hanging is an effective means of getting rid of most abominations."

"Not this one, my duke. The thing isn't a leper. It is an undead. A walking corpse." The sofa creaked as Wellan leaned back and rubbed his bearded chin. "It can't be killed by any means other than total destruction of the body."

Any hint of a smile disappeared from the duke's face. "Undead?"

"Yes, my lord."

"Childhood horror stories come to life. That's unbelievable, but it fits the rumors. I have heard the guards had trouble with them. I thought it odd, considering their sickness. Do you have any idea what they were doing inside my city? Do you have any idea why one was captured near my home?"

Wellan shook his head. "No, my lord. That's the main reason I'm so late getting back here with a report. I wanted to look through my archives and find out a few things about the undead before I reported to you."

"What did you learn?"

"Not a whole lot. Of course, I didn't have a great deal of time to study my documents because I was already late returning here to tell you what I had found. As soon as we're done, I'll return to my archives and see if there's any other information to be gained about these creatures. In the meantime, with your permission, of course, I would like to have the abomination's body burned and the ashes sent to me. They may aid me in learning what its purpose was. I would also like to meet with all the guards who were involved in the capture of the creatures."

"Of course, Wellan. I will make sure you get all the assistance you need." The duke rubbed his chin, gazed into his coffee, and whispered. "Why were they in my city?"

The question wasn't directed at Wellan. He didn't answer.

After several moments, Duke Renier reached out and grasped Wellan's shoulder. "You will inform me as soon as you know more about these undead creatures."

"Yes, my lord." Wellan nodded.

"Keep the truth of these creatures between us for now, my friend. If word of this reaches the public, it will only cause panic."

"A wise course of action, my lord."

Both men stood, the discussion ended. Duke Renier put his hand on Wellan's shoulder. "Keep me informed, my friend."

With a nod Wellan replied, "I will, my lord."

∞ ∞ ∞ ∞

"Get up."

Drummen's eyes flew open. He stared at the leg of his dining table.

"Get up."

He pushed himself off the floor, shaking like a newborn calf. Whiskey, blood, and bile covered the front of his armor. It clung to his beard and matted his hair. He didn't notice.

"Go."

He walked to the front door. His stride was no longer confident, shoulders drooped, head bowed. Limbs dangled at his sides. A crescent mouth moist with drool replaced his angry demeanor. Eyes that had once glared at the world now opened wide, a window into the shadow of a soul. He looked ahead, ignoring table and chairs as he shuffled forward. Nothing mattered. Everything became hollow and valueless. They weren't edible. They were meaningless.

A door. Closed. It blended with the rest of the barrier that surrounded him on all sides. He shuffled into it and stopped, clawing at the wood with stiff fingers.

"Lift the handle. Pull the door open."

Drummen's head tilted and rolled as he examined the door from top to bottom. He didn't understand. He only felt hunger, so much hunger.

"Lift the handle. Pull the door open."

His hand moved of its own accord. It found the latch. He jerked and yanked until the door opened. It slammed into his cheek. He didn't notice.

"Go."

He walked outside, into the night breeze. The distant smell of flesh rode the wind. Starvation clawed at his stomach. If there had been anyone around, he would have ignored the Voice and eaten, but the streets were dark and empty. He listened for food, but didn't hear any.

"Do as I say and you will eat. Do as I say and you will feed, but not now."

Drummen didn't care about the Voice, he wanted food, but the Voice couldn't be ignored. The Voice had to be obeyed.

"Good. Now go. I know where to hide you until it's time for you to feed."

Chapter 3

"It will begin as a single seed and grow among you, hidden from your very eyes. There it will nourish itself and flourish as the flowers in the spring until you realize it is among you, a great harvest. The harvest to end all harvests!"

~Secret Holy Scriptures of the Waken Book

"Are you using a new flavor of tea?" Malach asked his wife. A frown twisted his mouth.

She set a plate of scrambled eggs and buttered bread in front of him, wiped her hands on her apron, and answered, "No. It's the same tea I used yesterday. Why, does it taste bad?"

He set his cup down and stabbed a glob of eggs with his fork. "Well...it's just got an odd taste to it is all. A little bitter." He shoveled the food into his mouth and chewed.

Martha walked to the cupboard and lifted a canister. Grape leaves and squiggly vines adorned the front. All her canisters were decorated with leaves of one sort or another; it was the latest style in kitchenware. Martha had even painted the design herself. She had shopped around for pre-painted canisters, but the prices had made her balk. They weren't poor, but that didn't justify throwing their hard earned money away. "No reason to spend coin on things you can do yourself," is what Malach always said. She twisted open the canister and sniffed, drawing in a crisp herbal scent. The tea leaves didn't smell odd. She removed a leaf and stuck it to her nose, giving it a pinch to draw out some of the aroma. She sniffed again. It smelled fresh to her.

Malach frowned and spoke around a mouthful of food. "I didn't mean for you to start all that business. I just said the tea tasted odd is all." He pointed at her plate with his fork. "Now forget about it. Sit down and eat your breakfast. The market is gonna be busy today, and you're gonna need to eat something before we go."

Sighing, she put the canister back, making sure the leaf design faced toward the front. All of her containers lined up to form a chain of leaves across the top shelf of the cupboard. A smile teased the corners of her mouth. Her canisters were as fancy as the store-bought ones.

She sat across from Malach, but didn't touch her food. Instead, she lifted her teacup and took a sip. She pursed her lips. Her eyebrows came together in a frown. "I see what you're talking about. It isn't bad, but it does have a bitter aftertaste, doesn't it?"

Malach nodded without looking up from his food. He pointed at her plate with his fork as he wolfed down a piece of bread. He was always in such a hurry, not listening to a word she said.

"Okay, okay. I'm eating." She stabbed a piece of egg and brought it to her mouth.

They ate in silence. Malach was right about a busy day at the market. Soon the Festival of Gods' Day would occur. The citizens were preparing for a day of feasting, visiting, and giving thanks to whatever gods they prayed to. The holiday was created to keep businesses running despite over a dozen temples to different deities within the city. If it wasn't for Gods' Day creating a common holy time, every religion would have their own holiday throughout the year and things around the city would be sporadic at best.

They needed to be at the bakery before dawn, and they probably wouldn't leave until well after sundown. Through twenty-seven years of marriage, it had been the same, and Martha knew it would continue for the next twenty-seven. She didn't mind. The bakery was her life, and she knew that Malach felt the same way.

Only a few morsels of egg remained and a corner piece of toast when she put her fork down. She watched Malach as he carried his plate and fork to the washing tub.

She pushed her plate away and said, "Maybe it was the water?"

He set his dishes into a suds-filled bowl before turning to her. "What was the water?"

"The tea. Maybe the water's got sulfur or minerals in it this morning."

Without much interest he replied, "Yep, I suppose it could be the water. It very well could be."

Following Malach's example, Martha carried her plate to the washtub, scraped the uneaten food into a separate tub for the neighbor's chickens, and put her own dishes in with Malach's. She frowned at the mess. It would have to wait until they returned at dusk.

Wellan arrived at the training field moments before the morning sun crested the trees. Dew beaded the grass and soaked through his boots. The damp air clung to his robes in a thin film, causing goose bumps to rise on his exposed flesh. The morning walk felt good despite the chill, refreshing after a night spent stooped over a table reading tomes by candlelight.

He hadn't slept. Instead, after leaving Duke Renier, he had worked through the early morning hours studying books, scrolls, and clay fragments. Most of the text belonged to languages no longer used or even remembered by man. Wellan knew them. He could read most as easily as he read the common tongue; he had been looking out for mankind for a long time.

Unfortunately, his efforts had turned up almost nothing about the foul creatures that had invaded Renier.

As Wellan walked toward a line of soldiers, one of them broke away and came to him. The rest remained standing at attention. Though the young, sandy-haired man was the smallest of the group, his confident stride, almost a swagger, indicated he was their commander. He stopped, tucked his helmet under his arm, and saluted Wellan. In a formal military rote, he bellowed, "Sir, I have gathered the men who were involved in capturing the lepers."

Wellan looked around the field. "Where is Captain Patrell?"

"He commands the Day Guard, sir. He has worked two shifts back to back and went home to get rested before reporting for duty again, sir." The man's fist never left the armor that covered his heart. The salute would remain until Wellan ordered him to relax.

Wellan hated formalities. "What is your name, soldier?"

"Stiles, sir! Stiles Milo of the Night Watch."

Wellan put his hand on the young man's shoulder. The stiff leather was cool to his touch. "At ease, Stiles. There is no need to be formal with me." Wellan's gaze traveled to the other men. "Is this all of them?"

Stiles glanced over his shoulder at the guards. His tone relaxed as he replied, "Almost all, sir; my captain hasn't reported back yet. He was pretty upset about the whole thing."

Wellan frowned. "That would be Drummen?"

"Yes, sir. He left after dispatching one of the lepers."

"Yes, I heard about that." Wellan walked to the line of guards. "Were any of these men injured by the lepers?"

"No, sir. Not physically anyway. We're all a little shook up. We ain't seen nothing like that ever. Are all lepers that hard to kill?"

Wellan strolled down the line of men, using his eyes to probe for bites or scratches. "No. Normally a leper would be easy to kill. These were special, and that is why I am going to ask you and your men to do me a favor. A very large favor. One that I don't think you will like."

A smile lit Stiles' face. "We can do whatever needs doing, sir."

Wellan paused, measuring the character of the soldier. Stiles seemed ambitious, eager to please his superiors, almost too eager. *A sycophant perhaps?* He glanced at the soldiers again. He didn't see any animosity directed toward Stiles. They seemed anxious, curious, and tired. No, Stiles wasn't a boot-licker, just a young soldier trying to fill in for his commander. With a weary sigh, he said, "I want you and your men to incarcerate yourselves in the city dungeon…just for a few days."

The smile vanished from Stiles' face, and his eyes widened in surprise. His voice broke as he tried to find the words to reply. "But…but my Lord Wizard…we have done nothing wrong! We…"

The soldiers shifted and frowned at one another. Wellan grasped Stiles' shoulder and shook his head. "No…no, it isn't that you and your men have done anything wrong. Far from it. It is for your own good and the good of the city. I am probably being overly cautious, but the lepers may have been contagious. It will only be for a day or two. If none of you have shown any symptoms by then, you won't show any. You and your men will receive full pay. You can eat and drink as you like, play cards, almost anything you'd like to…"

"Ale?" an older man yelled. The comment put the men at ease as they realized that the next two days might not be as bad as they had thought.

"Women?" questioned another. The men snickered.

The comment brought a smile to Wellan's lips, a badly needed smile. "Yes, yes. You can have all the ale your hearts' desire. I will make sure a keg or two is brought down to you. The women…" Wellan shrugged his shoulders "I'm afraid that is out of my jurisdiction."

The soldiers laughed at Wellan's joke, the laughter of men who are not sure they should be laughing with a superior. He wished he had a spell that would allow him to fit in with the common folk. Feeling more relaxed and assuming the talking was finished, the soldiers fell out of line to joke and talk amongst themselves. Wellan turned and left, walking across the practice field with Stiles in close pursuit.

"The men are easily bribed with promises of pleasure, my Lord Wizard, but this contamination you mention bothers me."

Any humor that may have lingered on Wellan's lips quickly vanished. He hoped he sounded less tense than he felt as he replied, "Don't worry about it, my friend. I honestly believe that if any of you were going to be sick, it would have already begun."

His words appeased Stiles for a moment, then his brow furrowed and his eyes saddened. "Do you think my captain, Drummen, may have caught it?"

This man is definitely not a boot-licker, just a good soldier.

Wellan locked eyes with Stiles and said, "That is the next thing I am going to find out."

∞ ∞ ∞ ∞

True to his word, Wellan walked from the training field, through streets lined with stores and middle class homes. The residents of Renier had begun opening shops and getting ready for another busy morning of Gods' Day shopping. Dark clouds gathered to the south, over the open water of the Hismaer Sea. A breeze blew through streets that smelled of seawater and fish.

As Wellan moved further from the center of Renier's market area, the homes diminished in both size and grandeur. Stone mansions became wood homes. Large, carefully sculptured properties gave way to small, manicured yards. As he got closer to the dock area, the wooden homes withered away to shanties and shacks crammed uncomfortably together. Wellan found it hard to believe that a captain of the guard would live in such poverty.

He hoped to find that Drummen had simply shirked his duties. He didn't know him, but according to rumor, he behaved like a drunkard and a bully. Wellan didn't understand how the beating of a leper could cause such trauma in a man like Drummen. He abused liquor, fought with friends and enemies alike. He chased the women with little success when money wasn't involved, but he had never shirked his duties, not in his entire ten years of service. He hoped for the best, but feared the worst.

He pushed Drummen's fate to the back of his mind and focused on finding the captain's house. The homes were built almost on top of one another with hardly enough room to squeeze between them. Cracked paint, like wrinkled skin, indicated the lack of upkeep. Old boards nailed at odd angles patched many of the homes. Tattered plank chairs adorned several porches. Some held equally worn folk who stared as he passed, while others kept their heads down, glancing occasionally to make sure his business wasn't with them. Wellan's reputation made him an icon throughout the city, leaving him few places he could go and not be recognized. Normally, people didn't gawk so brazenly, but this was not an area that he frequented. Rumors would fly, but it couldn't be helped.

He found Drummen's shack deep within the poverty stricken neighborhoods of the docks. Only the lower denizens of the city, the riffraff, lived in the docks area. Surely a city guard of the lowest level could afford to live in a better part of Renier. The stench of fish was enough to make any sensible person want to live somewhere else. It did fit what Wellan knew of Drummen, though. On this side of town, he would be feared and respected. Of course it was also rumored that the man pissed off every coin that came his way, which would also land him here.

Wellan shook his head as he stared at Drummen's house, if anyone could actually call it a house. The entire wooden structure was smaller than Wellan's bedroom; he could fit two of the houses within his study. The porch planks had split and cracked with age, and the posts, made of sea flotsam, leaned in haphazard directions. The bark still clung in some spots, reminding Wellan of knobby legs covered in scabs. He reconsidered entering the structure after noticing the precarious angle of the roof. It was unfortunate that his path had led him here, but he had survived worse.

The boards groaned as he stepped onto the porch. *I suppose that's how Drummen knows when his neighbors are sneaking up to rob him.* The ungenerous thought crept into his mind. Wellan paused to take another look at the house. *No, maybe murder, but not robbery. I think his neighbors have more than he does.* Wellan heard that Drummen was a mean drunk and loved to gamble, but he never suspected such things could drive a man so low.

He reached to knock on the door and halted as the leather straps that served as hinges creaked in the ocean breeze. A gap indicated the door wasn't closed. Not a good sign, but after seeing the rest of the house, he assumed it might be normal. He held the flimsy door in place and knocked. No one answered. He knocked again. "Drummen?" Still no answer.

The door groaned as he pushed it open. The gap widened and the odor of liquor and vomit assaulted his nostrils.

He stood in the doorway and let his eyes adjust to the dim room.

Filth covered everything. Part of the room served as a kitchen. Plates, fuzzy with mold, sat next to a tub scabbed with dry suds. Past the tub sat a cot with stained sheets wadded into a pile. On the floor lay a pillow that Wellan wouldn't have let the duke's wolfhound's sleep on. A table took up the center of the room. A chair lying on its side gave the scene a menacing aspect, as of something started and left undone.

As Wellan bent to straighten the chair, he saw why the room reeked of liquor. A bottle of spirits lay on its side next to the chair. His hand wavered from the chair to the bottle and stopped. Blood crusted the floor in wide splashes, forming explosive patterns around the container. He pulled his hand back without touching the bottle and backed away from the table. More blood splattered its filthy surface, camouflaged by the dim light and variety of other stains.

Wellan backed out of the room without touching anything.

Drummen had been infected. Now he roamed freely within the city. Wellan's eyebrows gathered together as he considered what that meant for Renier. The man had to be captured soon or the situation would get out of hand, and Wellan didn't want to think about where that would lead.

First, he had to take care of the house.

Wellan stepped off the porch and onto the street. He raised his arms, as if hung on an imaginary cross. His fingers locked into claws and pointed at Drummen's home. Smoke flowed like wisps of steam from his palms. As the smoke thickened, his eyes rolled back and his mouth whispered unintelligible words. Onlookers backed away, not wanting to witness something so unnatural.

Wellan closed his eyes and saw the shack through his mind's eye. The structure became millions of tiny glowing specks too small for the naked eye to see. Millions upon millions of spheres stuck together by a force he didn't completely understand. He didn't understand it, but the magic within him did.

Within seconds, the house began to disintegrate. The wood blackened and charred, yet no flame appeared. More seconds passed and the roof collapsed with a thunderous crack. The walls crumbled to black dust that didn't drift with the breeze, but fell straight to the ground. Wood fractured into particles. The particles broke apart to become smaller, and then again and again until the shack became the most basic of materials. In moments, the home had become a pile of ashlike dust that stood untouched by the wind. It was almost enough.

Wellan brought his hands together in front of him. The black dust piled together as if mimicking the sweeping motion of his arms. His fingers interlocked. The ash compressed even more, forming a tight mound. He dropped his hands below his stomach, and the pile of ashes sank into the ground leaving a clean area of dirt, ready for a new structure.

When it was done, he opened his eyes and marched away. He needed to speak with the duke.

Chapter 4

"Mind your folk all your days,
If you don't there are ways
To make you suffer and make you pay
When the monsters come you cannot slay."
~Children's rhyme

he early morning sunshine shifted to twilight in a matter of minutes as Martha looked out the bakery's front windows. Light flashed, casting the streets and surrounding shops in black and white. Thunder shook the windows moments later. The sky grew darker and the drizzle became a downpour. Her stomach rumbled as she watched the people run, seeking shelter. *This is no time to get sick*, she said to herself. Her hand went to her belly as she placed a loaf of bread, still warm from the oven, into Olga Roth's basket. The store wasn't as busy as it should have been. Aside from Olga, the shop had no customers. *Must be the weather.*

She added two muffins to Olga's basket and thanked the elderly lady as she accepted several small coins.

Olga turned and mumbled; age made her voice quiver almost to the point of being unintelligible. "Bit o'nasty weather out there, it is."

Martha frowned as Olga pulled her hood over hair that reminded Martha of gray wool. With a fierce look at the dark heavens, the elderly woman stepped through the door and out into the wet streets. A bell tinkled as it opened. Martha watched Olga scurry across the road and wondered if she should start delivering bread to the elderly woman on her way home from the bakery. Malach wouldn't like that. He enjoyed walking her home at the end of the day, after they finished cleaning the kneading table, wiping the ovens and washing the dishes. Besides breakfast, the walk home remained one of the few things they still did together.

The bakery had been open for three hours. Usually, the day started out busy, folks purchasing something to eat on their way to work. The sweet breads led the morning sales, but the rolls and loaves of bread became the lead seller as lunch neared. By the afternoon, business would slow down until almost closing time, when mothers sent their children by to pick up a last minute loaf of dinner bread.

Business was slow. Only three other customers, besides Olga, had entered the store. That wouldn't do, not with God's Day around the corner.

Martha's stomach churned with an audible gurgle. It relieved some of the pressure, but a customer had already commented on her health because of the noise. It was terribly embarrassing. Mrs. Lodsworth, her first customer, seemed to suffer from the same malady. The woman had looked up in embarrassment as the gurgle of shifting bowels reverberated through the bakery.

Martha placed the back of her hand to her forehead and frowned. Her skin felt like a fresh buttered loaf, warm to the touch and damp with sweat.

She turned and walked toward the swinging door that led to the back of the building, where bread rose in Malach's ovens. The room spun, and she grabbed the counter to steady herself. The walls tilted and shifted, giving the bakery a surreal twist. Martha squeezed her eyes closed and tightened her grip on the counter. She focused on the wood beneath her palm: stable, smooth and suddenly comforting. She gritted her teeth. Her knuckles whitened as she willed the room to stop spinning. Sweat rolled down her cheeks like tears as everything tilted once more, and then stabilized. She released the counter, opened her eyes, and stood upright. Her legs quivered. Something was wrong. Martha would have to tell Malach she didn't feel well, not well at all. *He won't like it, but I can't work like this.*

"Malach," she called as she pushed through the swinging door. She froze in mid-step.

He leaned over the edge of the kneading table. His eyes bulged, ready to pop from his skull. His muscles knotted and strained his throat. He didn't speak, only hunched over with his mouth open and his face a deep red as a choked groan rumbled from the back of his throat. He stared at her with scared, pleading eyes. Martha forgot about her illness. Her husband couldn't breathe. His terrified gaze drove all other thoughts from her mind.

Malach convulsed as Martha stumbled to him. His head dropped to face the ground. With a roar, he spewed a yellow and brown soup from his mouth and nose. The stench of meat and bile filled the air. The floor became covered in a wet mixture of eggs and soggy toast.

Martha tried to run to him, but she swooned and fell against the kneading table. The room spun, reminding her of childhood when her brother would swing her around by her arms. The dizziness prevented her from getting her bearings. Her stomach heaved without warning and her breakfast splattered on Malach's back. He didn't notice. He had problems of his own.

She wanted to straighten, to help Malach, but her body rebelled. Her stomach clenched again as though an invisible hand squeezed then twisted. Eggs, toast and bile burned up her throat to splash across the floor. Malach echoed her actions nearby.

When the spasm ended, she straightened and grabbed a rag from the counter to help clean Malach. She felt terrible about soiling his clothes; he was so careful about looking clean for the customers. Martha had the towel in her hand when another spasm hit. She had nothing left to vomit. She doubled over as every muscle contracted at once. Her breath wouldn't come. Something deep inside gave way with a rip and Martha's mouth flooded with burning copper.

What splashed onto the floor wasn't eggs and toast. The syrup-thick liquid painted the floor dark red and trickled into the cracks.

She had enough time to look at Malach before another spasm clenched her belly. He returned her look, hand outstretched as if pleading for help, maybe asking forgiveness for all the lost time he should have spent with her. Blood covered his mouth and dripped from his chin, dying his white apron red. His terror-stricken gaze was the last thing she saw as she bent and sprayed blood over his shoes.

The couple collapsed to the floor, hidden from the rest of the world. The rain fell harder, drowning the sound of blood dripping from the kneading table.

∞ ∞ ∞ ∞

The drizzle started while Bolvar sat on the edge of a dock with his feet hanging over the side. He squinted at the dark sky. A mist of sprinkles fell onto his stubble-covered face.

"Awwww shit!" he grumbled, taking another swig of wine. The sorry crap was bitter and sour, well on its way to becoming vinegar. Bolvar didn't care. He drank the swill all day long, so he took whatever he could get. This batch didn't even come from a store. A teenager sold him the mulberry wine from a jug he kept in a warehouse. The boy brewed it himself and sold it cheap. All Bolvar's panhandling could afford was the cheapest of liquors.

The time had come to relocate somewhere drier. As he lifted his legs to leave, someone ran by and yelled, "Better get your ass under something, Bolvar. You stupid drunk!"

Bolvar staggered to his feet with his arm outstretched to the sides for balance. He hollered, "Oh go t'hell, ya sorry bastard!" but the tormentor had passed out of sight, disappearing into the haze of drizzle. He knew he drank too much, but so did a lot of the other guys. He didn't have a home like everyone else, nor a wife and family. He didn't have shit, but that was okay with him. He had freedom. Who the hell needed all that responsibility dragging you down? All he needed in his life was himself!

Hell no! He didn't need any of that other shit. Bolvar was a visionary. He had ideas. Sure, he was hung up at the moment, but that wasn't a damned problem. No, not a damned problem at all.

He stumbled to a group of dilapidated buildings and found a dry spot underneath the eaves moments before the rain began crashing down. "See there, I'm luckier than anyone gives me credit for. I'm one lucky sumbitch." He rewarded himself with another swallow of wine.

Oh yeah, he was lucky all right.

Bolvar sat for a short while, contemplating his good fortune and watching the rain. He listened as the individual drops splashed together. The noise undulated from a calm finger tapping to a watery cacophony. His bare feet became soaked, but he didn't have enough room to pull them in without having to sit on them or stand. He wasn't about to stand and a wet ass was the last thing he needed. *Oh well, my feet could use a good washing anyway.*

Something tickled his chin, crawling through his scraggly beard. He dug into the bird's nest of hair and pulled the culprit out. A small, black bug wiggled its legs and clawed the air as he brought it to eye level. In the distance behind the struggling creature, a gray form walked toward him in the downpour. He crushed the bug between his fingers, flicked it away, then took a swig of wine. He watched through squinted eyes as the fellow moved closer. It was a young man, maybe sixteen or seventeen. Sheets of rain buffeted him. It pasted his hair to his head and soaked his clothing as he splashed through the alley. He staggered toward Bolvar. *Hey, maybe a kindred spirit.* Bolvar smiled to himself.

The young man tottered underneath the eave and placed both hands on the wall. He bent over with his ass hanging in the rain and gulped air.

Being a gracious host, Bolvar held up his bottle of wine and gave the stranger a toothless smile, offering the young man a sip. The fellow looked at Bolvar then at the wine. He shook his head and turned away.

If the kid was too godsdamned good to have a drink with old Bolvar then to the abyss with him! He didn't want to share his wine with the little bastard anyhow.

Retching broke the rhythm of the drumming rain. Bolvar turned to the kid. The boy had doubled over, shaking and puking chunks against the wall.

"Hey, kid. You okay?" Bolvar wasn't that concerned about the boy. He wished the kid had picked another spot to make such an ungodly mess, but it was a polite question to ask. The rain would wash the vomit away in no time, anyway.

The kid turned to Bolvar. The poor bastard looked like a goggle-eye caught out of water, eyes bulging and mouth open wide. The boy tried to say something.

Not wanting to seem rude, Bolvar leaned closer to the young man and yelled over the rain, "What? Whacha tryin' t'say? I can't hear ya!"

The boy gasped for breath one last time before spewing blood and gore all over Bolvar's face and neck.

He fell back as the kid's dead weight fell forward. "Ya godsdamned stupid boy. Ya gots me all filthy." He pushed the limp boy out into the rain. The kid landed with a thud and lay with his eyes staring into the rain.

Bolvar stuck his head from the eaves and gazed into the boy's bloodshot eyes. The rain washed the blood and bile from them both, diluting it into the puddles around them. "Ay, kid? Kid? You okay?"

The boy stared at the heavens as rain splattered his face. He should have been blinking or something. Bolvar looked at the boy's chest. It didn't move. "Awww shit. Awwww shit!"

Bolvar stood over the boy and screamed into the dark as rain soaked through his tattered clothes. A gust of wind rushed through the alleyway. "Somebody help me! Somebody help this kid!"

He screamed and pleaded, but nobody came. When his voice grew too hoarse to be heard over the rain, he backed up under the eave and plopped down with his bottle of wine. He coughed to clear his throat then grabbed the bottle and took several generous swallows while looking at the dead kid.

Maybe he wasn't so lucky after all.

∞ ∞ ∞ ∞

Piet Lithor sat at the head of a banquet table and wondered what chef Roboldi had prepared for lunch. The chef was a soft-spoken man, and the Piet knew very little about him. He wasn't even sure if he worshiped Vaspar the Just. It didn't matter. The man was terrified of Piet Lithor and he liked it that way. Chef Roboldi was the best chef in the city—even better than that famous chef the duke had hired. Riboldi had a recipe for grilled quail that must have been handed down from Imarias, the prophet of Vaspar. It was that good. Piet Lithor would go so far as to say it was divine. Yes. *That is what I want today—the grilled quail.*

He lifted the silver bell and shook it vigorously. Tinkling filled the room. Piet Lithor waited.

That damnable wizard had infuriated him. The fool didn't treat him with the respect he deserved. He was the voice of God, an ordained priest of Vaspar, the Living God of Justice and Righteousness. The only man more powerful than the piet was the duke himself. Even that was debatable as far as Piet Lithor was concerned. It simply wasn't right that a heathen like Wellan should talk to him like that. *I am the high priest, the piet, for Vaspar's sake!*

The black arts had never impressed Piet Lithor. If great Vaspar wished, he could give the priest the power to crush that arrogant wizard. The almighty Vaspar must have some use for the man or he would have already struck him down for his insolence. Vaspar's plans and motives were hard to understand sometimes, but everything that happened occurred because of his god's master plan. Piet Lithor wished he knew what that master plan might entail. *Patience. Have faith. All will be made known in the Lord's time.*

Piet Lithor's stomach growled, scattering his thoughts and reforming them into more immediate concerns. He squeezed his hand between the table and his considerable belly and rubbed it. He looked, but didn't see the chef with his lunch. *What could be taking so long? The man knows I don't like to be kept waiting!* It wasn't like Roboldi to be late with his meals. No one, besides the duke, made him wait.

Piet Lithor thought back to the night before and his confrontation with Wellan. Furious, he had gone straight from the dungeons to Duke Renier. He had complaints about the disrespectful wizard. At first, the duke hadn't seemed happy to see him, but as the piet told the duke how poorly the wizard had treated him, and how he refused to call him by his proper title, the duke had smiled and said, "Yes, Wellan is a handful, isn't he? I will make sure he shows you more respect in the future."

He had expressed his concerns about burning a leper for running away from the city guard. A crime no reasonable person would consider being burn worthy. Duke Renier had seemed shocked. "I will have a talk with Wellan about that! After all, the man should at least get a fair trial.

Thank you for bringing this to my attention, Piet Lithor," he had declared.

Yes, the wizard's credibility would be damaged thanks to the piet's information. Duke Renier would make sure the sorcerer was properly chastised for his arrogance. The duke was a good man, a ruler who knew how to show a fellow leader the honor he deserved. He would make sure that Wellan treated Piet Lithor with more respect. Yes, the duke was a good man.

"Where's my lunch? That bumbling chef had better hurry and get it out here or there will be consequences!" He rattled the bell with more vigor, filling the room with an awful racket.

When no one responded, Piet Lithor screamed at the empty hall. "Chef Raboldi! Chef Raboldi! Where's my dinner! You're late with my dinner, Raboldddiiii!"

The piet's boy servant burst through the kitchen doors with an apron around his waist.

"What is this, boy? Where is Raboldi?"

The child bowed his head, his thumb and index fingers formed a triangle over the crown of his skull with his palms facing the high priest. A respectful moment passed before he dropped his hands and spoke. His gaze never left the floor. "I am so sorry, Piet Lithor. Chef Raboldi has gone home sick for the day. A-all of the kitchen staff is gone."

Piet Lithor's nostrils flared. "All of them sick? Oh, come now. They can't all be sick."

The boy raised his head, but didn't look him in the eyes. "Y-yes, Piet Lithor. I-I'm afraid they all started feelin' unwell shortly before lunch. Even the c-clergy are staying to their rooms."

That didn't sound good. It didn't sound good at all. Now who would prepare lunch? He wasn't about to prepare it himself.

The boy grabbed the edges of his apron and spread the material out in front of Piet Lithor. His face lit up with an awkward smile. "If it meets you're a-approval, Piet Lithor, I-I'll try and make you somethin' fer lunch. Course I ain't nearly as experienced as Mr. Raboldi with the herbs and seasonin's, but I can prepare a fairly good rabbit stew if given half the chance. 'Fore she died, my momma showed me how. Mr. Raboldi's been givin' me lessons too!"

Piet Lithor curled his upper lip and lifted an eyebrow. "Stew?" The boy's smile fell. "Oh come now, boy. You can do better than that. I am in the mood for grilled quail smothered in a tangy sauce."

The boy cringed. "Tangy s-sauce, Piet Lithor?"

"Yes. I don't know what it is, but Raboldi makes the sauce all the time. You should be able to make it easily." He gave the boy a sarcastic grin. "After all, Master Raboldi has been giving you lessons—or were you lying about that, boy?" Piet Lithor's grin turned cold. He smacked his lips in anticipation.

The boy swallowed, and held back the tears that shone in his eyes. "Yes, Piet Lithor. I-I will do m-my best."

Piet Lithor shooed him away, then sat back in his chair to wait for lunch.

It was odd that so many of his staff had become ill. Odd, but he could deal with that once his stomach was full of quail. Yes, he would deal with that after he ate.

∞ ∞ ∞ ∞

Drummen stood in the dark, staring ahead as drops of water fell from the ceiling. The water had risen halfway up his thigh in the last half hour, over the lip of his worn leather boots. That didn't concern him; he hardly noticed. Only food meant anything to him now. Only flesh could satisfy his hunger, and blood quench his thirst.

He couldn't eat yet. No, not yet. He had to wait. The Voice told him to wait for the others. They would arrive soon. The Voice gave him dreams to calm his hunger. Glorious visions. In these dreams he could feel his teeth sink into soft flesh. The taste of blood as it sprayed into the air and flowed around his mouth and gums, sliding, like thin honey, down his throat as he chewed and swallowed.

In the visions, his victims screamed as he ate them alive. The noise meant nothing more to him than the sound of the water dripping into the flow around him. They would find no mercy in him. He hardly had any compassion in life. Death gave it no meaning at all.

A hoarse chuckle accompanied the screams, the Voice laughed in the background. His victims struggled ineffectually as he grasped their shoulders, sinking his teeth into the side of their necks. He should have recognized his mother and the girl of his dreams, but they had become nothing more than blank templates, more food to appease his ever-growing appetite.

Perhaps the dreams weren't quite as good as actually feasting. He would know as soon as the others arrived. With the others, his brothers and sisters, he would hunt flesh. He would bask in blood, and he would suck the marrow of bones. His eyes rolled back, and he shivered as the dreams continued to give him an ecstasy he had never found in life, a fulfillment greater than drink and more erotic than sex.

It was unfortunate that he really couldn't understand any of it.

Chapter 5

"Your own counsel you should not keep,
neither take the counsel of those who are too eager to give it
for in their eagerness, they may lead you along the wrong path."
~ Secret Holy Scriptures of the Waken Book

Wellan sat with Duke Renier in their small conference chamber. The room was quiet and out of
the way, half-hidden in a corner of the castle.
They felt comfortable in the small chamber, a private den
shared between friends where they could relax and speak
their minds. The room had plain furnishings that allowed
them to discard all the flash and pomp that clung to the
duke like badly scented oils.

Wellan opened a small, black book, which rested on his
knee. Cracks lined the leather cover like a dry seabed, with
scrawling cryptic letters pressed into the hide. Time had
aged the pages, turning them dark yellow and coarse.
Wellan's tender touch kept them from crumbling as he

opened the book. Undecipherable scribbles that only he understood blended together in vertical columns, occasionally separated by diagrams and intricate illustrations.

Wellan read a paragraph in a hushed, almost reverent tone. "Thus do the necromancers' ilk walk the earth, created and used by the black arts of Syn. Syn doth grant the corrupt heart favors in this area, but the unholy god, the Keeper of all that Dies, doth require a great favor for the vile blessings which are granted unto such an evil heart. These favors are known not by any but he that requesteth the boon from Syn, and they dare not speak of it.

"A man must die in order for the boon to be granted. Such evil beings which shall be bold enough to ask for such a favor as this will have a heart of stone and will gladly find a victim to use as an unholy vessel of Syn. Once the victim is slain and given over to Syn, it shall lie dormant, without sign of life or spirit for a time. When the time has expired, the vessel shall still be dormant of spirit, yet it shall contain abominable life. With this life shall be only one desire. The desire shall be to feed. Bread shall it not want. Water shall not quench its thirst. The meat of the beasts of the field shall repulse it and make it ill, for the new creature is not of this world. Its spirit is not its own. The new being will be a vessel of Syn and require the flesh of its brethren to fill its hunger. The new being shall require the blood of its neighbor to quench its thirst. It eats not only the flesh, but the spirit also, and only the soul of men can sate its appetites for a time. The abomination will not see wisdom or reason. It will no longer work the hammer or plow. It will no longer create beautiful works or care for its fellow man. It will be a mindless ghoul, existing only to feed its hunger for flesh."

Wellan glanced from the book to make sure Duke Renier didn't need him to stop and explain any of the passage.
The duke sat on the edge of his seat with a stern look in his
eyes. His fingers rubbed his stubble-covered chin in
thought. He waved for Wellan to continue.

"It should be known throughout the world of men that
these abominations are to be greatly feared. No man shall
approach them for Syn, Master of the Abyss, holds a fate far
worse than any mortal death. Should a man contact an
abomination, he shall be burned within the hour, else he
also become abomination! Neither grab nor touch one such
as these, else ye become as they, an animate corpse, without
mind or spirit. Thou shall avoid them and flee. Neither iron
nor golden brass shall quench the beast's hunger. How
shall thou kill that which no longer lives? How shall thou
separate a soulless spirit from a body that no longer needs
it? Nay, thou shall not have the power to kill such a one as
this with mortal weapons. Only the plasma of fire or the
burning of acid shall destroy such a hideous thing. If any
but these are used, the abomination's hunger will live and
grow with each passing minute, a hunger no mortal can
understand."

The duke stared at the leather tome and crossed his
arms over his chest. Finally, he asked, "Is this true, Wellan?
These creatures can't be stopped with a sword or an axe?"

Wellan matched the duke's grim gaze and answered,
"No, my lord, they can be stopped with iron. Decapitation
or the removal of limbs will keep them from advancing,
though they will still hold the semblance of life. What the
passage said was that they can't be killed by anything short
of complete destruction of the body."

"Now I understand why you insisted that the 'leper' be burned to ash."

With a barely audible sigh, Wellan replied, "Yes. I wasn't sure until I saw the creature, but there was no mistaking what it was. It had to be destroyed completely."

The duke leaned back in his chair and his face brightened. "All five of the creatures were destroyed. The last one, the prisoner, has been cremated, so other than finding out why they were here in the first place, the disaster has been averted."

Wellan gently closed the book and shook his head. "No, I'm afraid not. The captain of the Night Watch, the one who reportedly went berserk in the streets when he confronted one of these things, never reported in for duty. I requested all of the men involved to meet me on the practice field this morning before they went home. He wasn't among them. When I went to his home, he wasn't there. Only evidence of his conversion remained."

"If he's loose in the streets…"

Wellan rose from his seat and tucked the tome under his arm. "Yes. He is loose in the streets, but he shouldn't be able to stay hidden. He probably won't even try, because they truly are mindless creatures, as the book said. I have the city guard looking for him, so I expect to see him in the dungeon sometime later today."

As Wellan backed toward the door, the duke grabbed his sleeve. "What if he has touched or…or bitten someone?"

Wellan put his hand over the duke's. "I don't know, my duke. Let's just pray to the gods that it hasn't happened."

∞ ∞ ∞ ∞

The roiling clouds released a torrent of rain as Madam Rachelle approached the palace walls. She had seen the dark skies gathering to the south, but the walk from her home wasn't far. Rachelle thought she could walk ahead of the rain. Unfortunately, she remained fifty paces from the entrance and shelter when it began pounding the street behind her in a wall of mist. There was nothing to be done for it now. She pulled the hood of her cloak over her head and quickened her pace to a brisk stroll. Her hard-soled boots sounded in sharp clicks, dress and scarves trailing like wet wings behind her. She wore several colorful layers of clothes, but the water seeped through and chilled her skin. She prayed she wouldn't slip on the slick stone road as she sped through the rain.

Lightning illuminated the sky with an ear-ringing crack, throwing her surroundings into crisp black and white as she arrived at the guard station. The portcullis of the Cutter Path Road gate sectioned the entrance into rectangular blocks. Her whole body tensed a second later as another crackling burst of sound assaulted her ears.

Two burly guards stood in a sheltered area next to the gate; not a drop of water shone across their boiled leather armor. Smirks twisted their faces as she ran under the eaves of the gate.

Madam Rachelle pulled her soggy hood back and wiped water from her face. Her black hair stuck to her forehead and cheeks in thick, wet strands. She fought to keep a quiver from her words as her voice rose to be heard over the rain. "I need to see the wizard, Wellan."

One of the guards raised an eyebrow and glanced at his partner before turning to her. His snide gaze traveled from her hair to her waist, lingering on her breasts. An uncomfortable feeling of anger and embarrassment contorted her emotions as she returned the guard's stare. She felt as if she were livestock at an auction. When his sneering eyes returned to hers, he folded his hands across his chest and asked, "Is the Duke's Wizard expecting you?"

She didn't think to easily get an appointment to see the wizard, and the guard's sarcastic tone, not to mention his wandering eyes, made her feel less confident about her chances. "Please. It's important. I have information the wizard needs."

The other guard had been staring at her also, but his eyes shone with curiosity rather than lust. "Aren't you the fortune teller, Madam Roquelle or something like that?"

She didn't know if her reputation would help or hinder her. Many of the citizens of Renier loved and respected her, but just as many called her a charlatan and a witch. With a hint of hesitation in her voice, she answered, "Madam Rachelle. Yes, I'm Madam Rachelle, the seer."

The guard turned to his sneering partner and whispered something to him, but the pounding rain forced him to raise his voice so that both his partner and Madam Rachelle could hear. "Dale, we had better find out if the wizard will see her."

Dale turned to the other guard, looking like a child who was told he can't play in the mud any longer. "What do you mean? No one's told us the wizard's expecting any visitors today. If Wellan wanted his palm read, I'm sure he would have mentioned it to the captain."

"She said she has important information, and besides, my wife knows her. If we don't at least find out if she can talk to Wellan, and my wife finds out we just sent her on her way, she's not gonna give me any..." He glanced at

Madam Rachelle then looked to Dale, whose frustrated frown had turned into a toothy grin. "...dinner for a month."

Grinning and trying to hold back his laughter, Dale replied, "Okay. Go find out if Wellan will see her. Wouldn't want you missing *dinner* tonight."

When he turned back to Madam Rachelle, the grin vanished. "Just wait right here. We ought to know if the wizard will see you within half an hour or so."

She nodded to the other guard, ignoring Dale. "Thank you."

The kind man nodded in reply and walked through the small guard entrance as Dale responded. His snide gaze returned to her wet clothing. "You're welcome."

She folded her arms over her breasts and prepared to wait for the man to return.

∞ ∞ ∞ ∞

Stiles sat on a small cot and watched water trickle down the wall. *Must be raining outside*, he thought, then turned to watch and listen as the other men drank their ale, rolled their dice and told their tales within each of the four cells. There were fifteen men in all. Three of the cells held four men. Stiles only had two other guards with him in his cell. His cellmates laughed as they exchanged exaggerated tales.

Stiles didn't laugh. Waiting in a prison cell under quarantine didn't amuse him at all. He envied the other guards' ability to carry on despite their circumstances.

Migel turned to Stiles as soon as old man Oswald finished another one of his stories. "You sure you don't want anything to drink?"

Stiles smiled. Migel wasn't really asking if he wanted ale; he was asking him to break in so he wouldn't have to listen to another of Oswald's tales. The old soldier loved to tell stories of his adventures, and they became grander with each retelling, but Stiles wasn't in the mood to join in and ease Migel's aggravation. "Don't feel much like drinkin'."

Oswald, who was well on his way to being falling-down-drunk, plopped himself on the cot next to Stiles and slurred, "Man, yoos sick?" He had a bad case of tooth-rot and his breath reeked. The sour smell of ale made the odor even worse. Stiles shook his head and turned his face away from Oswald's foul grin.

"Yeah, Stiles, it ain't like you to pass up a free drink. Everything okay?"

"I'm fine. I just don't feel like drinking is all." He wanted to say more, maybe ask how the rest of them could get drunk while there was a chance that they could be contaminated. Images of the lepers kept flashing into his mind, reminding him that he could become one of them. If they had contaminated him, he would start rotting away, a little bit of himself dying each and every day, the community shunning him, his family sending him away. He prayed to the gods that he wasn't sick, but if the leprosy did get him, he almost hoped Wellan would have him burned before his family and friends could see him, could shun him. He imagined his mother, despair warping her features. The thought didn't put him in much of a drinking mood.

He continued to mull it over as Oswald started another tale of his grand adventures.

"Godsdamned lazy bunch o' bastards!" The barred door to the main chamber burst open and their guard stormed in. He was a slovenly man, even by city guard standards. His bulbous gut stretched his soiled uniform almost to the breaking point, making Stiles wonder why he didn't request a new one, one that would fit his portly frame a bit better.

Oswald leaned an arm out of his cell, an ale mug in his hand, wanting a refill.

"Hey, Sharky, I thought your shift was over?" Horn bellowed from a cell across the chamber.

The portly guard stared at the man with disgust, a venomous look that made the ugly man look like a troll. "Godsdamned right my shift is over. Bunch o' lazy bastards."

Jamee chimed in from another cell. "Well, what the hell are you still doin' here? Shouldn't you be home bangin' the missus' or somethin'?" Stiles could always count on Jamee to see a sore point and poke at it.

Some of the men laughed.

The comment didn't bother Sharky, but a wicked gleam twinkled in his squinting eyes as he replied, "Keep it up, jail-bait, and when I get off, I'll go to your place and do a little bangin' on your missus'."

The men roared with laughter. Jamee scowled and gave Sharky a rude hand gesture.

When the laughter died to quiet chuckles, Sharky continued. "Nobody showed up to relieve me. Can ya believe it? I've been down here over twelve hours watching these cells, waitin' on you assholes like a barmaid for the last three of them hours, and nobody comes in to relieve ol' Sharky."

Stiles sprang off of his cot and strode to the bars. "Nobody came in to relieve you?"

Sharky spat on the floor. "Not a damned soul."

Jamee, seeing a chance to redeem himself, grinned through the bars. "Hey, Sharky, maybe they quit doing shifts by hours and started going by how hard you work instead. Hell, you're liable to be here for another twelve hours."

A few nervous chuckles followed his comment.

Stiles stuck his head to the bars and yelled, "Shut up, Jamee. This might be a real problem." He turned to Sharky. "You need to find your commander and ask him to check on those men."

Sharky's fat lips formed a frown. "Awww, I figured I would give 'em another hour and then I would…" Sharky swayed back and forth, reaching out to steady himself.

Stiles' hands tightened on the pitted bars. "You okay, Sharky?"

The man raised his hand to his cheek and gave it a little rub. "I…I don't know. Feel hot as the Abyss. Just sorta came over me." He turned and walked toward the main door. His steps wobbled. He drifted back and forth as if he had been the one drinking ale. Before Sharky had gone halfway across the room, he tripped and caught himself on the ale barrel. Mugs tumbled and fell to the floor in a cacophony of crashes, but he stopped himself from falling.

Stiles had to lean his head further into the bars to see Sharky's back. "Sharky, what's the matter?"

Everyone stopped and stared. Cards and coins lay on bunks; ale mugs sat forgotten.

Sharky hunched up and retched. Something wet splashed onto the floor. The noise stopped, then started again. Sharky tried to push himself off the keg, but another convulsion struck him, doubling him over and sending him crashing to the chamber floor. When the convulsions stopped, the room went silent. Everyone stared at the prone form. The keg hid his head and the puddle he lay in was covered in shadows. Stiles didn't need to see the puddle. The odor of rancid stomach acids filled the room. A few of the men looked queasy themselves. The smell of vomit didn't bother Stiles. What bothered him was the faint aroma mingled in with the vomit, the trace of a scent that he was too familiar with, the smell of blood.

"Sharky...Sharky, you okay?"

Chapter 6

"The afterlife doesn't hold the promises of Heaven
if we submit to the will of our gods,
nor the Hells we should suffer if we rebel.
The afterlife is something totally...different"
~ Dokkien the Wise

adam Rachelle browsed through the impressive collection of books lining the walls as she strolled through the vast room. She felt like a bee in a hive of knowledge. The shelves rose from hand-carved wooden cabinets a foot above the floor and didn't stop until they touched the ceiling, well over her head. Thousands of books, more than she had imagined the entire city possessed, all meticulously organized by subject and author. Their topics ranged from blacksmithing to complicated mathematical algorithms. Her only disappointment was not finding any books on the subject of magic. She wasn't surprised, given the little she knew about the wizard. Legend had it that the man, if he was truly a man, had been sent by the gods and entrusted with the welfare of mankind. The wizard's sorcery erupted from his soul, not from the knowledge in any book. Still, it would have been nice to see a tome or two of spells and their workings.

No one knew a great deal about Wellan. Madam Rachelle spent a good portion of her time uncovering anything she could concerning him, with little success. Her casual curiosity had grown to a hobby, but as she discovered little tidbits here and there, her pastime became an obsession. Maybe her obsession grew to such a driving force because the Wizard remained a mystery that had yet to be unraveled. Maybe she was simply nosy, a busybody like the women who stood around the corner well and gossiped. Her curiosity had more substance than common gossip, though. The sorcerer had lived in the city since its founding, but few knew more than his name. Many folk whispered that he had meddled in man's affairs since long before Renier existed, maybe since the creation of man. A guardian and guide sent by a higher power. Whatever he was, he seemed to be the only one who could help. He had to be warned of her visions.

Her fingers trailed behind her, gently touching the books she passed. The wizard had knowledge unknown to most mortals, of that she was sure. He would be able to interpret what her gift had shown her. He would know why she saw the terrible visions. He would tell her why death glazed the faces of everyone she met. He might even prevent her visions from manifesting. She had to try.

"Hello, Madam Rachelle."

Her heart fluttered and skipped a beat as the strong yet quiet voice spoke behind her. She turned to see the Duke's

Wizard standing in the doorway. Black hair with sprigs of gray framed his face, making his piercing blue gaze more vibrant and mysterious. He held a silver tray with a carafe of tea between his slender hands.

He smiled as he set the tray down on a reading table. The room filled with a spicy aroma as he filled two cups with the dark, steaming liquid. "I am terribly sorry to keep you waiting. I had some other business to attend to."

Her nerves overwhelmed her and stole her voice. Her heart raced and her face flushed. She stood speechless, all the things she had imagined saying to the mysterious wizard suddenly disappeared, a vanishing trick brought on by the awe of his presence. She felt as if she stood in a dream, a dream her tongue-tied nervousness swiftly turned into nightmare. After a short but awkward pause, she mumbled, "The wait was short, my lord wizard."

He shook his head, giving her a gentle smile. "Please, call me Wellan. Titles don't mean a great deal to me." He passed her a cup of tea. "Now, Madam Rachelle, the guard said you had some important information to share with me."

She set her cup on the table. It would only shake in her nervous hands, distracting her from what she had to say. Taking a deep, trembling breath she gazed at the cup as though it held the answers to the meaning of life. She whispered, "Since we are being informal, please call me Rachelle."

"All right, Rachelle, what was it that you needed to tell me?"

She didn't know where to begin. The speech she'd planned for two days became a jumble she could no longer recall. She had imagined herself speaking with eloquence and logic, but her voice died in her throat. Finally, she gave up, speaking more bluntly than she had intended. "Everyone I see will die in the next few days!"

Wellan's cordial smile vanished. "Why do you say that?"

She paused and took a deep breath to calm herself. "I don't know if you know anything about me, but I'm a fortune teller, a seer. I run the little business from my home, reading cards, palms, bones, tea leaves…anything that will allow me to interpret the signs Aoruza Jus Tor, Lady Fate, graciously gives me. I can also see auras, colorful mists that seem to radiate from everyone. The color can tell me what sort of mood they are in, what has taken place in their past, and what might be in store for their future. It's a gift…a gift I don't take lightly."

Rachelle took a seat at the corner of the table, afraid that her legs would betray her. Wellan sat in a padded chair at the end of the table, his own tea forgotten. His eyes filled with concern as he asked, "When you see these auras, how can you tell whether they reflect the person's mood, past or future?"

She put her hands around her cup and twisted it back and forth, watching the tea swirl, unable to bear looking into the wizard's eyes. "I ask them questions."

"Questions?"

"Yes. I use the cards, bones, tea leaves or anything else I happen to have to focus my concentration, and I ask them a question. For instance, I might ask if they have ever been in love; love is the most popular reason I do business. I might see a dark red glow telling me that there are strong emotions here and they truly were once in love. The props aid me a little in narrowing down the possibilities of the telling, and they make it all seem more real for the customer, but…but I mostly rely on my aura sense."

Wellan placed his hand over Rachelle's. The comforting touch drove away some of her nervousness. She stopped twisting the cup and looked up into his face as he said, "You see auras, but what does that have to do with all of these deaths you are talking about?"

A knot formed in her throat and tears misted her eyes. She wiped the tears away with the back of her hand as Wellan pulled a kerchief from his robes and handed it to her. It smelled of pipe smoke and leather. "I...I don't always see the auras. The props help me focus and then the auras come easier. Sometimes they come all on their own, and sometimes they won't show up at all. Earlier in the week, two days ago, a customer came in to have her fortune told. She asked the usual questions, one was about her husband loving her more and will she find happiness in her future. I used cards for the reading. When I looked up at her, she glowed...she glowed black."

Tears freely streamed down Rachelle's face. Forgetting about the kerchief, she wiped them away with her forearm, sniffled, and continued. "It means...it...death. Black always means death. I couldn't tell her the truth. I couldn't tell her she was going to die, or maybe it was her husband, or children, but death walked by her side. I told her I couldn't see anything. I lied. She...she left and an hour later, another woman came by. I was still upset about the first customer, but I met with the next one hoping that they might have a bright future. Again, I saw black. Black!"

She hunched over and wept as the sudden flood of emotions overwhelmed her. Rachelle hated to break down in front of the wizard, but seeing the disturbing auras was a burden she could hardly bear. She wanted to run out of the room and hide under a rock.

Wellan leaned over and put a comforting arm around her shoulder. "It will be okay, Rachelle. They won't die. I won't let that happen, I promise."

She sat up in her chair as he leaned back in his. "What can you do?"

Though he obviously tried to hide it, she could see that he didn't know what to do. He patted her knee, attempting to be kind to her, to comfort her.

She saw something else that terrified her, made her want to scream. Smoke surrounded the wizard, the black smoke that only she could see.

A kind smile arched Wellan's lips as he reached out to brush the moisture from her cheek. "Don't worry, Rachelle. I don't know what is causing these black auras, but I will do my best to look into it and stop anything from happening."

His words brought her little comfort.

∞ ∞ ∞ ∞

Piet Lithor cowered beneath satin sheets in the shadows between his bed and the wall. His breath wheezed through his throat and his heart pounded with a quick rhythm. He could hear each beat as the blood passed his eardrum; unfortunately, the sound wasn't loud enough to drown out the banging coming from the door or the scrape of fingernails against wood.

The terror began as the boy brought the piet's grilled quail to the table and placed it before him. The quail was dry and overcooked. Piet Lithor cuffed the boy across the temple with an open hand. His mouth parted to tell the child to return the tray to the kitchen and try again. His angry comment withered in mid-breath as Brother Somners shuffled into the room. The man was hardly fit to be seen in public, wearing only his nightclothes, soiled nightclothes at that!

The piet's mouth snapped shut and then opened again, ready to tell Brother Somners to make himself presentable in the presence of the piet. The sleep-clad priest turned toward him and the words died in his throat. The blank stare in the priest's eyes grasped the piet's spine in a hand of ice. Brother Somners raised both arms and shuffled forward. Somners' head twitched with a nervous tick. The splattered stains on the night clothes shone red, a dark red.

The boy shrieked. Lithor's heart banged against his chest. He stumbled out of his chair. The ornately carved furniture crashed to the floor as he backed away from Brother Somners.

Other priests and house staff stumbled into the room behind the bloodied priest. All of them wore an odd assortment of bloodstained clothes, more suitable to the privacy of their homes than the grandeur of the piet's dining room. They stumbled toward him, arms outstretched as if begging for help, aid far beyond the piet's ability to give.

He recognized every face. Brother Moyes, the record keeper of the order, shuffled around the corner. Black ink speckled with red blood blotted the front of his robes. A quill grasped like a club in his ink-stained grip. Mina Trey, his personal housekeeper and occasional caretaker of his more base needs, hobbled slowly at the back of the crowd, her ankle twisted at an impossible angle. Little Gorkis Rowe, a fine young man working to enter the priesthood, and a whirlwind at the races, hobbled past the slower bodies. Blood covered his mouth and hunger shone in his eyes.

It was too much for the piet.

He turned and ran, slamming into the boy and knocking him to the ground. He didn't even glance down as he stepped on the child in his haste to get away from the dining hall.

He raced down the corridor to his room, leaving the boy to his fate. The child's high-pitched wails spurred him on.

His priests had become abominations. He heard their shuffling from the other side of the door, a door barricaded by a dresser and overturned bookcase. Every sound sent a shiver down Piet Lithor's spine. The shuffling and banging spoke volumes to him. The priests told him that they wanted him, desperately had to have him.

For what purpose? Did they want Piet Lithor to join their ranks and become one of them, a new dark priesthood in the service of death? Though the boy's screams had ended minutes ago, he could still hear the high-pitched screeches within the dark recesses of his mind. Childish screams filled with terror and pain.

"Leave me alone!" he shrieked at the barricaded door.

His plea only increased the intensity of their assault. The feet sliding across the floor became more erratic; the pounding grew louder.

He prayed for Lord Vaspar's protection, but the dead continued their assault upon his sanctuary. With a sob, the piet realized that he stood on his own. His god wouldn't help, or hadn't noticed his plight. Surely Vaspar the Just wouldn't leave his high priest to be taken by his clergy. He had to get his attention.

Piet Lithor crawled to the end of the bed where an immaculately polished and carved table sat. In a glass case on the table rested a sword, a holy artifact. Centuries ago, the sword belonged to Tyrmra the Just, a saint of justice and purity. Righteous symbols etched its gleaming blade. The intricately wrought handle called for his grasp, promising comfort and hope.

Rising to his knees, he fumbled with a set of keys. His hands shook. The keys looked alike. He sorted them out until he found the right one. With a sob, he jabbed it into the slot and twisted. The latch released. He threw open the case and grabbed the artifact by its golden handle then scooted back to his hiding spot behind the bed. He knelt with the sword between his clasped hands, as if in prayer. The blade pushed against the tiled floor. His sweaty forehead pressed into the pommel.

In a frantic whisper, he pleaded, "Oh mighty Vaspar, the Just and Righteous, you who rights the wrongs of mankind, giving your faithful righteous strength and punishing the unholy. I, your humble servant, ask you to deliver me from this nightmare. Destroy those who wish me harm and save me from the vile clutches of the unholy, so that I may continue to lead men in your righteousness."

The banging of the unholy grew louder, the sound of his prayer driving them on.

Piet Lithor lowered his voice to a minor vibration of his vocal cords. "Oh mighty Vaspar. Please, please save me from these abominations. I will do anything you wish, anything. I will…"

The crack of wood interrupted his prayers. The door facing began to split.

The piet gasped as his bladder threatened to give way. His knuckles turned white against the pommel as he squeezed tighter and continued his prayer in silence. *I will give you my life. I…I realize I have become…arrogant. Pious. The…the boy… It was wrong to leave him, to push him down. I treated him…poorly, putting myself first, thinking I was better than a street urchin.*

82

With a clarity that he had never before experienced, he witnessed himself as he trampled over the boy. He saw every detail of his cowardice, how he plowed into the child then stepped on the boy's chest as he fled to safety. His vision showed him things that he had been too afraid to see in the heat of the moment, such as the look of fear and betrayal in the boy's eyes. Finally, he relived the child's scream, his final plea. The piet shuddered as it echoed through his mind. It yanked at his heart and made him want to die of shame. Tears flooded his eyes and wet his cheeks. He forgot his fear, the abominations, and his safety as he shrieked, "What have I done? Lord Vaspar, what have I become?"

The piet's voice lowered, not out of fear of the abominations, but because gasping sobs overtook him. "Oh Lord. I don't deserve to live. I am a vile coward, an arrogant and self-righteous fool."

He wanted to say more, to tell his Lord Vaspar to let the abominations in, to end his life before he could cause any more harm and bring more disgrace upon his Lord, but his remorse overtook him, silenced him. He gasped and his back shook with sobs as self-realization overcame him. He didn't deserve to live. Seeing his true self, he didn't want to continue on.

The banging stopped. Piet Lithor sensed disappointment underlining the unholy quiet, as if the vile creatures were being denied their sole purpose.

Within seconds, their shuffling faded away and only silence remained.

Weeping, he hugged the holy artifact of Vaspar the Just to his chest.

After meeting with Rachelle, Wellan walked the silent woman to the gates at the palace wall. He led her to the gate through corridors and passageways to keep her out of the rain. Rachelle remained silent as he reassured her that the people of Renier wouldn't come to harm. She strolled beside him, but didn't speak. Several times, her hand rose within the cowl of her cloak to wipe her eyes. He said he would get to the bottom of things and prevent her visions from becoming reality. He tried to sound convincing, but her silence told him she remained certain about the fate of those around her. Her confidence scared Wellan. Rachelle was a seer, known throughout the city for her accurate predictions. He hoped he would be able to stop disaster from falling, but her strong convictions overwhelmed his sense of security.

At the gate, he wished her well, trying to sound more convincing than he felt. The guards stood at attention, eyes fixed on the trees across the road. She nodded her head once, turned, and walked away. Within moments, she had disappeared into the downpour.

As Wellan turned back, one of the guards cleared his throat and stuttered, "Eh…excuse me, sir."

The other guard rolled his eyes, as if to say, *Here it comes!*

"Yes."

With a nervous quake in his voice, the first guard said, "Dale and I..."

Dale turned to his companion and glared, forcing him to start over. "Well, sir, you see...I was wondering if you know what's goin' on today?"

Wellan's eyebrows drew together. "What do you mean?"

The guard scratched his wiry beard and said, "Nobody's come into the gate today, other than that seer. Usually, we got at least a dozen people by now. The rain don't even account for it. That, and...well, we've been hearin' hollerin' all over the place. We would've checked it out, but it's hard to tell where it's comin' from with the rain and all, plus we can't leave our post, and nobody has made their rounds to see if we need anything, or we would've reported it."

Fear's icy fingers crawled up Wellan's spine as the implications became obvious.

"Shut the gates until I return." He frowned at the guard who had spoken. "Go back to the palace and find your commander. If he isn't available, then go straight to the duke. Tell him the palace needs to be searched for dead bodies or sick people. The dead bodies need to be locked away or burned, and the sick need to be quarantined. I will be back within the hour."

The guards looked at one another and hesitated; uncertainty and fear clouded their faces.

Wellan put a hand on each of their armored shoulders and spoke, keeping himself as calm as he could. "Hurry. It's important that the palace be sealed as quickly as possible."

The first guard spun and ran toward the palace while the second man closed the heavy ironbound doors. Wellan turned and stepped out from the palace wall. Within seconds, the rain soaked through his cloak. It chilled him, but not enough for him to deviate from his task.

Rain pummeled his robes as he walked. It narrowed his senses so that he could only detect things in a small area around him. Trees could be seen to either side of the road, but only as grayed silhouettes. He wondered if the sudden

driving rain might have more purpose than nature intended. *Maybe to hide a vile horror from the eyes of those who might
be able to stop it.* The thought unsettled him.

He pulled his cowl tighter and widened his stride.

Within moments, the market opened before him.
Wellan stopped.

Each morning, vendors brought their wares to this part
of the city and set up colorful tents and booths, hoping to
fill their pockets with coin before the day ended. On a
normal day, the market bustled with activity. With God's
Day nearing, people should have been packed together
shoulder to shoulder, even with the rain. The sight before
him was far from normal. Several booths and tents could be
seen, buffeted by the downpour, but the buyers and vendors were missing, their wares ruined by rain. Pots, hung
from wires, clanked against one another in the wind while
banners twitched and flapped. The weather accounted for
some of the lack of participation, but it wouldn't explain
why the booths sat completely empty. Not only that, but
the market stood in eerie silence, other than the constant
patter of rain and the wind flapping fabrics back and forth.

Wellan pulled his cloak around him and walked further
into the market, toward the well in the center.

Everywhere he looked he saw the same thing: empty
booths, wet goods—and no people.

As he approached the well, he saw a pair of boots. They
protruded from the backside of the stone and mortar pipe,
the heels faced toward him. The boots didn't move.

He ran to the well, splashing through puddles with
every step. Death assaulted his nostrils. A heavy-set man
lay by the well, eyes glazed open in terror and skin fish-
belly white. Wellan squatted next to the man and reached

down. The thought of contamination crossed his mind, but he shoved it away. He felt for a pulse. The cool skin told him there was no need. Oddly enough, the smell of death slackened as Wellan knelt beside the body. He bent down and took another whiff. The putrid smell was faint. He stood and sniffed again. The smell became stronger. Realization flooded his mind and he bent over the well and took a deep breath. The putrid stench wafted up from the black opening.

Wellan slammed his open hand against the stone lip of the well. "Damn!"

The city's water supply had been poisoned with the infection. He suddenly understood why the "lepers" had been found mutilated. They had done it to themselves, using their own bodies as a poison, a plague against Renier. Everyone used the city-supplied wells. Despair twisted his stomach to the point of nausea. Most of Renier would be infected.

Shuffling footsteps splashed through the water. Wellan spun around. Five corpses staggered toward him. Others stumbled forward between the booths. They were dressed in merchant attire, men and women who woke up thinking that they would have another day of business as usual. The pallor of their skin and blank look in their eyes told a different story.

Surprised, Wellan stepped back. The corpses advanced.

Repulsed by the sickening creatures, not considering who they may have been a few hours ago, he pulled his arm back, drawing in air. Magic took over his vision, revealing the life giving gasses around him in shades of red, and the inert gasses in blue. With the speed of thought, he separated the two. Wellan slung the red gas forward like an invisible rock, drawing in the energy and heat from around him to create a spark. Hell burst from his open palm and incinerated three of the five corpses.

Seven more stumbled in to take their place. Wellan exhaled a fog of chilled air as he drew upon the heat and gasses around him. He bared his teeth, pulled both arms back, and let loose.

Chapter 7

"...and while the righteous gather in their temples,
seeking the protection of their gods,
the children shall rise up against their parents
with unrighteous vengeance and hatred."
~Secret Holy Scriptures of the Waken Book

"What we gonna do if he don't get up?" Horn pressed his wide head against the bars of the cell and nodded in the direction of the motionless Sharky. Two of his cellmates crowded around to either side. The ever-cocky Ash sat on the bunk and glared through the bars. Their troubled faces reflected Stiles' fear.

Stiles could always count on the burly warrior to break his concentration, but Horn did have a point. Sharky was the only person they had seen since being locked up, and he should have been relieved hours ago. When he collapsed on the floor, they had yelled and beat their ale mugs against the bars, but no help came. As the minutes passed, Stiles' sense of impending doom grew. Something wasn't right.

"I ain't worried none. The relief guard'll get here any minute an' all this'll sort itself out," Gorney said, his tone relaxed, as though he didn't have a care in the world. He sat on the stone floor in the cell adjoining Stiles with his elbows propped on his knees. Straw stuck to his britches and an empty ale mug perched in his lap. The soldier made a habit of sailing through life with a slow, carefree attitude.

Oswald slid next to Stiles and pushed his scrawny head between the bars. He waved a drunken hand in Sharky's direction and belched. His speech slurred as he mumbled, "I...I ain't so sure dat ol' Sharky's gonna make it tru dis one. Looks ta me like a feller I knew when I was sailin' wit those mariners. We comes up to dis island and one of da feller's gots himself stung by dis little flea lookin' t'ing. Next t'ing we know, the guy's all pukin' up blood and gaspin' fer air and..."

"Shut up, Oswald." Stiles couldn't take another one of the old soldier's stories.

"But all I was sayin..."

"Yeah, and I'm telling you to shut up."

"You ain't my cap...captain. You just barely outrank..."

"Shut up, Oswald," Ash whispered from a bunk across the room, in a cell he shared with Horn and two others. Ash didn't voice his thoughts often, but when he spoke, everyone listened. Though Stiles outranked everyone in the room, he still hesitated when giving orders to Ash. The lanky man had a cold disposition, distant and self-confident. Stiles had sparred with Ash on the practice field and he knew the man's confidence wasn't misplaced; he was a quick and deadly swordsman.

A frown twisted Oswald's face. The old man's mouth opened then snapped shut. He looked at the ceiling as if in deep thought, then dropped his eyes back to Ash. Again, his mouth opened and again, it suddenly closed. Stiles waited to see if he would say whatever he had to say, though he expected the old man to cower down. Instead, Oswald threw his arm toward Ash and swept his bleary gaze across everyone as he mumbled, "Awwww...ta hell with ya all!" Then he dropped onto the cot, folded his arms across his chest and glared at the floor.

An awkward silence blanketed the room. Everyone leaned against the bars or sat on the cots. No one had anything to say that would change the fact that they were locked in a dungeon with no way out, so they said nothing.

A scraping sound broke the tense silence. The noise wasn't loud, but it got everyone's attention.

Sharky's foot twitched and slid across the floor.

Horn grasped the bars with his beefy hands and pushed his wide head against them, "Aye, Sharky. You okay?"

Sharky didn't respond. Instead, he dragged a knee to his waist and scooted forward into the open area past the barrel. His chest and face slid against the cold stone, mouth open and lips pulled taut. Soundlessly, he placed his hands by his shoulders and pushed his torso up. His head hung as though his neck were broken. Strands of blood and gore dangled from his open lips.

Stiles stepped back, away from the bars. In the next cell, Gorney said, "Let us out of here, Sharky. Give me the keys, and we'll get you some help."

Sharky's head snapped up. He looked over his shoulder at Gorney with cloudy, boiled egg eyes. He rose on legs that wobbled under his weight and staggered across the dungeon toward the cell Gorney shared with three others.

Stiles' stomach clenched with panic as Gorney stood and stuck his arm through the bars, his hand open to accept the keys. He couldn't identify the source that caused his fear. It was more than Sharky's clouded eyes and bloody drool. Something seemed horribly wrong. It was nothing obvious, nothing that Stiles could place. Still, there was something all too familiar about the events unfolding before him.

Sharky reached forward and grabbed Gorney's hand; the jailer's other hand clasped the soldier's elbow. Gorney grunted as Sharky jerked him forward until his chest slammed against the bars. He pulled the soldier's forearm to his mouth and sank his teeth into the flesh until they snapped together. Gorney screamed and yanked his arm back. Blood gushed over Sharky's lips and nose. He wouldn't let go.

Arolyn, Blade, and Wolf ran to Gorney and pulled him back as Sharky chewed and swallowed. His head lowered for another bite. Stiles grasped the bars in a white knuckled grip. He watched helplessly as Sharky clung to his victim's arm while the three men pulled him free.

The pale, dull-eyed man didn't give up. Both arms reached through the bars. His blood-covered hands grasped for the men standing at the far end of the cell; his mouth constantly opened and closed, snapping at empty air. Red gore stained his teeth and covered his lips and chin.

Stiles knew why he had an uneasy feeling about Sharky. The snapping teeth brought it all back. The lepers had acted the same way. The behavior had seemed vicious and bloodthirsty for men who seemed so blank and empty. He couldn't forget the raw violence of the lepers, violence that lacked purpose. The sort of violence Sharky had suddenly displayed.

"What the hell's wrong with Sharky?" Horn bellowed.

"Can't you see? He's got the leprosy!" Owl shrieked from the cell across the room.

Migel grabbed Stiles' arm and twisted him around. "What we gonna do?"

Stiles couldn't think through the terror and shock. One thought stood at the forefront of his mind. *It's contagious. The stuff is contagious! Just a breath or a touch and I might catch it. A drop of blood, a trace of spit, or breath on the wind might have given us the sickness. Any of us could have it now and not know it. I could be rotting from the inside out at this very minute...*

Migel shook Stiles. "Sir...what are we gonna do?"

Like a man waking from a dream, Stiles snapped back to the present. *We have to get those keys!*

He turned to the four guards. Three of the men stood with their back against the wall of their cell, as far away from the snapping and grasping Sharky as they could get. Gorney sat with his legs splayed across the floor, glaring at Sharky and holding his open wound while blood dribbled between his clenched fingers. "Arolyn, Blade, grab Sharky's arms and pull them into the cell. Hold him tight, so he can't move. Wolf, when they get Sharky pinned to the bars, you grab the keys from his belt."

Stiles had trouble calling the deranged guard Sharky. The man had always been gruff and mean, a necessity when employed as a dungeon guard, but not insane.

Though Sharky acted like a brute in the dungeon, he had a wife and a young daughter that he doted over to the point of spoiling. The blood-hungry stare, grasping hands and chomping mouth had transformed him into another creature. Not a man any longer, but a wild thing, something violent and hungry, a rabid beast. He had to remind himself that the vicious thing was still Sharky and he needed help. The man might be cured if they could get him to a healer.

Arolyn and Blade moved forward. Both were good soldiers and didn't question orders.

They had only taken a few cautious steps when Stiles stopped them. "Wait. Don't touch him with your bare hands. Use the sheet."

Arolyn turned and yanked the sheet from the bunk. He handed one end to Blade and they advanced on Sharky. The jailer didn't dodge or try and pull his hands away as they wrapped his flailing arms together in the sheet. His hands grasped and jerked between the bars. Using the sheet to protect themselves, they pulled the man tight against the cell until his cheeks pushed against the bars. Their proximity maddened Sharky. He slammed his head against the bars, grinding his cheeks into the cold steel. His jaws snapped with savage force and blood flowed between his crooked teeth as he bit into his tongue.

Wolf slid between Arolyn and blade as they held Sharky against the bars. Cloth ripped as Wolf jerked the keys from the guard's belt. He tossed them to Stiles and backed away from the deranged man.

Stiles caught the key ring and turned to unlock his cell. He stopped and spun back to the men holding Sharky. "Don't let him go. Hold him tight so he can't get away. I'll let everyone else out and then we will deal with him and get you out."

They nodded and tightened the sheet around Sharky's arms, pulling him forward until each of his shoulders pressed against a bar.

Stiles struggled with the lock, but the third key opened the door and, within minutes, the guards, except for the ones holding Sharky, stood outside their cells. The man thrashed and slammed his head against the bars, silently biting at the freed men. With the prisoners free, he fought and raged worse than ever, struggling to get to the men behind him, the ones not protected by the iron bars.

Stiles tried to reason with him, standing a safe distance away. "Come on, Sharky. It's us. We want to help."

He snapped at Stiles, biting his tongue in half. The bloody mass bounced off his shoulder and fell to the floor. Without a tongue to pad his bites, Sharky's teeth snapped together with loud clicks. Blood ran over his bottom lip and speckled his mouth with every bite.

"Stop it! Quit or you're gonna bleed to death."

The madman kept biting and fighting, paying no attention to Stiles' pleas. He didn't struggle to free his arms. He ignored them. All his attention focused on the men. His thrusts and jerks came not so much from a desire to be free as a need to get to those around him.

Oddly, after the initial burst of blood, his tongue stopped bleeding. A ragged stump of meat glistened with each snap of his teeth.

Stiles grabbed Horn's broad shoulder. "Get another sheet off a cot and stuff it in his mouth. If the bleeding starts again, the cloth might slow it down. Use what's left to cover him up so we don't have to touch him."

Horn nodded, then ran to a cell and came back with the linen. He wadded a handful of material into a tight ball and, between bites, he shoved it into Sharky's mouth, then threw the rest of the sheet over the man's head and shoulders. Horn grasped Sharky around the chest in a bear hug. The guard wiggled like a netted fish against his captor.

Stiles turned to the four men still trapped in the cell. "Blade, help Gorney up and get ready to run out of the cell. Arolyn, prepare to let him go."

A frown curled Arolyn's lips. He didn't look happy about the order, but he nodded.

Owl and Blade helped Horn hold Sharky while Stiles unlocked the cell. "Arolyn, let him go."

Arolyn pulled the sheet from Sharky's arms. The moment his limbs came free, he reached back and tried to grasp the men holding him against the cell. Owl and Blade grunted as they pinned his flailing hands to his side. Horn pulled the struggling man backward.

With the doorway cleared, the four prisoners ran from the cell. Once they were out, Horn shuffled to the door and pushed Sharky in. As the guard fell into the cell, Stiles slammed the door closed and locked it.

Sharky stumbled, blindly making his way back to the door. He looked like a drunken ghost as he stumbled around the cell with the sheet covering him from head to waist. He slammed into the bars with a clank and stuck his arms through; his hands clasped and grabbed for the soldiers again. The sheet squirmed around his mouth in a puckered red dimple, but didn't fall off.

Horn spoke first. "Look at that. He ain't even bothering with the sheet. It's like he don't notice it."

Stiles turned to Gorney. "Royd, bandage Gorney up, then we'll get some help for Sharky."

When a tourniquet had been put on Gorney's arm, they walked up the stairs to the front room of the dungeon. A wooden door stood between two dirty windows that faced the training yard. The rain had slowed to a fine drizzle. The windows let in a drab light that painted the room in deep shadows. A table sat against one wall with a deck of cards strewn over its surface and a half empty mug of ale. Their weapons and armor hung on the opposite wall.

Stiles walked to the door and stopped as a woman passed by one of the windows. She wasn't a soldier and didn't belong in the training yard. Her chin and the front of her pale blue dress glistened in the midday sunlight. Both were coated in blood.

He ducked below the window and motioned the others to do the same. As they squatted, he crawled to the opening and peeked over its edge.

The woman had her back to him as she shuffled toward the walls of the training yard. A dozen other people aimlessly shambled back and forth around her. Most of them were soldiers, but none looked like they knew where they were. A distant scream broke the silence.

"What da hell was dat?" Oswald blurted from his prone position near the stairs.

Stiles glared over his shoulders at the man. Between clenched teeth he hissed, "Shhhhh." He peeked over the windowsill again. The woman had stopped with her head cocked to one side as if listening. Her tongue snaked out to lick her lips. She clawed at the air then continued her ambling gait toward the wall.

Blade crawled next to Stiles and looked through the window, then gasped, "What's going on? Is the whole city infected?"

Stiles turned and sat with his back against the wall while Blade took in the scene. Like scared children peeking at the local haunted house, the other men crawled toward the windows for a look. Oswald stayed near the stairs and sulked, keeping to himself.

A decision needed to be made, but he couldn't make it lightly. Stiles had no idea how much of the city might be infected and he didn't want to enter the training yard only to be swamped in crazy people. He also asked himself if they had the right to hurt those people. They were sick and needed help. If there was a chance for them to get well, he couldn't take their lives. On the other hand, he couldn't let them attack him or his men. Hell, he didn't even want them touching him or his men.

Even if they did get through the training yard, what then? He hadn't seen any of the city watch dealing with these people. He had to assume, within the few hours they had been incarcerated, the entire city had fallen prey to the strange illness. If that were the case, then the best thing for him and his men to do would be to get away from the city and into the sparsely populated countryside.

He peeked over the window's edge again and looked toward Castle Renier. It sat just beyond the wall of the training yard. It stood higher than the other structures and was easy to spot. He didn't see any movement and almost gave up looking for anyone who wasn't infected, but a flash caught his eye. Someone leaned out of a tower window, looking down into the city. He couldn't see much from where he crouched, but the person seemed to have his wits about him—gazing upon the carnage Renier had become.

Stiles sat and leaned against the wall. "There are still people at the castle."

"So?" Gorney muttered. Sweat coated his face and caused his pale skin to glisten in the dim light. Stiles didn't reprimand him for his outburst; it was the pain talking.

"We've got to get to the castle. The duke may need us."

∞ ∞ ∞ ∞

Madam Rachelle stumbled through the streets of Renier in a daze, a bundle of cloth grasped to her chest. Little legs dangled from the material and swayed loosely as she walked, one foot bare and the other wearing a small leather shoe.

After leaving the castle, she had returned home through empty, wet roads as the rain beat down on her. The city was silent except for the crackle of rain on her cowl. The shops and houses were dark and lifeless. Even the pets and livestock seemed to be in hiding; not a bark or chirp interrupted the patter of the rain. She didn't notice the deserted streets. Her mind roamed elsewhere, focusing on every detail of her conversation with the wizard.

She thought about how foolish she must have looked. Over and over again, the thought repeated itself. *I finally have the chance to talk to him and I ruin any credibility I may have had by blurting it out like a follower of Rosh screaming about the end of the world!* Rachelle tried to see the situation through his eyes and all she saw was a hysterical madwoman, inarticulate and full of false worries. She hoped he didn't ignore her warning. The city would suffer greatly if he did.

When she reached her home, she brushed through the door and froze; water dripped from her cloak and puddled on the wooden floor. Mia lay face down in the middle of the living room. Rachelle had asked the young girl to watch after Tanilla while she spoke to the wizard. She didn't often ask anyone to watch after her daughter, but she had to deliver her warning to the wizard and she couldn't do it with Tanilla at her side.

Mia's head lay in a pool of vomit and blood, terrified eyes open and staring at the leg of a small table. Her hair formed a black halo around her head, making her face even whiter by contrast.

Rachelle ran to the girl and rolled her over. Her voice quivered as she cried out Mia's name. She touched the girl's cheek; cold flesh told her what her eyes refused to believe.

Tanilla!

She stood. Her legs trembled. A lump of terror gathered at the base of her throat as she raced to the child's room. Her worst fears were confirmed when she saw her five-year-old daughter lying on the floor, arms outstretched as if reaching for the door. Bloody vomit smeared behind her, creating a red smear from the girl's chest to the base of her bed. A shriek burst from Rachelle's throat. She ran to her daughter, picked the child up and held her close. The cold little body slumped against her chest; arms dangled at her sides.

She had raised Tanilla by herself for the past three years, since Raman had gone out on a merchant boat and never returned. The loss of her husband had been devastating, but she didn't have time to wallow in self-pity. She had a daughter to raise, a little girl who depended on her for everything. Rachelle had to be strong for her daughter's sake.

There's no reason to be strong now, she thought as she cradled her daughter's limp body in her arms and cried. Tears streamed down her face as she laid the child on her bed and tenderly wrapped her in a blanket before pulling her close again. Her breath hitched in her throat as she walked through the house and out the front door, her daughter's small body pressed tightly against her. Rachelle went through her actions automatically, pure instinct without thought. Reasoning had buried itself deep within her. Unable to face the bitter truth, her body took control and simply walked. She had to see to the needs of her precious baby.

The world vanished. Her feet acted of their own accord, slowly carrying her daughter back to the castle. She barely noticed the shambling corpses that stepped out of houses and stumbled from alley ways and stores. They moved as blobs in her peripheral vision. More and more slinked out of doorways and between houses with each step she took. Rachelle continued down the road, ignoring the people as they grouped together and shuffled behind her, slowly gaining ground and numbers. She ignored everything until her cherished bundle began to shift and squirm.

The movement yanked her mind back from the void. Her heart filled with hope that she didn't trust. With trembling arms, she lowered her daughter to the cobblestone road. As she bent down, she noticed the crowd of people behind her, men and women with blank eyes and blood coated mouths and clothes. She recognized some as neighbors and clients. Temporarily ignoring the shifting bundle in her hands, she willed her vision to focus into another spectrum, a spectrum of life and death, love and hate, future and past. The people's auras stood out like holes in the fabric of the universe. These auras were worse than the smoky shading of death. They stood out like black shadows thrown from a hundred suns. Dozens of ebony silhouettes tottered in her direction, forming an undulating dark wave.

With a cry, she willed her normal vision to return.

Not understanding, but refusing to lose her baby twice in one day, she hugged the child to her again and ran down the road toward the castle. The bundle she carried fought and squirmed against her grasp. "Shhhhh...it's gonna be okay, baby. Mama's got you."

She stopped, frozen in place as more bodies stepped out of the manicured forest on each side of the road ahead of her. She stepped back, but with the others advancing from behind, she had nowhere else to go.

"Leave us alone!" she screamed, knowing it would do no good. Hope drained away, replaced by gut-wrenching fear and despair.

Rachelle dropped to her knees. She pulled Tanilla's head to her shoulder and stared at the ground as tears fell to the road.

Pain flared through her shoulder. She pulled the bundle away and looked at her squirming daughter. Little arms fought against the constraining blankets. A small circle of cloth opened and closed in the center of the girl's head as her mouth chomped up and down.

She needed to see her daughter's face, hear what she tried to say. With quivering hands, Madam Rachelle unwrapped Tanilla from the blanket. She shuffled backward and gasped as baby teeth snapped together behind bloody lips pulled back in a snarl. Her short arms reached out for her mother, but not for a hug. The sight that hurt Rachelle the most was the lack of recognition in the solid white eyes that had once been brown, eyes like small white grapes.

Rachelle held the struggling girl at arms' length as her mind retreated again, going behind the dark door of her consciousness where none of these events were happening.

Suddenly, the girl's hair wafted up with a hollow thunk and a spray of red. A steel arrowhead dripped blood onto the child's shoulder. A feathered shaft stuck out from her daughter's other temple. The girl stopped struggling.

"Don't just sit there. Run!" a colorfully dressed man screamed from between two trees while nocking another arrow into a short bow. A similarly dressed woman released an arrow into the crowd that steadily closed in on Rachelle.

Her mind snapped. Her daughter slid from her hands as she stood. Rage enveloped her. Rachelle's world glowed with auras, came alive with them. The diseased crowds were a black mass of waving forms, the trees a patchwork of bright greens with golden sparkles that flashed and danced. Houses swam in a neutral gray haze, and the man who shot the arrow through her daughter glowed a deep, pulsating red, the object of her hatred.

Her left hand curled into a fist, fingernails cutting bloody crescents into her palm. Her head rolled back. Open eyes faced the cloudy skies. A chilling scream erupted from her throat, an inhuman howl. Her hand flashed toward the man and a wave of blue energy burst from her fingertips and streaked forward, blasting into his chest with a crack of thunder. He flew into the air and slammed against a tree where he slumped to the root covered ground.

Rachelle collapsed to the street. Her thoughts retreated to the safe place behind the door within her mind.

Chapter 8

"The righteous will scatter before the unrighteous
like dust blown from an ancient book."
~Secret Holy Scriptures of the Waken Book

Piet Lithor stood on the balls of his feet in the entryway of his home, one eye shoved against the peephole in the door. He studied the fish-eye view of the courtyard, where Brother Rayne and Brother Foster aimlessly shuffled through the drizzling rain and short grass. Neither priest noticed the other. They looked foolish, tottering back and forth on bare feet. Brother Foster's small hat, a symbol of his divine authority, had slid down his brow, covering one eye and adding to the ludicrous appearance. Their bloodstained robes reminded him that there was nothing funny about them.

Only an hour ago, the sight of Brother Foster sloshing through the rain-drenched grass with his hat covering his eyes would have infuriated Lithor, possibly earning the man a beating. Appearances and respect were important qualities in his home and he would not have tolerated his priests looking like court jesters. Since renewing his commitment to Lord Vaspar the Just, he saw the world through new eyes. His chest constricted with grief. The sight saddened him. He empathized with the shame Brother Foster would suffer if he knew he sloshed through the rain looking so peculiar. Lithor's eyes clouded with tears as he became consumed in an emotion he hadn't felt since childhood—pity.

He looked past Brother Rayne to the front gate. His priests always locked it at dusk and unlocked it at dawn. He needed to know if the gate had been opened before his world had fallen into the abyss. The sculptures of saints surrounding the well partially blocked his view. Age didn't help. His vision blurred when he tried to look at distant objects and the small lens warped the edges of his vision. He rubbed his eyes and moved his head sideways, but the courtyard remained blurry through the small peephole.

"Blasted well!" he growled in frustration, momentarily forgetting to remain silent. He cringed and looked over his shoulder, making sure no one heard. The house remained silent other than the drip of water from the eaves. He didn't think anyone remained.

Looking down the hallway brought back memories. He thought back to the consuming fear that filled him. A quiver ran down his back as he remembered the terror that had flooded his heart to the point of bursting. He had cowered in his chamber, trembling between the wall and bed of his chambers, shaking like a puppy in a thunderstorm.

He thought back to the fear that had slowly ebbed as he gained enough courage to leave his room. The mansion had stood empty of both the living and the dead. He hadn't heard the shuffling footsteps of deranged priests or seen them stumbling about. Only the boy remained. The child lay in a pool of blood, his insides strewn about, his mouth open in a silent scream. Piet Lithor had never seen so much blood. He hadn't realized the human body could contain such a quantity. Though the boy stared at the ceiling, Lithor felt as though he gazed at him. Accusing him of being a coward and not the holy man he claimed to be. Lithor felt it was a well-deserved accusation.

He felt remorse for the boy, and shame at his actions. What a terrible person he had become. A man who would knock a child down in the midst of such horror and leave him there to die without so much as a look to see if he had gotten up. *I'm a self-centered coward, not a man.* He didn't even know the child's name, always referring to him as "the boy" and sometimes worse.

Months ago, Lithor had bought the boy from a poor family. The child had several brothers and sisters, more than his parents could support. They felt that they were doing their son a favor, giving him a chance to get more out of life. Little did they know that Lithor only wanted the boy as his personal slave, someone he could dominate over, boosting his ever-inflating ego to new heights. He hadn't even bought the boy better clothes, preferring to keep the child humbled and humiliated.

With a heavy heart, Lithor knelt next to the boy's torn body and said a silent prayer to Vaspar the Just. He made the sign of peace, said the words of ascension, then touched the Yawai tattoo just above his ear to emphasize the prayer's importance. Lithor placed the boy's arms over his chest then closed his horror filled eyes. He gave his small body as much dignity as he could under the circumstance. The eyes had torn Lithor's heart the most. In the child's face he saw the horror he'd caused, and knew that the boy's last thoughts consisted of terror and abandonment. Before getting up, he kissed the boy's forehead and whispered, "I don't deserve your forgiveness, child, but if you can find it in your heart…please forgive me and know that the man who did this to you is gone."

After asking forgiveness, he stood and scanned the room to make sure none of his priests were sneaking about. The room remained empty and quiet. With a last look at the boy, he turned and crept to the front foyer.

Putting the memories behind him, he turned away from the corridor and faced the entryway. He lifted his arm to his eyes and wiped away the tears that brimmed there.

One last look through the peephole showed that none of the priests were near. With a short prayer to Vaspar, Piet Lithor cracked the front door open. Though the sound wasn't loud, the creak of the hinges reverberated through him like a hammer on a gong. He cringed and peeked through the crack to see if the priests heard the noise. Brother Rayne had fallen and struggled to push himself upright. His shoulders wobbled and tipped precariously to the side. Brother Foster had walked out of Piet Lithor's line of sight.

"Have faith in almighty Vaspar. He saved me once, and I doubt he did it just to let me die an hour later on my doorstep," he mumbled.

Piet Lithor opened the door enough to squeeze his portly body through. Brother Rayne struggled on his knees, hands in the grass, still working to push himself into a standing position. Lithor had seen him in this submissive position every day for the past seven years as the priests prayed together to Lord Vaspar. The memory both saddened and terrified him, reminding him that the man kneeling in the grass hadn't been a mindless killer twenty-four hours earlier.

He still couldn't find Brother Foster.

Cocking his head to the side and stretching as far as he could reach without leaving the safety of the entryway, Piet Lithor looked toward the front gate. He could see around the well, but even with it out of the way, the drizzle and his poor vision worked against him. The blurred portcullis may have been open, but the fuzzy shadows made it impossible to tell. He would just have to go and hope for the best.

He stepped into the drizzling rain and stopped. Five feet to his right, hidden by the edge of the entryway, stood Brother Foster. The hat-wearing priest no longer appeared ludicrous. His hands rose. His mouth opened in silent hunger.

Piet Lithor stumbled backwards and lifted the holy sword of Tyrmra between himself and the priest. The blade glowed with a foggy blue light and the handle quivered as if appalled by the abomination before it.

Brother Foster's head turned aside. His hands lifted to cover his face, as if ashamed of what he had become. Piet Lithor held the sword before him like a shield. His eyes shifted between the sick man and the other priest. Brother Foster's eyes followed him, but he never dropped his hands or turned his head.

Piet Lithor sidestepped around the priest until he stood between Brother Foster and the gate. He turned and ran.

His heavy frame bounced and jiggled. He hadn't moved so fast in years. Before he had run halfway to the well, he gasped for breath, pushing his free hand against the ache that stabbed into his side.

The pain became unbearable as he reached the gate. He wanted to stop and catch his breath, but he had to make every second count.

He turned to see if the priests followed. Brother Rayne, his bloodstained robes now filthy with mud and grass stains, stumbled toward him. Brother Foster followed close behind. Other priests, ones that Piet Lithor couldn't see from the entryway, shuffled through the yard in his direction. He knew each blank face that swayed toward him, and felt a twinge of betrayal. He had known them for years, and now they wanted his flesh, his blood, maybe even his soul. After all of the things he had done for them year after year, this was the payment he received.

He shook his head and pinched his lips together. *No*, he reminded himself. Some malady had taken them, made them into monsters. They couldn't control their actions. They needed prayer and forgiveness, not hatred. He took a deep breath and turned to the gate.

The portcullis blocked his exit.

He had never opened the portcullis before; that task belonged to Brother Craige, who must have succumbed to the illness before the task could be done. If Brother Craige could open the gate, then he shouldn't have a problem with it. He backed toward the wall, watching the priests as they lurched forward. If he could find the gate mechanism, he could still escape before they reached him.

As he turned, he noticed a small wooden door set into the support pillar of the gate, intricately carved in the likeness of his god. He opened the door with a pull on his god's nose, shaking his head at his own sacrilege. Behind the door sat a recess with a plate-sized steel wheel with a wooden handle at the top. *This is going to be easier than I thought.*

He held the sword behind him to keep the priests at bay as he reached in and pulled the handle. The wheel didn't move. He pushed it. The wheel still didn't move. He trembled as he looked over his shoulder, his heart firing rapidly in his chest. The priests shuffled toward him, but they had a ways to go before they would become a threat. Lithor leaned the sword against the wall and grabbed the wheel handle with both hands. He pushed again, and it began to move. The portcullis lifted an inch. Pushing the wheel took all of his strength. He fought to get the wheel to turn even one revolution. Footsteps at his back spurred him on. Sweat mixed with the constant drizzle as he turned the wheel until the portcullis sat a few feet above the ground, high enough for him to crawl beneath.

He pulled his hand from the wheel and it spun backwards, dropping the portcullis half a foot. He dove into the box and grabbed the handle with both hands.

"Oh blessed Vaspar, aid your humble priest." It was a statement he mouthed whenever a project exasperated him, and this particular chore had him exasperated beyond measure.

With both hands in place, he lowered his head to his sleeve to wipe some of the sweat and rain from his eyes. The damp sleeve didn't help.

Water splashed behind him. Piet Lithor's neck crackled as he twisted to look over his shoulder. Brother Rayne tottered thirty feet away. He needed to use the sword, but if he let the wheel go, he would be trapped. With teeth gritted together, he swung back to the wheel and looked for a latching mechanism. His gaze darted over the shadow-cloaked box, but he didn't see it. *Surely there is some way to latch this thing...* Suddenly, he saw it. The dark line of a bar flush against the side of the box. He let go of the wheel with one hand and slapped the bar down, wedging it against the handle. The portcullis dropped an inch and hung in place.

Piet Lithor didn't stop to congratulate himself. Driven by fear and necessity, he grasped the Sword of Tyrmra and wheeled around to face the threat that stumbled toward him. A blue glow erupted down the blade at Piet Lithor's touch. He swung the artifact up, creating a barrier between himself and Brother Rayne, a blue arc of light like the afterimage of lightning. The glow dissipated swiftly, but Brother Rayne cowered before the sword, turning his head aside and holding his hands before his eyes. Piet Lithor backed toward the portcullis.

When his shoulder touched the gate, he squatted down with the sword held before him. Behind Brother Rayne, the other priests advanced. With a final glance at the men he had known for years, Lithor lay on the ground and scooted beneath the gate. Gravel bit into his stomach while mud and grit stained the front of his white morning robe.

The bottom of the fence bit into his back, but he would happily have removed a layer of skin to put some distance between him and his priests.

Moments later, he stood on the other side of the portcullis, appalled at his filthy appearance. He reached up to wipe the grime from his robes and frowned. Mud covered his hand. With a sigh, he wiped the grime against his hip. *Better a dirty robe than having that foul muck on my skin.*

A hand stretched between the portcullis bars and raked his arm. He yelped and stumbled back.

Brother Rayne forced his head between the bars. His neck stretched out, and his teeth cracked together like a wolfhound on a chain. Lithor took another step back, then turned and ran up the tree-lined road as fast as his tired body could carry him. Before he lost sight of his home, he looked back. The priests crowded behind the portcullis, hands reaching through the iron bars like refugees begging for food. He didn't know whether to laugh or cry as he realized that none of them had the sense to crawl under the portcullis, even after seeing him do it.

Their ignorance brought a half-hearted smile to his lips. It vanished as he reminded himself that they were once his priests, his responsibility. Men who had broken bread with him, prayed and worshipped with him. They were priests of Vaspar the Just who had looked to the Piet for guidance. Some had aspirations that would never come to pass while others had simply taken joy in the service of their god. *Why have I survived while they didn't? Surely any one of them deserved to live more than I did.*

He shook his head in wonder.

Leaving his home behind, he continued on. He had to reach the duke's palace and report the horrid affliction of his priests. The duke would send guards to capture the sick priests, and hopefully, a cure could be found. If not, he would have to send a message to the order and have new priests brought in. He hated training new men. It would take months to show them how to perform their duties to his satisfaction.

Within minutes, he reached a fork in the road. He bent over and gasped for breath. His tired body begged for rest, but this business had to be taken care of as quickly as possible. He turned to the northeast road, toward the castle, and began walking. The south road led to the holy temple of Vaspar. He was intimately familiar with both roads.

Rain soaked his clothes, chilling him with each breath as the air wheezed in and out of his lungs. Soon the walls of Castle Renier appeared between the trees, gray in the drizzle-filled distance. Relief coursed through him. His pace quickened, though his feet ached and his calves felt tight as stones.

As the palace grew near, he noticed blurred forms wandering across the road. They moved back and forth along the wall. *Odd. I wonder what's brought so many people out on such a foul day?*

A guard stepped out of the woods and onto the road a stone's throw in front of him. Piet Lithor waved his arms and called in a breathless croak, "Guard…guard. I need your assistance!"

The man's head shot up. His arm lifted and his mouth opened wide to reveal blood-coated teeth. Piet Lithor stumbled backward. His relief dissolved like sugar in hot tea. His call not only gained the attention of the guard, but also a dozen others who stumbled in his direction. *No! This can't be happening. Has the entire world gone mad?*

With a cry worthy of any five-year-old girl, he turned and fled. Fear overrode his exhaustion. He forgot about his muddy robes and his pride as he ran, stumbling down the road. His generous bulk jiggled beneath his muddied robes like loose sausage within a mud-basted casing. He continued to blindly run through the drizzle as it grew into a downpour. The sword of Tyrmra was clasped in his hand and slapped his leg with each stride. His wet and filthy robes clung to him like a second skin, a discomfort he hardly noticed. He had to get away, somewhere safe, somewhere sane. Safe...*Is there such a place, a place where the deranged masses can't go?*

Vaspar. The holy temple of Vaspar. If the temple had fallen to corruption, all was lost.

Through the sheets of rain, ghostly outlines became visible on the road ahead—shambling, gray silhouettes.

Piet Lithor stumbled from the road and into the trees. Limbs and damp leaves slapped against him as he plowed through the underbrush. The foliage formed a canopy that lessened the downpour as he lumbered across the leaf-covered earth. His side threatened to burst and his lungs never seemed to get full enough. He refused to let the pain slow him down as he dodged around trees and over roots. The run through the forest shortened his distance to the temple. Within minutes, he broke through the underbrush and onto the open road.

The temple sat on a field of living green trimmed in carefully manicured shrubbery. Trees shrouded the structure, coating the beautiful stonework and stained glass in shadows. Lithor couldn't remember the building ever looking so ominous. Usually, the temple practically glowed with candles and torches. Brother Cylus made sure of that. The old priest took great pride in the stained glass, often saying, "The brighter, the better."

Between Lithor and the temple, a group of people stood. They formed a line at the edge of the community well, a popular gathering spot for the parishioners. They stared at the temple and swayed as if waiting in anticipation.

Lithor looked past the line of people. Within the temple, faces peered out through the narrow openings of the windows. Fear masked faces. He recognized Dray, the winemaker. His wide eyes stared out at the well. Lana, the wife of the blacksmith, said something to him and pointed to one of the well people. Dray ignored her.

Why don't the people at the well go into the temple? Piet Lithor didn't fool himself. The well people had obviously gone mad and even if they hadn't, he wouldn't chance it. Something about their calm stance didn't seem right. They stood as if held back by an invisible barrier. The thought nagged at him only a moment before he realized what it all meant. *Holy ground!* The ones at the well were inflicted by the vile curse and they couldn't approach the temple because it sat on consecrated soil. The ones inside were like him, normal and sane. That had to be it.

He took one last look at the human line standing behind the well and made his decision. Awkwardly holding the Sword of Tyrmra before him with both hands, he took a deep breath and ran toward the crowd of madmen. As he approached, the sword burst into blue luminescence. The crowd turned. Their blank eyes gazed into his very soul with a madness and hunger he never knew possible. He stumbled, but didn't slow as he crashed into their midst. Lithor barreled through, knocking one poor soul to the ground. He stormed past the invisible line, almost tripping as he stepped on the stomach of the fallen woman. He didn't slow or look down. Seconds later, he reached the steps. Behind him, he heard the mindless woman thrash against the ground. He looked over his shoulder. Water and mud splashed into the air as the woman convulsed. Her hands clawed at the sky and beat the ground.

He reached the door and pounded it with the pommel of the holy artifact.

Morbid curiosity forced him to turn to the thrashing woman. Her skin blistered and smoked.

The door opened. Hands pulled him into the temple.

The woman's convulsions subsided into weak flinches. Her skin dissolved over her skeleton and dripped to the ground in smoldering puddles.

"Thank Vaspar you made it here safely, Piet Lithor!" a tear filled voice said.

In front of the temple, the woman's flesh smoldered and dissolved away from a blackened skeleton.

Chapter 9

"The laws of man, rules society place upon itself in order to be called civilized, separate the human race from the other creatures of nature. Justice and fairness. These concepts don't apply in the real world, the fierce realm outside man's control. What should the world be like without the laws of man, only following the chaotic laws of nature, of the beasts of the wild?"

~Dokkien the Wise

Wellan's long strides ate up the distance as he walked to the war room to meet with Duke Renier. Exhaustion threatened to overtake him, but he had to tell the duke about the fall of his city.

Wellan spent a large portion of his powers in the battle at the open market, leaving smoldering corpses in his wake. Still, the dead had continued to come from every corner of the market, flowing from the nearby homes like a flood of ants taking down a wounded cricket. He fought a battle he couldn't win, so he ran, fleeing back to the castle walls. The undead had swarmed to every side of him, stumbling out of the forest and into the road.

He walked with his head tall and proud, but his march to the war room was a mild deception for the living. Drained. Exhausted. It wasn't very often he felt his age, but as joints creaked and his eyes blurred, he remembered how ancient he truly was. It took every bit of his will to maintain the prideful posture, but he couldn't show weariness, couldn't show fear. Fear was contagious, a plague of its own, but hope and pride could be spread almost as easily. He just had to maintain the farce a little longer.

His weary mind wandered, returning to the battle and the surprise he'd discovered once it ended.

The palace walls had risen above him at the end of the road. The duke's standard waved in the wind against gray skies. He was almost to the gate when the mystical energy burst over him. Its power radiated across his skin like a puff of sand in a gust of wind, abrasive and raw. He couldn't ignore the feeling. Wellan had turned and run through the woods, sidestepping the shambling undead that he could, blasting the ones that stood in his way. He had to know what had caused the phenomena.

He hadn't traveled far before he burst through the trees and saw Madame Rachelle. She lay in the middle of the street, face down, one arm over her head and the other tucked beneath her stomach. A child lay before her, an arrow fletching stuck from the girl's head like a barrette. Blood puddled beneath the child's cheek and wove through her blond hair. The undead closed in around Madame Rachelle. Within the palm of her open hand, a blue ember of magic glowed, dwindling before his eyes.

Only Wellan could see the smoldered power, and a spark of hope glimmered within him.

A brightly clad woman knelt over a half-conscious man. She pulled on his shoulders, trying to help him up. The man stumbled forward, dragging the girl with him as he fought to stand on legs that wouldn't support him.

Wellan hurled bursts of flame into the undead that surrounded Rachelle, using up the last of his power. Each roar of flame weakened him a fraction more. His flames no longer reached as far or burned as hot, though he remained a force to be reckoned with. He needed rest to rebuild his magical reserves.

Some of the undead burst into flame. Others stepped back from the heat. A few were thrown from their feet by the force of the concussions. The moment a gap opened in the undead mob, he ran to Rachelle and scooped her into his arms. He wore a scowl of determination as he turned to the colorfully clad woman and bellowed, "Come with me."

She didn't argue. Tears glazed her eyes as she nodded and gripped the man tighter. The woman held the man upright and stumbled forward as they followed Wellan to the castle gates. The dead shuffled behind in pursuit, block by block fading further into the drizzling rain.

They soon outdistanced the shambling corpses and reached the gate. The guard's hands trembled as he worked to open the gate.

Black smoke billowed into the sky from behind the palace walls. The smell of burning wood and searing flesh filled the air, an ominous sign that things had changed in his short time away from the palace.

The guard slammed the gate shut the moment they passed through. It shook as iron met iron. He cringed as the noise reverberated in the entryway like a gong.

Wellan turned to the guard as he passed and said, "Make sure that door stays shut and don't let anyone else through."

"My lord wizard, what if someone..."

A hand pushed through the small gate window. It slapped the back of the guard's armor in a pathetic attempt to pull him to the gate. The man leapt forward with a girlish screech and turned, sword half drawn.

"What the bloody hell..."

Wellan stopped just long enough to turn and nod his head at the gore-coated arm. "That's all there is out there. Make sure they stay on that side of the wall."

Wellan and his companions walked to Castle Renier. In the courtyard, several piles of corpses burned. Arms and legs crackled like firewood. Dead eyes stared out from the flames. The makeshift funeral pyres sent black smoke and the sweet aroma of cooked meat into the air. Guards dragged mangled bodies across the yard. Servants held one another as tears streamed down their faces.

Wellan wanted to vomit.

He still carried Rachelle, though his legs burned and felt like they would give out at any second.

The woman supported the man. Her arm wrapped around his waist, his arm crooked around her shoulder. He seemed to be improving, though still dazed and wobbly. They walked in silence, too stunned to speak, too tired to even try.

When they reached the palace foyer, the duke's personal servants greeted him with sullen glances, huddled together in the main entranceway. Some cried and wailed while others stood quietly to the sides. They all looked to Wellan, waiting to hear what was happening to their beloved city.

Dom Aubrey, the lead house caretaker, questioned Wellan. The other servants stood behind her and listened. Though cantankerous, Wellan liked Dom Aubrey. She was a short and stocky woman. Her flaming red hair, meticulously bound into a hair net, matched her fiery personality. At times, the woman could be overbearing, but she meant well, a mother hen for the servants of the palace. All questions ceased when she noticed the injured woman in Wellan's arms and the colorfully dressed girl supporting the groggy man. She snapped her fingers and ordered the servants to find a spare room and a healer. She then ordered one of the male servants to take Rachelle from Wellan's arms, and another to help the woman with her burden. Wellan watched them until they disappeared around a bend in the hallway.

He never answered any of Dom Aubrey's questions. He didn't know how. Instead, he thanked her and walked down another corridor, the one leading to the war room.

As Wellan pushed open the heavy wooden door, he thought about Rachelle and what had caused the outburst of power. He frowned. He didn't have time for distractions. Madame Rachelle's power was a matter for later, when time allowed. For now, he had to meet with his duke.

Duke Renier looked up from a great oak table as Wellan walked through the open doors. Spread out before him was a city map. The duke looked angry and tired. Crow's feet trailed from the corner of his eyes, giving him the appearance of a much older man. A middle-aged guard stood next to the duke. The man straightened and stared at Wellan as he walked through the door, fear and self-doubt evident in his wide eyes.

The duke nodded to the guard. "That will be all, General Rancor."

The young man stumbled over his own feet as he tried to choose between saluting the duke and leaving the room. He performed a clumsy combination of both and backed out of the room, pulling the doors shut behind him.

Wellan waited until the door closed, then turned to the duke and frowned. "General Rancor?"

Duke Renier gave Wellan a weary sigh and shook his head. "He's the highest ranking...living soldier I've been able to find. A hell of a promotion, too, from major to general in one fell swoop." He stooped over the table, his shoulders bunched in rage and his hands balled into fists, knuckles white with pressure. "What are we to do, Wellan? In just a few short hours, this...this plague has swept through my city, killing everyone without mercy. Dead! Dead for a short time and then they are back. Back to...to..."

Apparently, a lot had happened in Wellan's short absence.

The duke turned and faced Wellan, eyes swollen, red and glossy. "Some died right here in the castle. Here in my own home. We tried to find help, but even as we did, they came back. Not as the men they were, but as maniacs, intent on killing...and eating those they killed!"

Wellan remained quiet and let his friend speak, allowing him to release the anger and frustration that filled his soul. "I had to kill my own men, Wellan. I had to cut them up with the very sword that is sworn to protect them. Even that didn't stop them. I had to remove their heads." He wailed. "I had to remove their heads and still they snapped like rabid dogs." Duke Renier looked to the ceiling with his lips pinched tight. "I then had to order the rest of my men, the ones who weren't afflicted, to kill their comrades, decapitate them and burn the bodies. Is *this* what my city has come to? Is *this* where I have led my people?" He looked down at the table and raised a hand to wipe his eyes. A sob shook his shoulders. "Is this what I've done with the responsibility that I've been entrusted with, my friend?"

Wellan grasped the duke's shoulder and squeezed. His voice shook as he whispered, "No, my friend. This was unavoidable, an unprovoked attack. You had no way to know this would happen, and no way to defend against it."

Duke Renier lifted his head and stared at the far wall, his voice hardening with resolve. "What are you saying, Wellan? Who attacked my city, my people?" His gaze locked onto Wellan's.

Wellan returned his stare. "I don't know, my lord, but this has the stench of necromancy. I fought those creatures by the Open Market almost an hour ago, and I could feel the dark power radiating from their souls. This is no natural disease. It's a thing of darkness and magic."

∞ ∞ ∞ ∞

"So...how do you plan to get to the castle?" Horn asked the question that raced through everyone's mind. "I mean, we can't just barge out there, swords swinging. Look at 'em all! There's enough to handle right here in the trainin' yard where there ain't supposed to be civilians. Gods only know how many is out on the streets. Stiles, you know I ain't scared o'nothin', but fightin' a whole city is suicide."

Stiles rubbed his temples as if that could ease his pounding headache. They had been waiting for an hour, watching as people roamed around the training yard like sleep walkers. Some bore horrendous wounds, fatal wounds—bloody arm stumps and huge bite-sized chunks of flesh missing. Oddly, the wounds didn't seem to bleed. Others appeared relatively sound other than the glazed look in their eyes and the lack of purpose to their walk.

The city was quiet. Only the gusts of wind and rain could be heard, along with an occasional terror-filled shriek that tore through the city. The distant screams made Stiles think of the cry of a cat in the deep woods or the screech of an eagle in the far off distance. Some of the shrieks cut through the air from just beyond the training yard wall, destroying the illusion that the horror happened somewhere else, distant from them. The pain and terror of the close screams sent a shiver of ice down Stiles' spine.

Each time the men heard a wail, they glanced at one another without saying a word, their eyes wide, their lips pinched tight. None of the noises sounded like an organized attack, no shouts of command, no roars of victory. Only the occasional distant shrills of terror.

They couldn't remain in the dungeon foyer, but he didn't know if they could make it anywhere else. They would be going to the castle blindly, without enough information to create a solid plan, but it couldn't be helped.

"This is what we're going to do." Crouching below the window had begun to hurt his back. He straightened, careful to stay to the side of the opening while looking at each of the men. "Ash, Wolf, Tarl, Arolyn, and Owl. You are the best with the bows, so grab all the arrows you can find in the storage lockers and bring them with you. We're going out that door in a diamond formation with the archers at the points. They will drop the...uh..." Stiles didn't know what to call the enemy. Were they civilians? Infected? Residents? What could he call a hostile force that had been friends, neighbors and loved ones only hours before? *No. I need to be honest with myself and the men. At this point, it's us or them.* "...enemy if they get within forty feet. We will warn them off at fifty. If they continue to advance, then we'll have no choice but to treat them as hostile."

The men looked at one another, each set of eyes contacting another, silently asking if they could do it, wondering if there could be some alternative to what they were about to do. No one thought about making a smart comment or cracking a joke; most had never had to kill anyone before.

Without saying a word, the guards crawled deeper into the room and returned moments later with their borrowed bows and a meager supply of arrows. Stiles gathered everyone at the door. The anticipation and fear in the room became palpable as they crouched around him in silence, careful to stay below the windowsill and out of sight. Stiles' heart thrummed in his chest. Every muscle in his body tensed with anxiety. His arm froze with his hand on the door handle. Once the door opened, there would be no turning back. His mind raced through the possibility of consequences, but it had to be done. They had no other options.

He took a deep breath and let it out in a slow hiss. Tension eased as his lungs deflated. Before the anxiety could return, he turned the handle and opened the door.

None of the people in the training yard turned their way until the group had passed through the door and took their positions. The archers formed the points of their crude diamond formation while the other men stood between them with weapons drawn. Oswald and Gorney took position in the center; Gorney, because of his injury, and Oswald on the premise of helping Gorney, though in reality he was simply too drunk to hold a decent formation.

The men advanced through the yard at a steady pace. Their swords trembled. Horn's axe jumped back and forth between his hands. They hadn't been trained for this; maybe a lecture or two on crowd control, but not for this.

Brown puddles littered the yard. As the men splashed forward, the slack-jawed intruders changed their direction and maneuvered toward the guards from all directions. Their feet slid through mud, leaving jagged grooves behind them.

Within seconds, the formation halted as a woman advanced within fifty feet of the guards, blocking their path to the gate. The archers lined their arrows on her. Their eyes darted back and forth, watching the other people gathering closer.

"Ma'am, I order you to halt!" Stiles impressed himself. His voice didn't quake, though fear threatened to overtake him.

The woman shuffled forward. Her long nightshirt trailed through the mud. Her knees didn't bend as she stepped. She reminded Stiles of a wooden puppet controlled by invisible strings. The scene was all too familiar, but on a much wider scale. Stiles thought back to the leper. Drummen had tried to stop them verbally, but his commands fell on deaf ears. Even knowing the woman's newfound nature, he still couldn't bring himself to give the order to shoot her. Only hours ago, she had been someone's sister or mother, a loving daughter or wife.

The gap closed by another ten feet, bringing her into the agreed upon kill zone.

"Halt!" A mumbled "please" that only he could hear crawled its way from a throat that felt tight and dry with anxiety. *I don't want to kill you. Please don't make me kill you.*

She stumbled forward, closing the gap by another ten feet. Stiles froze; his mind worked frantically to find a solution that didn't involve ordering the men to shoot an arrow through her skull. *It's a woman. I can't order the men to shoot a defenseless...*

An arrow punched through her chest. She stumbled backwards. Her head twitched and her arms jerked, but she continued to advance as though nothing had happened.

As if the first arrow were an order to fire, three more sliced through the air. Fletchings suddenly appeared in her chest, pointing in different directions. One punched through her arm, pinning it to her side. The wounds were nearly bloodless, reminding Stiles of the dummies they often trained with. She tipped back, almost fell, and then resumed her march forward.

The arrows punched through Stiles' fear, converting it to anger. He turned and shouted, "Who fired without an order?"

Ash stepped forward, nocking another arrow. His ice blue eyes looked upon Stiles with disdain. "Me, *sir*." The sir hissed out and dripped with sarcasm.

"Uh...sir?" Horn's deep voice went unnoticed as the two men faced off.

"You don't do a damn thing from now on without an order from me. You got that?"

"Sir?" A small word, yet filled with frantic implications.

Ash pulled the arrow back, forming a V in the bow-string. "You weren't gonna give that order. You..."

A scream tore through the training yard, redirecting Stiles' attention.

Oswald broke rank and ran at the arrow-pierced woman, his sword drawn, held high over his head. As he neared, the woman raised her arms to grasp him. The arrow-pierced arm shook then pulled free from her torso. The arrow ripped flesh and scraped bone on its way out. The old drunk ignored her and brought his sword down on the crown of her head with a crack of bone and spray of blood. As she dropped to her knees, he yanked his sword free and ran past the collapsing woman, toward the gate in a screaming frenzy.

Oswald's violence cut through the men like a wolf's howl in a herd of sheep. Five of the fifteen guards broke ranks and ran behind the drunkard, their weapons forgotten in their white-knuckled grip as they sprinted for the gate.

Stiles froze, taken by surprise at the turn of events. Though his body refused to move, his mind worked to figure out another way to gain control of the situation.

The five men zigzagged through the people, driven by panic like cattle stampeding through a crowded city. Ash released another arrow into a man who had gotten too close to what remained of the guards' formation. The other men turned to Stiles. They needed orders, direction. His mouth opened, but no words came forth. He didn't know what to do.

Stiles remained frozen with indecision as Oswald ran through the gate, screaming and babbling as he disappeared behind the wall.

A piercing scream tore through the drizzle. The men running behind Oswald halted. They saw something that Stiles couldn't, something he knew he didn't want to see. They raised their weapons as they looked back and forth along the opening of the gate. Their eyes widened, and their mouths opened in silent terror.

People poured through the gate like water released from a dam. Many shuffled through the opening dressed in their nightclothes, some with no clothes at all. Others wore the everyday outfits of merchants, the sparse clothing of dock workers and the long dresses of wives. They trampled over one another in their mindless haste to reach the guards. A single thing remained common—blood covered their mouths and chests regardless of their attire or social status.

The guards at the gate stepped back, overwhelmed by the mass of clawing flesh, thrown into the thick of battle without a chance to retreat.

The remaining guards didn't wait for a command from Stiles. They followed Ash as he dropped his bow and ran forward with sword in hand to help the overwhelmed men at the gate.

Stiles stood frozen as Ash sliced his way toward the men with the grace of a master swordsman. Shame washed over him as he watched the man cut his way to the gate. Stiles had command, but Ash held the men's respect. He pushed his doubts and shame to the back of his mind and drew his sword to join his men in battle.

He dodged the stumbling civilians and raced to the gate. He wanted to slice through them as Ash did, but he didn't have the heart for that sort of violence, nor did he have Ash's skill with the blade. He knew he would have to kill to get to the castle, but he would avoid killing until he had no other choice.

As he neared the gate, he saw how pointless the struggle was. Hundreds of deranged men, women and even children funneled through the opening. Their blank eyes held no fear of the men who slashed and hacked a bloody trail through their midst, a bloody trail where there were few real casualties. Men and women took disemboweling slashes and continued to advance. Arms were severed from bodies, but they stumbled on. Some lost legs, yet they crawled forward though the blades as the guards hacked their numbers to pieces. His men didn't stand a chance against such a numerous and relentless enemy.

He stopped, looking over the muddy training field for other options. There had to be another way, something he hadn't thought of yet. He saw the short stone fence facing the road, the huge wall protecting the outer courtyard of the castle and the stony face of the Barclave Mountain blocking off everything to the north. Inside the training yard, large stakes stubbed out of the ground like saplings and straw dummies stood like scarecrows. The guardhouse merged into the side of the mountain. The entrance they'd come from that led to the dungeon, but nothing that would save them.

Giving up hope, Stiles turned to join the battle when he saw them. Soldiers ran along the top of the castle's outer wall, ropes coiled in their hands. His world had changed so drastically in the last few hours that he didn't associate the men with an escape, but when they stopped and unrolled the ropes down the side of the wall, hope returned.

He spun toward his men, mouth open to sound the retreat. His voice died in his throat as he saw Migel fall.

One of the contaminated, legless and dragging its bloody thigh stumps through the mud behind him, crawled forward and grabbed the guard by his ankles. Hands grasped his arms and head as Migel fell into the crowd. He screamed as they pulled him into the mass of bodies and out of sight.

"Fall back! Fall back!" Stiles screamed.

The guards stepped back, out of the people's reach, then turned and ran toward Stiles. Only Ash and Horn continued the battle, giving the others time to gain distance between them and the growing crowd.

Gorney also stayed behind, but not by choice. He turned to run, made three wobbly steps and fell in the muddy yard. The crowd pounced on him. They pulled his limbs in separate directions. They gnawed at his legs as they tried to bite through the thin leather that protected him. Blood gushed from his arms as their teeth sank through skin and tore away muscle. Gorney screeched as they pulled his arms out of their sockets. Spurred on by the scream, they pulled harder until his flesh ripped and blood sprayed the ground. The human tug of war ended. The ones in front fought over his severed arms while the others dragged him backwards through the mud until he became lost in the maw of gray, thrashing flesh. He looked sick and dazed, like a man too far gone to care.

The guards dashed past Stiles as he stood and watched Ash and Horn. Ash's blade slashed and arced through flesh with amazing speed and agility while Horn's axe, the one he jokingly referred to as his Cleaver of Death, tore through meat and bone with all the force the huge man could wield.

Stiles ran to them screaming, "Ash! Horn! Fall back!"

They rent and tore into the horde like madmen. Blood sprayed into the air around them, adding a splash of red to the drizzle.

Stiles had almost reached them when Ash bellowed, "Okay, Horn. That should buy us enough time. Let's go."

He slashed at the flailing arms one last time then turned and ran toward Stiles. Horn's battle with the crowd remained too intense for him to simply turn and run. He stepped back, but a hand reached out and grabbed his breastplate.

Stiles' legs wouldn't move as he stood by and watched. He silently formed the word "run" over and over again as Horn turned back to the mass of people. They were too numerous for Horn to fight alone. A dozen hands reached out and grasped him, pulling the beefy man further into their midst. He roared and raised his axe to slice off the arms that prevented his escape, but the mob had gotten inside Horn's defenses, too close for him to properly use the bulky weapon. Another hand grabbed his arm, further hindering him. More of the wretched beings surged forward, burying him in a pile of flesh. The people grasped and tore at the giant man, ripping at his skin with their bare hands and teeth.

"No!" Ash screamed. Stiles reached out and grabbed Ash, stopping the guard from throwing his life away.

Ash jerked his arm free of Stiles' grip and fought like a caged tiger.

A roar ripped through the air.

Horn pushed himself to his feet. People clung to his bloody armor. Teeth sank into his neck. Others bit chunks of meat from his arms and legs. Stiles watched in horror as they began devouring him alive. Horn made two hard fought steps forward then collapsed to the earth under a mound of thrashing, biting bodies.

"It's too late, Ash. We can't save him."

Ash glared at Stiles. Hate burned from his eyes. His nostrils flared with anger and battle lust. He didn't say a word. Instead, he shoved Stiles back and ran for the castle wall.

Stiles turned to the heap of bodies covering his comrade. He watched Horn's final convulsions as they tore him apart. His body twitched under the retched flesh. The others swarmed around the pile, like a stream of water flowing around a stone.

He ran for the ropes.

Most of the men stood safely on the top of the wall. Four others climbed the two ropes while Ash waited his turn at the bottom. He glared at Stiles as he jogged up to the other rope.

"You couldn't have saved him."

"Shut up," growled Ash.

Stiles shook his head as he grabbed the rope and began climbing to the safety of the castle wall.

Chapter 10

"The party's over, the night's done.
Let's go home, we've had our fun."
~A popular bard closing

Shannai stood in the back corner of the room, arms folded across her chest. She leaned against the wall and studied the sleeping woman. She waited in the shadows, not wanting the woman to see her when she awakened. The woman was dangerous. She knew that the moment the witch had used magic, throwing her brother thirty feet through the air. Shannai also suspected why the woman had done it, but she needed to talk to her to know for certain. Things would need to be patched up if her suspicions were correct.

She couldn't believe how bad everything had gotten. The whole city, lost. Shannai and her brother trapped within the palace, unsure what tomorrow would bring.

She and Marchas, her older brother, had been in Renier for almost a week. They entertained the crowds at the local taverns with their music and stories. They were bards. She sang while her brother played the mandolin. He often blended in a wild story or two, acting out the parts and captivating the audience with his performance. Their life was unlike any other. No day-to-day job for them. No family to root them to any one spot. They were free in a way that few people could ever imagine.

She and her brother received coins for doing things they loved to do. Every night they danced at the center of a party. They didn't pay homage to any man, god, or employer. They lived a free life, and she thought they held a firm grasp on their destiny. That misconception had faded away in the mid morning hours when they woke up to a city of the dead.

Being bards, they kept late hours and slept late into the mornings, lying in rented beds until lunchtime. The morning the city died was no different, except for the piercing scream that woke her at mid-morning, several hours before her usual lunchtime awakening.

Her eyes had snapped open. Her hand darted to the dagger tucked beneath the pillow as she listened for more noises. Silence. She released the dagger and sat up. It must have only been a dream. Hell of a way to wake up, though.

Marchas lay in the bed next to hers. His growling snores attested to the amount of alcohol he had consumed the night before. There would be no getting back to sleep with that ruckus filling the room.

If his snoring is gonna keep me awake then he's getting up too, Shannai thought. Her lips twisted into a lopsided smirk. She reached for the water pitcher on the nightstand. Only a little liquid remained, sloshing in the bottom of the pitcher, but she slung the water at him anyway. She aimed for his face, but missed, sprinkling his bare chest and blanket. The rhythm of his snoring quickened into a series of rapid snorts then grew louder as the water soaked through his blanket, but he remained fast asleep. Her smirk turned into a frown. *Guess I'm gonna have to do this the hard way.*

Picking up one of her boots from the side of the bed, she leaned back and tossed it at Marchas' head. His snoring became a growling snarl as he sprang up. He held a dagger in front of him, wide-awake and ready to combat thieves.

"Rise and shine, you lazy bastard!" Though the words sounded harsh, her mischievous smile let him know she didn't mean it.

He rubbed the back of his head in feigned hurt and replied, "What did you get me up for? We don't have to be anywhere until this evening." He stretched and rubbed his goatee.

"Had a nightmare that woke me up, and I couldn't fall back to sleep on account of your snoring. Figured this would be a good morning to see why everyone raves about breakfast."

"Had it once. Trust me, it ain't all that special." He grinned, tossing her boot back to her.

Fifteen minutes later, dressed in their colorful gypsy clothes, they walked down the stairs to see what the inn-keeper served for breakfast. Shannai wasn't fond of the brightly-colored clothing. Her tastes ran more toward earthy browns and shades of gray. Her outfit consisted of red and purple stripes. Marchas wore his yellow and or-ange outfit. She often called it his squash clothes. She wore the outfit because the clothing announced her occupation as a bard and often brought unlikely clients to them.

The main room of the inn contrasted with its appearance from the night before, empty of both patrons and noises. The sweet smoked aroma of bacon filled the air. It piqued her hunger and made her wonder why she didn't eat breakfast more often.

Marchas took a seat at one of the small tables, looked around the room and commented, "Sure doesn't look like it did last night, does it?"

"Nope, but it smells better. I didn't realize how hungry I was."

"Yeah, it's been a while since I chowed on any bacon. I remember that aroma, though. Smell goooood!" He smacked his lips.

Shannai laughed. She leaned back in her chair until only the back legs supported her, and looked into the kitchen. She wanted to catch the attention of Bos Talle, the tavern owner. Her laughter ceased. A frown took its place as she saw smoke drifting through the kitchen.

"What's wrong?"

She shrugged and leaned her chair back down. "I don't guess it's anything. There's just a lot of smoke in the kitchen. I guess they burned something."

Marchas propped his elbow on the table and supported his chin on his hand. "Maybe that's why nobody's out here yet to serve us breakfast?"

"I'm sure..."

Shannai jumped in her seat as metal crashed together in the kitchen. She leaned back again, hoping to see what had fallen.

Shannai looked at Marchas. He began to shrug, but as his shoulders rose, his eyes widened in shock. She turned her attention back to the kitchen.

Bos Talle lumbered through the doorway; his apron trailed flames, and a frying pan dangled from his left hand. Grease dripped onto the wooden floor. He didn't seem to care about the flames, or the slimy puddles of grease that marred his clean floor.

Marchas leapt from his seat and ran to Bos Talle. He knocked the portly man to the floor. Burnt cloth and seared flesh replaced the smell of bacon. Shannai remained in her seat, frozen in shock by the flaming innkeeper. When Bos Talle hit the floor, her brother grabbed him and rolled him back and forth, putting out the fire. She breathed a sigh of relief as the flames flickered and died. Smoke drifted through the air in a thin fog.

Her relief vanished as the frying pan clattered to the floor and Bos Talle grabbed Marchas' arm, his teeth closing around the colorful sleeve. The material ripped away as Marchas leapt from the ground. He backed away, leaving a pumpkin-colored tube of cloth dangling from the innkeeper's mouth. Bos Talle's jaws opened wide and the cloth fell to the floor as the man pushed himself off the ground.

Marchas' voice shook as he asked, "Bos Talle, are you okay?"

The man didn't reply. His mouth opened. A trail of thick saliva dribbled down his stubbled chin.

"What's wrong with him?" Shannai screamed to her brother.

Marchas' turned, perhaps to give her one of his flippant replies, but before he could say anything, Bos Talle lunged and grabbed him by the shoulders, his head darting forward to take a bite out of her brother's neck. Marchas' hand flashed up. He grabbed the innkeeper by the throat and held his head back, inches away from his neck. His other hand slapped the bar, blindly looking for a weapon. Before Shannai could run to Marchas' aid, his hand grasped the neck of a jug. He swung it around, shattering it against the man's temple. Shards of pottery slit his skin and water sprayed Bos Talle's face. He crashed to the floor without a groan.

The innkeeper pushed himself up until he stood on wobbly legs.

Her brother screamed, "Stay back!"

Bos Talle reached for Marchas. Her brother's foot lashed out. His boot, orange with yellow stitching, caught the man under the chin. He crashed backward in a spray of blood and teeth. The innkeeper lay on the floor facing the ceiling, neck turned at an impossible angle. His mouth opened and closed like a fish pulled from the water as his eyes rolled around the room and fixed on Marchas. Bos Talle's tongue twitched out, past his lips. Jaws slammed shut, nearly biting the thick flesh in half as blood squirted across his nose and dribbled from the corners of his mouth.

Her brother stepped back. His eyes locked with Bos Talle's, blank and cloudy. Disgust contorted Marchas' features.

Shannai's stomach churned, and she had to look away.

Marchas stared at the innkeeper and whispered, "Let's get our stuff. We're getting out of here."

"What happened to him? Why did he attack you like that?"

"Don't know."

"Are you okay? Did he bite you?"

Marchas turned to her. His usually happy face was hard with resolve. His nostrils flared and he growled, "Quit asking so many damned questions, Shannai. We have to get out of this city, and we have to do it quickly, before somebody stops us."

Shannai's eyes blurred. Tears glazed her pupils. "It was self defense. He attacked you."

He looked back at the innkeeper, and his voice cracked. "We are roving bards, gypsies as far as the law is concerned. Do you think for one minute that they aren't gonna punish me for this? I just killed a city Bos, a respected merchant. Now, let's get our stuff and go."

"But, they can't..."

His voice rose almost to a shout. "They can and they will."

He turned and ran up the stairs. Shannai stared at the innkeeper. His head lay in a pool of slowly coagulating blood, his ruined mouth opened and closed, chewing on her from the floor. She looked up the stairs and shook her head. She had to trust her brother. Marchas always knew what was best for them. She wiped the tears that crested at the edge of her eyes and followed her brother up the stairs to get her things.

It only took a few moments to gather their meager belongings, then they raced back down the stairs and opened the front door. Marchas stopped in the doorway.

Shannai adjusted the straps on her pack and asked, "What's wrong? Why are you stopping?"

"There's nobody on the streets."

"Isn't that a good thing?"

He shook his head, eyes never leaving the silent road. Water stood in potholes, reflecting the cloudy sky. "Yeah, normally it would be, but something just doesn't seem right about this." With a shrug, he stepped into the street. She followed close behind, looking from side to side, but seeing no one.

Other than the wind whipping through the empty road and the drip of water from the drizzle, the city sat eerily silent. Their boots clicked against the wet stone as they traveled through the streets. They walked close to the buildings and under the eaves; staying out of sight and the weather. As they crossed an alleyway, Shannai glanced between the stone walls. A black cloud of smoke rose in the distance, deep within the forest of buildings. She stopped her brother and pointed. He glanced at it and shrugged. *Not our problem.*

A splash drew their attention. A man stumbled across the road, staggering in their direction like an early morning drunkard. The drizzle made him look like a gray silhouette. He approached another ten feet before Marchas stepped back, pulling Shannai behind him. The man's throat glistened red around a hole where his Adam's apple had once been. Tendons and flesh worked up and down within the bloody cavern. His mouth hung open. His eyes, their moist shine coated in a dull film, stared at them. His stiff movements reminded Shannai of Bos Talle.

Marchas kept his focus on the stranger as he reached back and grasped her arm, his grip painfully tight. He pulled her to him as he raced under the eaves, away from the grisly sight. The man followed, but his wobbly gait couldn't keep up. Within moments, he became a faint shadow within the drizzle.

After running several blocks, Shannai stopped. "What's going on, Marchas?"

He shook his head and ran his fingers through his damp hair. "I don't know, but something is seriously wrong." His gaze moved from her to a nearby shop. Carved into the door was the symbol of a bow and knife, painted in red and black—a weapon smith.

He walked to the store, put his hand on the handle and turned to her. "I think that this would be a good time to get some better weapons."

Stopping didn't seem like one of his better ideas, but she followed him into the store anyway. She ran into his back as he paused in the doorway. Her mouth opened to grumble a complaint, but she froze as she looked around his shoulder.

A thin man slumped over the counter. His bald crown glowed like a boiled egg in the dim light; his face lay in a pool of thick blood. She put her hand over her mouth to stifle a scream. The world swam around her, and she didn't know if she were about to vomit or pass out.

Marchas pulled her through the door and pushed it shut, drawing her focus from the man and allowing her to regain her bearings. "Stay right there," he said, and strode to the counter.

He placed the back of his hand in front of the man's mouth. "He's dead. It looks like he almost turned himself inside out with his vomiting."

She still had her hand over her mouth as she stared at the ceiling, trying not to look at the bloody sight, fighting not to be sick. She studied the wooden planks above her to focus on something besides the bloody chunks that covered the counter, but even with her hand over her mouth, she could smell the meaty aroma, the man's breakfast sautéed in blood. She became thankful she had missed eating breakfast.

Shannai observed her brother as he moved away from the body. Several short bows hung from the wall at the far end of the counter. He grabbed two of them, then ran to another wall, grasped two empty quivers, and filled them from a barrel of arrows sitting by the counter.

She didn't say a word as he strung the bows, and neither did he. She knew by his silence that he was brooding about what needed to be done. Her brother was a kind and jovial man, but when stressed, he could quickly become vicious with his comments. She decided to let him work instead of starting a fight.

He handed her one of the bows and a cylinder of quivers, then slung the other over his back. She shouldered the quivers, but kept the bow in her hands. She didn't want to waste any time if she needed it.

He either didn't notice her nausea or pretended not to. *Yeah, he noticed. Marchas doesn't miss anything. He just can't deal with that right now on top of everything else. I should follow his lead and get my act together.*

On the way out, he stopped and grabbed a sword prominently displayed with a plaque on the wall. The blade was a beauty. Runes engraved each side of the blood groove. The hilt had been painstakingly crafted in a wolf motif. Bronze fangs held the blade within the wolf's maw. The handle formed the wolf's neck covered in black leather. The shopkeeper obviously had taken pride in the sword, enough pride to prevent Marchas from ever having enough coin to purchase it.

He pulled the blade down from the wall, admiring its craftsmanship. With a quick glance at Shannai, he grabbed a sheath, pushed the sword inside, and buckled it around his waist.

Neither she nor Marchas had stolen anything since their young days as street urchins; even then it had only been to survive. Considering their current situation, she couldn't fault her brother for snatching the blade. They had returned to survival mode.

The wet streets remained silent as they stepped out of the shop.

"We'll go to the South Gate. It's the closest one I know of," Marchas whispered over his shoulder and began walking, staying near the buildings.

Shannai looked at the quiet structures, and a nervous flutter crept into her stomach. She wanted to cower in some safe and hidden spot where nobody could find her. Cower there and never leave. The crack of stiff joints made her look back into the shop. The storekeeper stood, his face a blood-caked mess. Blood and gory chunks clung to his beard and cheek. He looked around his shop like someone waking from a dream. His eyes fixed on her. His mouth opened and his arms rose. He stumbled forward.

She gasped and grabbed the door, slamming it shut with a thunderous bang.

Marchas twisted around. "What in the hell did you do that for?"

"The shopkeeper...he...he got up...he was coming for me...he..."

The anger in Marchas' face melted away. His hand grasped hers with a reassuring squeeze as he turned around and pulled her behind him. They continued, hand in hand, just like they had as children. Behind them something slammed against the door. Shannai turned, not slowing down as her brother dragged her along. The weapon smith's door rattled in its frame as something pounded on it from the inside.

Marchas didn't turn, ignoring the sound. Shannai bit her lip and followed close behind.

Something was wrong in Renier, seriously wrong. The fluttering in her stomach grew with every step until she thought she would freeze with terror. She saw a ghoul in every shadow, a walking corpse in every alley, felt a cold hand grasp the back of her neck with each gust of wind. They needed to get out of the city as quickly as possible. She released her brother's hand. His reassuring gesture would only slow them down.

They had only gone two blocks before a noise caught her attention. She stopped. Seconds later, Marchas halted and turned. A *what the hell's wrong now?* look covered his face. She put her finger to her lips and cocked her head to the side, listening.

A faint clanking, the sound of a muffled bell, drifted through the air. The cowbell sound repeated again and again. It grew louder with each recurrence. Shannai frowned at her brother, who shrugged and looked into the distance, toward the odd noise.

As the sound grew, Marchas stepped forward, pulled his bow from his shoulder and notched an arrow. He nodded to Shannai to do the same.

With arrows notched and pointed at the ground, they waited.

Shapes took form in the misty rain. The outline of the damned stumbled forward. They became clearer as the group marched toward Shannai and her brother. A dozen pale bodies shuffled through the drizzle. The bell noise became obvious as an indentured servant, scarred with the half moon and triangle shoulder branding of a slave, shuffled with the crowd. A length of chain shackled to his leg was dragging behind him.

Marchas raised his bow, then lowered it. He grabbed Shannai by the elbow and pulled her away from the slow-moving mob. "There's got to be a better way than this! I'm not shooting anybody till I have to. We run. We run till we don't have a choice, then we'll do what we have to do."

Shannai nodded; fear filled her with anxious energy as though chipmunks were scampering in her stomach. Tears clouded her vision.

Her memories became a blur of rain, running, and terror as her brother led her through the city. The crowds of people forced them to move deeper into the metropolis, north, toward the Barclave Mountain and Castle Renier. Her brain blocked out everything around her, turning her into a sleepwalker with one thing in mind—following Marchas. She could ignore the corrupted humanity around her. She could pretend the city wasn't a lair for the damned. She could just continue to follow her brother and everything would be all right. He would take care of her. He always did. Good old Marchas—Shannai's big brother, protector, and best friend. She blocked everything out except taking her next step...

"Don't just sit there. Run!" Her brother's voice burst through her half conscious mind with explosive force, breaking her from her stupor. At first she thought he screamed at her, but he faced away, toward a lady sitting in the middle of the road. The woman cradled a small child in her arms.

Marchas screamed at the lady as he nocked another arrow.

Shannai blinked. It all felt like a dream. *Why is Marchas nocking another arrow? What happened to the arrow he already had?* Minutes had passed, events had transpired, and she had no recollection of them. Tears streamed down her face as she raised her bow and released an arrow into the crowd. She didn't look to see whom she hit, if she even hit anyone. As soon as the shaft left her bow, her gaze focused on the weapon and she nocked another arrow.

Suddenly, everything changed. A scream. A burst of blue light. Her brother flew through the air.

Her memories blurred as her eyes filled with tears. When she blinked them away, she stood back in the room with the witch woman, the woman who could shoot bursts of power from her fingertips.

How did you do that? she asked herself as she stared at the sleeping woman.

Just when she thought they were about to be initiated into the ranks of the dead, the wizard had shown up. Like a demon fresh from the Abyss, the wizard had come in and saved the day. He cleared a path through the crowd with bursts of blue hellfire. He had picked up the witch while Shannai helped her brother stand. Then they raced to the front gate of the castle and safety.

The door to the small room opened, breaking her thoughts. She straightened as the wizard walked through. He looked at the sleeping woman, then at Shannai. A smile crossed his face, and he waved her into the corridor. She pushed herself from the wall and followed.

"How is your brother?"

She shrugged, not looking the wizard in the eyes, "A little sore, but he'll live." Shannai gazed at her feet, not sure what she should say. Finally, she mumbled, "Thanks for saving us out there."

He gave her a fatherly grin. "Think nothing of it. I felt Madame Rachelle's burst of power and couldn't help but follow it to its source. You saved her, and I helped to save you. It looks like we were both at the right place at the right time."

"Yeah."

His grin melted, replaced by a more serious expression. "What are you doing in Madame Rachelle's room?"

She didn't look up from the floor, watching her boot toe make short arcs across the stone. "Nothing...I just...I was wondering why she did that to Marchas. Why she slung him against that tree like that...and how."

His comforting smile returned. "I'm here to ask the same question. To at least find out how she did it. As far as why...did you see the child, the one near her when she fainted?"

"No. I was too busy helping my brother." She lied, an initial reaction that she immediately regretted. Tears blurred her vision and her tiny voice shook as she asked the question. A question she feared she already knew the answer to. "Wh...who was she?"

His smile fell, replaced by a sad frown. "I will have to ask her to know for sure, but I believe it was her daughter." He held up a small pendant on a gold chain. "I found this around the child's neck. It is Madame Rachelle's symbol."

A tear rolled down Shannai's cheek. She wiped it away, looked at the wizard, and whispered, "I don't think I need to speak to Madame Rachelle when she wakes up."

Before he could reply, she turned and ran down the corridor. Shannai didn't look back as she said, "I'm gonna check on my brother now."

∞ ∞ ∞ ∞

Piet Lithor looked out the window. The crowd of people outside the temple had grown. Hundreds of blank eyes stared back, all milky white with small black specks for pupils. Hundreds of torn and ragged arms grasped out with cold, gray fingers, as though they could reach through the yards of empty air, past an invisible line they couldn't cross. Hundreds of mouths opened, their hungry maws biting the humid air. He imagined their breath released a stench of decay and rot, a silent affront to the few remaining men and women trapped within the temple.

"Look at all the people gathered around the temple, Brother Cylus. It reminds me of the days when Piet Pearson preached the gospel. Oh, but he could draw a crowd."

Brother Cylus walked up to stand beside Lithor and look out the window. "Yes, Piet Lithor. Piet Pearson did have a way with the masses."

A baby cried from among the pews while a mother rocked it back and forth. Moments passed before the child calmed and grew quiet.

"Yeah, you got a hell of a crowd out there, Piet." The angry voice belonged to Lurok Bos Spielter, a local merchant mariner and owner of a dozen ships. His tithes had paid for many of Piet Lithor's excesses. Now he looked as though he planned to make Piet Lithor earn the money.

Brother Cylus bristled and opened his wrinkled mouth, ready to give Bos Spielter a lesson in manners, but Piet Lithor halted the angry priest with a grip on his elbow and a wave of his hand.

Bos Spielter twisted the end of his thick mustache. His eyes shifted from the old priest to Piet Lithor as if Brother Cylus was of no consequence. "I don't mean to sound rude or speak heresy here, Piet, but exactly what have my tithes bought me? Year after year, I dumped coins in your lap in the hopes of gaining some favor from the almighty Vaspar, but I got up this morning to find that your god left me with nothing. No family, no servants, and nobody to crew my ships. Nothing! Got any answers, priest?"

A day ago, Piet Lithor would have ruined the man for saying such things. He would have given the businessman the sign of the unholy and said a special prayer for his damnation. He would have crushed Bos Spielter's reputation. His clients and peers would be told of his heresy and the duke would know of his disrespect. The words still infuriated Lithor. He wanted nothing more than to throw the arrogant merchant out of the temple and into the ghastly crowd.

But now, he saw the situation in a new light. He saw a reflection of himself in the man's ranting heresy. An example of how others must see him. The men reeked of arrogance, self-righteousness, and contempt for others. His anger turned to disgust, more at his own tainted soul than at Bos Spielter's words.

None of that showed as he looked the merchant in the eye. His voice rolled with more authority than he felt. "You are still alive, Lurok. Maybe those tithes bought you an ending that is better than those out there. Maybe all those coins bought you salvation from a fate that is worse than death."

"Yeah, Piet? Well, I look out there, into that crowd, and I see a bunch of faces. Some faces I even recognize. I look out there, and I see that we're a little school of minnows surrounded by sharks. My wife and kids are out there, priest! They stumble along with the rest of those abominations. So, you will have to forgive me if I miss the *blessings* that the almighty Vaspar has bestowed upon me."

"He has made this ground holy, Bos Spielter! He has given us sanctuary." Brother Cylus spoke, an angry quiver in his voice. His hand rose over his head, index finger and thumb pinched together on each hand and connected thumb to thumb, creating the infinity symbol of blessings in the air. The man was far too quick to throw up both blessings and curses. They were so common that they didn't mean anything to anyone, especially him. It was his nature. Piet Lithor couldn't fault him for it. Most of the time, he found it amusing.

Bos Spielter waved his hand in the air, mocking Brother Cylus, or possibly brushing the comment away? Piet Lithor hoped for the second choice.

"He's given us a beautiful tomb, priest; a place where we can starve to death in the holiness of his presence. I don't know about you, but I don't feel all that fortunate right now."

Before Brother Cylus could argue the point any further, an ear-ringing gong sounded throughout the temple. Everyone cringed at the unexpected noise. The baby wailed with renewed vigor.

"The bell of Saint Renando. Someone is ringing the bell." Brother Cylus's voice shook with fear.

The temple bell rang again. The sound shot terror up Lithor's spine, as though the gong reverberated from the base of his neck.

Bos Spielter twisted his mustache all the harder and growled. "Someone better get up there and stop whatever idiot is pulling that cord, or we're gonna have everyone in the city waiting outside this temple to get in. Though I'm not really sure if it matters at this point."

The three men rushed to the stairs leading to the bell tower. Piet Lithor led the way. The bell chimed again.

He ran halfway up the stairs. Sweat dripped from his nose and into his eyes as air heaved in and out of his lungs. He halted and wiped the sweat from his brow as he braced himself against the wall, and yelled, "Stop ringing the bell! You're calling them all down on us! Stop ringing the bell!"

An excited voice, not yet deepened by puberty, called down to him. "Piet Lithor! There are men moving around on the walls of the castle. Guards, I think."

The bell stopped ringing, but the youth continued to chatter as Piet Lithor climbed the rest of the stairs to the open bell tower. It rose above the trees, giving a bird's eye view of the entire city. Red tiled roofs rose up through the trees and gleamed with a wet sheen in the dim sunlight. Roads created wide gaps between the trees. Buildings towered up in a forest of stone. The sea lay to the south, disappearing into the mist. Ship masts made another type of forest in the harbor.

A young man stood with the bell tower rope in his hand. He held it taut and pointed toward the castle. Though his eyes lacked the strength they once held, Piet Lithor looked across and saw guards rushing along the top of the outer castle wall.

"Is that rope they are carrying?"

Piet Lithor had no idea how the merchant could see such details through the haze of drizzle that thickened the air between the temple and the castle. Maybe it was a seaman trait. Not that it mattered. What did matter was that men still occupied the castle, and guards at that. They still stood a chance of rescue if only someone would notice their presence.

He turned back to the young man. "What is your name, my son?"

The boy blushed and smiled proudly, "Tollis Mayer, son of Royce Mayer."

Piet Lithor gave the young man an equally wide smile and replied, "Well, Tollis, keep pulling that rope until someone spots us." He turned back to watch the guards on the castle wall and said, "You may have just saved all our lives."

PART II

SIEGE

Chapter 11

"Can we understand good without knowing evil?"
~Secret Holy Scriptures of the Waken Book

General Faygen placed his feet on the ground for the first time in two weeks. After an extended trip on the rocking ship, the dock felt solid, stable.

During the ten-day sea voyage, he had remained in the hold, staring at the plank ceiling and pondering his resurrection. He had done little else as the ship dipped and rose upon the ocean's surface. When the craft docked in Renier, he had remained in the hold for two more days and listened to workers as they yelled back and forth across the docks. He waited in the hold while the five lower undead entered the city to perform their terrible deed.

It felt good to have land underneath him once again. He hated the hold. While out at sea, the ship reminded him of a fishing cork as it rose and fell. It had been more stable since they docked, but nothing could beat the stability of soil under his feet. He hated the hold for another reason. It was a dark and humid place that fed the gasses within him, making his innards gurgle and swell.

Thankfully, he couldn't smell his gaseous expulsions or the rotting carcass he had become. The senses of taste and smell hadn't returned to him with his resurrection, though his other senses worked just fine. His skin itched constantly and made him wish his sense of touch had been deadened as well. Scratching only peeled layers of skin away, exposing rotting meat that would soon harden to jerky. He tried not to scratch. The decomposition caused much of it. The wiggling knots of larvae rooting beneath his skin caused the rest. Occasionally, he would catch one as it bore through his flesh, or cough one of the little white buggers up as it tickled the back of his throat. He took his frustrations out on the tiny vermin with a pinch of his fingers, smearing the planks with their biological paste.

The rain began fourteen hours earlier. The screaming started shortly after that. Within hours, the screams had died to an occasional screech. The noises broke the rhythm of the rain as it pattered against the deck of the ship and trickled in across the walls of the hold. He ignored the distant cries and concentrated on his mission. He heard the screams and tried to block them out, willing them away. He had enough self-loathing to deal with; he didn't need the added guilt of more victims he couldn't help. The screams of men, women and children as they transformed into his mindless army were more than he could bear.

Twelve days in the hold gave him time to reflect on his situation, both his first life and this new one. Death had claimed his soul almost a thousand years ago. Evil had restored a twisted version of that soul to his body only weeks ago.

He had died a warrior's death in the glorious battle of Sipha. Outnumbered two to one, the Croshans still claimed victory, thanks to General Faygen's military genius. They won, but at a staggering cost; almost two thirds of his men never walked away from the battlefield. He received a sword through the back and died moments after victory had been proclaimed. He couldn't complain. It was a glorious end, a warrior's death.

Faygen's last moments consisted of terrible pain. It felt like fire and electricity ripped through the flesh between his shoulder blades as bone and muscle parted. Steel grazed bone and he drowned in his own blood. Darkness. Not only the absence of light, but smell, sound, touch, self…everything. A thousand years of nothing. Time had no meaning in death. A thousand years seemed like minutes or an eternity. No glorious warrior's greeting by Roke, the God of war. No grand fortress for the great leader of the Croshans. No gold. No jewels. No beautiful concubines. No friends or family. No reconciliation with his daughter. No forgiveness. Nothing.

His god had granted him a thankless death for years of service and loyalty.

Consciousness. No great swirling lights or a voice from heaven, only self-awareness. One moment nothing, then a glimmer of existence. A dim thought, the spark of a cell bursting to life in the center of his mind. *I am.* The thought grew into complex ideas, then foggy pieces of memory that fit together to form the pieces of a puzzle, of a person's life. The puzzle came together and displayed a man with friends, comrades, lovers, and a daughter. A man named

Faygen. A general who defined his worth by service to his king and the men around him.

He became aware, but darkness still held reign over his vision. No sounds. No smells. No feeling, no pounding of a beating heart to contrast the silence. Even in his panic, he felt no thump of a heartbeat. *Am I still dead?*

The pain began as pinpricks in his joints. The stinging grew and multiplied until burning torment flooded his body, focusing where bone met bone. He twitched and convulsed. The movements ground his joints together and intensified the torture. He realized he could feel, though he wished he couldn't.

His eyes snapped open, grating his corneas like sandpaper rubbed over a grape. His eyes burned but didn't moisten. Through narrow, fog clouded vision he saw two mummified arms. The skin cracked, dry as bark. They rose and fell, slapping against a hard surface. A dim beat came to his ears, wood striking stone. The arm rose for another strike. Through slowly ebbing pain, he willed the arm to stop. The appendage stayed in the air, thin fingers outstretched like twigs. He willed them to flex and they twitched with a pop, dust puffing out from the crusty joints. Fresh tendrils of pain raced to his throbbing mind. He cried out. His throat burned with dry fire. *My fingers. My arm. What have I become?*

The deep rumble of laughter, low and mirthless, erupted to his right. His hearing hadn't completely returned and the laughter sounded as though it came through a thick wall. He willed his head to turn. His chin swung an inch to the right. Pain knifed down his spine from the base of his skull to the middle of his shoulders. Popping vertebrae crackled like thunder; it traveled through his dry flesh, directly to his ears. An involuntary gasp escaped his mouth. The attempt to move air through the withered bags of his lungs created a new torture from deep within his chest, the burn of a blacksmith's bellows. Dust filled his burning throat.

"Hurts, doesn't it?" the voice whispered with a smoker's rasp. A grating groan, a growl, two rocks being rubbed together to create words. A face leered over him, hidden within the shadows of a cowl. Only a wide smile showed, filled with yellowed, wolfish teeth.

Fear of the pain stopped Faygen from nodding his head in reply. He rolled his eyes to the side and looked for the cloaked creature. Even that movement brought with it a throbbing pain behind his forehead.

The creature understood. "You awakened sooner than I expected, though I really shouldn't be surprised. After all, it is the mighty General Faygen that I have brought back from the Abyss. I will try and work quicker to make your entry back into the land of the living more accommodating."

A hand reached from a black sleeve and lay on his forehead. The other hand grasped his knee. The hand that grasped Faygen's forehead was black with rot. Knuckles stood out like the smooth ends of cypress roots, stretching the skin until it looked ready to rip. Hundreds of small boils covered the creature's flesh; their pus-filled heads lightened the dark skin like mushrooms growing in rich dirt. Veins and tendons snaked beneath the surface of the skin like shallow burrowing earthworms and worn roots.

He didn't want the vile thing touching him.

The creature began to chant in a guttural language that Faygen didn't understand. He tensed as ice filled his veins. It ran from where the creature touched his forehead to the other hand at his knee, like a river of ice within his blood-stream. A pain far greater than any he had yet experienced crackled through his body. His back arched and his fingers clenched against the chill. He didn't notice the aching in his

joints. A greater pain had taken its place. The hands stayed on him, holding him down against the torment until warmth began to melt the ice. Like the freezing chill, the heat began at the hand on his head and flowed down his body, thawing the icy pain and replacing it with warm relief.

The chanting stopped. The diseased hands pulled away.

"Feel better now, General?" When Faygen didn't turn his head or respond, his healer said, "You can look at me now. The pain is gone and your body is restored to its former state."

He turned his head and faced the thing that had brought him back. It stood hunched over a few feet away, surrounded by walls of stone. Tattered gray robes covered the creature's body; its face remained hidden within a deep cowl.

In a low voice, the diseased thing said, "I think you should know what has happened since your demise. How the world has changed and how I expect you to help me change it even more."

Before Faygen could reply, the creature mouthed another guttural word and the room suddenly became overlaid with images. Events that had taken place over the past thousand years flashed across a backdrop of stone. Thousands of images, important events, everything of significance he had missed while sleeping in the Abyss. Then he saw the future, a future where his resurrector controlled everything, a future of death where the undead became ghouls like him. Most roamed around as mindless things, performing simple tasks or stumbling forward until given instructions. Others were more like him, with the capability to think, but everyone could be controlled at any time by the horrid creature—a world full of abominations.

He didn't try and fool himself. He hadn't escaped death. No heartbeat, no breathing. He had been made into a ghoul by the creature's black magic, an abomination in the eyes of the gods.

Next, the creature showed him a city named Renier, a city full of undead waiting for a leader; an army in need of someone who could breach the walls of the castle, piercing the heart of the once beautiful city and claiming it for the necromancer.

He wouldn't do it!

The fanged smile widened. Images of his daughter flooded Faygen's mind. Eyliasa! Her body lay on a stone table much like his, but unlike him, she had been completely restored to her former beauty. His precious fifteen-year-old daughter.

The creature had her as surely as it had Faygen!

Guilt wracked him.

Years before the battle of Sipha, Eyliasa had been abducted by the Ryshans. They were a barbaric people, men who would hold a fifteen-year-old girl for ransom as blackmail to assure their victory, men who sent pieces of the girl as evidence of their brutality. With each piece of her body, they included taunting messages, telling how they abused her in every way imaginable. Even for the sake of his own flesh and blood, he wouldn't give in to them. His heart had felt like it would burst through his chest, but he hadn't given in. The good of the kingdom weighed heavier than the abuse and murder of a single girl, even his only daughter. Or so he kept telling himself. He wanted to believe it, but underneath the hard exterior, it tore his soul apart.

Six months later, her head was mounted to a staff at the forefront of the enemy formation. Her blank eyes gazed up to the heavens through tangled hair, the pole of the stake shown black behind the oval of her open mouth. He made them pay for the abuses. With tears wetting his cheeks, he fought like a demon of the Abyss. He tore into the enemy with a berserker rage, heedless of his own safety. When the battle ended, corpses littered the field three deep. They showed the enemy no mercy. He had their villages razed and their people killed down to the last child. Even the livestock became sacrifices to Faygen's fury. The vengeance only fueled his self-loathing, but he couldn't make himself stop, torn between a mercy he refused to give and hatred he couldn't end.

General Faygen had his revenge, but it didn't matter. His enemy had been annihilated, but it hadn't brought his daughter back. He had wanted to die. A boon he didn't receive until decades later.

The creature threatened to resurrect Eyliasa and use her as a bargaining chip. He couldn't live through her torture again. Undead or not, he couldn't exist with that burden renewed.

He raised his clouded eyes and glared into the necromancer's cowl. Hatred burned in his heart that he hadn't felt in ages.

The wolf smile widened, fueling Faygen's rage.

The creature motioned him off the table with a wave of his hand. "Despise me all you want, General. I wouldn't expect any less, but act on that hatred and you will find your daughter's head once again left on a pike. Now, do as I told you and stand up."

His daughter's plight broke his will. He kept a firm grip on the stone to support himself as he slid off the table and stood on legs that shook and threatened to fold beneath him, legs that hadn't been used in centuries. He would obey.

He pushed the dark memories to the back of his mind and watched his two companions step off the ship. They were an odd pair.

The first one looked like a wolfhound that had been crossed with a saber tooth tiger, a massive creature whose shoulders stood almost chest high. The beast carried itself like a predator. Its shoulders swayed with each step. It sniffed the air and constantly glanced back and forth as if in search of something to hunt. Huge fangs stretched its lips and jutted far below its lower jaw. Faygen would have thought it was alive if not for the gray, mold-covered skin that showed through the creature's thin hair. Its milky eyes didn't miss anything.

His other companion seemed to be more wraith than human as it glided down the gangplank to the dock. Cloaked like its dark master, nothing could be seen of the creature beneath. Unlike the necromancer, it gave nothing away within the blackness of its cowl. Neither the eyes nor teeth gleamed. The robe contained a moving void as far as Faygen could tell.

I wonder if that demon has some hold over him, something the wraith would do anything for, or is the creature helping for its own ends?

During the voyage, they had stayed in their separate quarters in the hold. Faygen could sense everyone on the ship, the five lower undead and these other two, as if their return from death created a bond in their souls, shining like a sickly green beacon in the darkness. None of the undead made any attempt to communicate with the others. He hadn't expected the lower undead to even try. They only lived to feast on living flesh. Of course, he hadn't expected the mutated wolfhound to try and communicate either, but he had expected more from the wraith creature. His new-found sense, the feeling that allowed him to know where the undead were without seeing them, told him that the wraith had a mind of its own. The creature was like him, having desires for things other than the destruction that the necromancer pursued. The wraith had cunning and intelligence. It would make a dangerous enemy.

He turned away from his companions and followed the dock along the waterfront to Renier's Port Gate. For the last two days, he heard men working on the dock, ships coming in full of cargo or fish. Now all he heard was the lapping of the water against the pylons, the wind gusting over the ocean, and the creaking of the dock. The boards groaned as the heavy wolfhound followed behind him. The wraith didn't make a noise. *Are they following me, or do we just happen to be going in the same direction?*

He didn't know their purpose and didn't really care. He only knew they had nothing to do with him directly. No orders had been given to him concerning them.

Within minutes, the three stood before the Port Gate. Faygen saw a silent city, a dead city. If his ancient tear ducts hadn't dried up centuries ago, he would have cried.

A thing that had been a man trudged through the drizzle further down the road. It aimlessly wandered down the street in a haphazard, zigzag pattern. Faygen sent out a mental command. *Come.* The thing stopped, its bald head turning toward the three. It lurched and stumbled toward

169

Faygen, eyes locked on the general. The creature didn't zigzag or deviate, walking straight to him. The ghoul's feet dragged along the ground, making even the straight path take some time. After several moments, he stood before Faygen.

He had just started to turn, to see what his companions were going to do, when the wolfhound bolted around him and grasped the mindless undead in its wide jaws. Bone cracked and popped as fangs sank deep into its skull. The wolfhound swung the undead back and forth, snapping vertebrae and slinging half-congealed blood. The beast slung it several more times before allowing the corpse to fall onto the ground. Without a pause, the creature's head dove to the ghoul's stomach. Massive teeth bit into the soft flesh and pulled. The corpse jerked up and down with the movement of the wolfhound's head until flesh ripped and a stew of organs oozed out of the ragged hole. The beast swallowed the loose flap of skin then dove into the quivering innards. It yanked out a length of intestine and devoured it, as any dog would do to a string of sausages.

Faygen knew the sight should have sickened him, but he felt nothing, or at best, puzzled. *Why would the creature kill one of the undead? Is the beast that vicious, or does it need food before continuing its mission?*

He turned to the wraith, hoping to get an answer, but the mysterious creature simply bowed his head and walked down the wall, away from the gate.

The wet snapping and swallowing continued for several moments before the beast lifted its bloody muzzle and trotted after the wraith.

Faygen watched the hooded figure glide down the wall with the beast lumbering behind until they disappeared around the corner, toward the mountains at the back of the city. Their presence would remain a mystery until another day.

Without sparing any more thought for his companions, Faygen walked into Renier. He had an assignment of his own to complete.

Chapter 12

"Mage: Sorcerer/Spellbinder/Warlock/Wizard/Witch
A person with the inborn and/or learned ability to alter reality
in ways that defy nature."
~The Book of Knowledge, Library of Cromwell

"Come here, Tanilla. Come to Mommy."

The baby took a wobbly step forward. A pudgy hand stretched out, narrowing the gap between mother and toddler. The baby's other hand stayed on the chair seat, not wanting to let go of the stable anchor.

"Come on, honey. Let go of the chair and come to Mommy." Rachelle motioned the baby to her; arms open, enticing the child with the promise of a hug.

She smiled. Her heart swelled with pride as the toddler took two awkward steps then stopped. Tanilla looked left and right. She turned and cocked her head at her mommy as if to say, *where seat go?* The baby glanced over her shoulder at the chair. She tipped back and forth, but maintained her newfound balance. Tanilla turned back to Rachelle. Her face lit up with a triumphant grin, all baby teeth and slobber. *See what I did, Mommy?* With a squeal of delight, the baby bounced and gave herself a single clap. The movement almost tipped her over. She looked at her feet to verify the truth of matters and her grin widened, eyes crescents of delight.

Darkness crossed the room. The golden glow of sunlight shifted to the hazy light of dusk. Shadows crawled across the floor and walls, giving the quaint room an ominous appearance.

Tanilla's head snapped up, far quicker than a baby should have done. Her happy, cashew-shaped eyes narrowed and turned completely white. The dim hint of pupils floated beneath a layer of milky film. None of the blue showed. Saliva turned to blood. It coated her mouth and dripped from her chin. Small lips pinched together in an ominous grin, jagged and deformed by two rows of crooked, narrow teeth. The toddler opened her arms and walked toward Rachelle. Heal to toe, heal to toe. The unsure stagger was gone. The child strolled forward like a predator. Her mouth opened, revealing dozens of narrow, bloodstained fangs. More teeth than could possibly fit within the baby's closed mouth. In a deep voice that reverberated throughout the room the child screamed, "MOMMMMMMEEEEEEEE!"

"Madame Rachelle. Are you all right?"

She jerked away from the voice. Her body bounced across a soft surface. Cloth pulled tight about her shoulders and prevented her from moving any further. Her heart pounded. A scream threatened to leap from her throat.

Wellan stood over her. His eyebrows furrowed together with worry. One hand reached out to comfort her and stopped in mid motion by indecision.

She sat up in the bed. Tears dribbled from the corners of her eyes and became diluted in the sweat that covered her cheeks. The gray light of dusk shone through the window. It filled the small room with long, menacing shadows.

Wellan's knobby hand gently touched her shoulder. Rachelle jumped. "You must have had a bad dream. It's not surprising...considering..."

She pulled the covers to her chest and held them tight, a thin wall against the horrible nightmare, against a world gone mad.

The wizard's voice softened to a gentle whisper, "I...I need to talk to you, to ask you a few questions. I know my timing is terrible, but...it's necessary. Are you up for it?"

She turned away. *My baby. Tanilla. Gone. Taken away by disease, a plague...or the man with the bow. No, she was gone before he shot her, but...she had moved. I felt her move within the blankets. I saw her stand. I saw her try...try and...bite.* Fresh tears trickled down her cheek. A flow began that she couldn't stop; a flood of grief that couldn't be dammed away with glad thoughts or logic. Her shoulders shook. Her breath hitched in her throat. *My baby lost her soul.*

She shook her head. *No, Wellan. I can't talk right now. I just lost the only thing that meant anything to me and I'm having a little trouble putting it behind me right now. If you could come back in say...a year or two then maybe, just maybe, I will have something to say.*

Though she faced away from the wizard, she sensed him nod his head in disappointment. Urgency and need radiated from him tempered by empathy and sadness. "I understand. I will come back later when you feel better."

The wizard's robes rustled like dry leaves blown in the wind. Each step echoed across the room as he walked away. His steps matched the rhythm of her heart, bringing her closer to despair with each footfall.

The door creaked open.

"Wait." The whispered word left her mouth before she could stop it. She didn't want him there. She didn't want to speak with anyone. She couldn't bear sharing her grief, but she couldn't be alone. Her grief smothered her in contradictions and confusion. The thought of not having someone near frightened her more than letting him see her pain.

"Do you want to talk?"

"No...Yes...I...I just don't want to be alone. Not right now."

"I understand."

She paused and stared at the floor; she needed to tell him something, anything. Nothing came to mind, nothing but her baby lying on the floor of her cottage. The look in her eyes as she came back to life, the hunger. She couldn't just sit and stare at the wall. Wellan had more important things to do than console her.

Rachelle's thoughts raced back over the last few hours. Dead-eyed people emerging from the shadows. She remembered her baby reaching for her with hunger in her eyes, an arrow plunging through the side of her daughter's head. Gore. Bone. Rage had consumed her, filling her heart, flowing through her like lightning. When it had burst from her fingertips, she felt her soul, her life force, flow away with the energy. Her mind spun in a circular pattern. She experienced the scene over and over again, living through each horrible moment. She wanted to screech and slam her hands against the wall. Rachelle wanted to die. Surely in death she would be released from her internal Abyss. She didn't scream or die. Instead, she sat and stared. Her eyes pointed to the corner of the room, but she only saw her horrid memories.

She focused on the dark corner and tried to clear her mind of memories. She needed to let it out, to talk. Rachelle had to tell her story before it could consume her.

"My daughter. I found her in my house. Dead."

Light footsteps followed by the rustle of robes; a chair creaked. "I'm so sorry."

She thanked him for his sympathy with a nod. Her eyes closed. The darkness took away the distraction of the dim light that shone through the window. She didn't want to see the texture of the wall. She didn't want to see anything ever again. Madame Rachelle visualized the morning again as she spoke, stepping through every heart-wrenching moment. "I raised Tanilla by myself. Her father disappeared at sea when she was small. Maybe he's dead. Maybe he just didn't want to be a father. I don't know and I don't suppose it really matters. She was all that mattered, the only thing I cared about. Now she's gone."

"Madam Rachelle, I—"

"I picked her up, held her close. Cold. She was so cold. I don't know how long I sat like that. I lost track of time. I wrapped her in a blanket, the blanket that Miss Whorton made. It had little animals all over it. Tanilla loved animals. I wrapped her up like a baby, like an infant, with only her face showing. Tanilla would have hated that. She was always reminding me that she was a big girl, but at that moment, she was my baby. I think I wiped the blood from her mouth. I'm not sure.

"I carried her outside. I don't know where I planned to go, maybe nowhere, maybe to bring her to you. I don't know. I just walked. People, blood covered people, followed us. I became afraid. I thought they would try and take my little girl. I couldn't allow that, but I couldn't prevent it. She started moving, struggling beneath the blanket. My heart surged with hope. I think I set her down."

Seconds passed in silence. Madame Rachelle wiped her closed eyes with the palms of her hands. The memory of those next moments twisted her stomach. A fresh wave of despair washed over her. Her shoulders shook with renewed sobs.

Finish the story. Get it all out. It will consume me if I don't release it.

"I don't remember...I...her face. Her eyes, the dead eyes, they looked at me with a need, a hunger. Like...like an addict. I can't explain the feeling that came over me. Fear. Shock. Despair. It was then that she...her head...an arrow. That...that's all I can remember." She turned to the wizard, her eyes swollen and bleary with tears. She moaned. "That's all I can remember."

"Madame Rachelle, I'm so sorry."

She nodded and turned away.

"I do have some news that might make you feel better."

Air stuttered into her lungs. New tears trickled down her cheeks. She hadn't thought there were any tears left.

"I think the...the situation awoke the magic within you. I think you could be a wizard."

She didn't smile. She didn't care.

∞ ∞ ∞ ∞

"How long are we going to sit here and wait?" Lurok Bos Spielter grumbled over the noise of the tower bell. He squatted on the tiled altar steps with his hand propped under his chin, staring at his feet. Lithor didn't care for his choice of seats, the altar being the holiest of ground. Under the circumstances, he didn't think it worth mentioning. Brother Cylus, on the other hand, fumed and glared at the merchant from his seat near the podium. His mouth had even opened once or twice to say something, but the rant never got past his wrinkled lips. Bos Spielter didn't move and no one, not even Brother Cylus, wanted to start an argument that wasn't necessary.

The incessant gong of the tower bell had started to give Piet Lithor a headache. Even his teeth had begun to hurt. The continuous clang hadn't done much to ease tempers. Lithor thought about asking the boy to stop for a while, but decided against it. The racket of the bell took priority over everyone's short tempers and throbbing temples.

"If Duke Renier is still alive, and I have no doubt that he is, then help will come as soon as he can arrange something." Though Lithor spoke to the group with confidence, his words were said to comfort himself as much as the others.

When no one replied, Lithor walked to the window. He could only take so much of the merchants' growling and complaining. Thank Vaspar the man had finally tired of his own grumblings. He desperately wanted to put the merchant in his place. He wanted to do what the old piet would have done, but he didn't want to become that man again— the one who ran. He never wanted to see himself cowering behind a bed again while a child, an innocent in his care, stood in his place against the forces of evil. No, he wanted that man to be gone forever. If he had to sacrifice his pride in order for that to happen then so be it. The loss of his status would be one of the many penances he planned on paying for a lifetime of sin and arrogance.

His hands tightened on the windowsill.

I don't even know the boy's name.

He watched the mass of pale bodies meander aimlessly back and forth at the edge of the safe zone. Their numbers had decreased, but not knowing where the missing ones had gone bothered him more than watching them stumbling about in front of the temple. *Maybe they will get bored and find somewhere else to haunt. Or should I be doing something? Did the lord Vaspar save me and give me a weapon to combat them? If so, then why do I cower behind the walls of His temple? What does He have destined for me? What is Your will, my lord?*

Brother Cylus' liver-spotted hand grasped the window frame, interrupting Lithor's thoughts. His raspy voice asked, "Why do they stay? What are they waiting for?"

"Us, I think."

Two of the bodies walked into one another's path. Each turned to avoid a collision.

"Why don't they attack their own?"

Lithor dropped his hand to the pommel of his sword. His thumb slid up and down the golden hilt, tracing deep grooves and cold metal. His eyes focused on the crowd. "I don't know."

"Why do they hate us?"

Because I deserve to be hated.

He pulled his gaze from the window and looked at Brother Cylus. He didn't have any real answers, but he had to try to rationalize the madness taking place around him. "I don't believe they do. I looked into their eyes and only saw a void. I didn't see hatred—longing, perhaps. Hunger, desire, need maybe, but not hatred. I believe I even saw fear or revulsion when they looked upon the holy sword, but hatred...no, that I haven't yet seen."

"Do you think they still have souls?"

Lithor returned his gaze to the window. Since entering the temple, he had asked himself that question over and over again. He wanted to think they still had souls, a part of themselves that could be redeemed and brought back. He shuddered to think that they could be lost in the void, wandering the Abyss without any hope of return or salvation. Or worse yet, trapped within those mindless bodies, forced to watch themselves commit atrocities they couldn't control. He told himself that they were still in there somewhere, blind to their actions and desperately trying to escape the prison of their own bodies. He wanted to see them returned to the lives they had lived only hours earlier. He wanted to put the world back where it had been less than a day ago.

Though he wanted to put everything back like it was, he couldn't imagine how things could be put right as he watched them aimlessly stumble through their environment. They ignored everything. They walked around objects and, occasionally, into them, and only became motivated in the presence of the uninfected. Violence and desire seemed to be their only drive.

Piet Lithor didn't care to think that those people couldn't be redeemed. He refused to believe that they couldn't find forgiveness in the eyes of Lord Vaspar. They seemed to be a reflection of his own soul, before Lord

Vaspar showed him the light, a tainted spirit, totally oblivious to the damage it caused.

No, he wanted to believe that they could be redeemed, but as he watched, he realized they were far beyond reach.

"Piet Lithor, do you think they still have souls?"

"I wish I could tell you that they do, Brother Cylus. I truly do, but to be honest with myself...I don't think so. I don't know what evil causes them to hunt us, but I think their souls are gone. I only hope that they are in a better place and not devoured by the force that created them."

"Where do..."

"Please, Brother Cylus. No more questions. I'm..."

The bell ceased its clanging. The priests turned away from the window. Everyone stared at the archway leading to the tower.

Footsteps pounded on the bell tower stairs. Both priests turned as Tollis raced down the steps.

Everyone stood. The newborn let out a whimper in his mother's arms. Two hands clasped as the newlywed couple tried to comfort one another. A mother pulled her two sons close to her sides.

Tollis looked at each person, searching. A grin lit his face as he found Lithor. "They want us to wait."

Bos Spielter growled, "What are you talking about, boy? Who wants us to wait?"

His smile faltered. "The guards, Bos. The guards want us to wait."

Lithor spoke up before Bos Spielter could snarl at the boy again, "How do you know this, Tollis?"

"A sign, your Excellency. They spelled out W-A-I-T on a sheet and unfolded it down the side of the castle wall."

Lithor turned to Bos Spielter. "I told you the duke wouldn't let us down."

∞ ∞ ∞ ∞

Stiles stood before the War Room door rubbing his temples. The War Room. He had never been within the palace walls prior to being rescued from the training yard. Just a day ago, he had been a lackey for Drummen. Now, he stood in the palace waiting to be called to a private conference with the duke and his top advisors. *I bet Wellan's in there.* Assuming the wizard would be in attendance comforted him, but there would also be generals and maybe even that haughty priest, Piet Lithor. Thoughts of the piet stole any comfort Stiles may have gained from imagining the wizard's presence.

What if they think I did a terrible job of getting my men out of the dungeon? What if they want to demote me, put me under Ash, or even throw me out of the city guard all together? He pulled his hand from his temple and rubbed up and down the leg of his britches instead. His stomach twisted into a knot.

He had botched the dungeon breakout. Stiles was man enough to admit it when he did something wrong. He hesitated when he should have known what to do and acted. Ash shouldn't have been the one making the decisions. Stiles had the responsibility of keeping his men together, keeping them from being killed. *Maybe I should step down, suggest to the duke that Ash be put in charge?* Ash had the men's respect. He didn't hesitate, didn't crumble under pressure. Ash was a natural leader.

What if they have another assignment for me? Maybe they want me to sneak out and get help? The thought didn't ease his anxiety.

He spun around as the clang of armored footsteps raced toward him. A soldier sped past him, dressed in full gear, boiled leather over chain mail, topped off with an open faced steel helmet. A thick black mustache protruded from each side of his head gear. The man stopped in front of the oaken door. He gave Stiles a quick nod then hesitated a moment to straighten his helmet. When all was in good order, he beat on the door with a glove-covered hand.

"Come in," a muffled voice ordered from behind the door—low and commanding, yet tired.

The guard pushed the door open and strode into the room. Stiles peeked around the corner. Inside the room sat a large table with a map of the city laid across it. Painted wooden markers stood at different points across the map. Three men leaned over the table, the duke, Wellan, and an upper-ranking guard that Stiles barely knew, but not a general, and no piet.

The guard snapped his hand to his chest and gave a quick bow before speaking in a winded voice. "My lord duke. The...uh...people are moving away from the palace, further into the city."

The duke straightened from his bent position over the table. His eyebrows came together at the bridge of his nose. "They are retreating?"

"To be honest, sir, we're not sure what they're doing. About ten minutes ago, they turned and started walking away from the palace. The areas around the walls are cleared of them for the moment."

Duke Renier turned to Wellan, a *What do you think?* look on his face. Wellan shrugged. The duke turned back to the guard. "Groyce. Your name is Groyce, isn't it?"

"Yes, my lord."

"Well, Groyce, did you see where they went?"

"No, my lord. The drizzle is starting to slacken, but with the sun beginning to go down, visibility is still poor and the surrounding trees and buildings hid them from us pretty quickly."

The duke turned to Wellan. "Well, my friend, do you have any idea as to what may be happening?"

Wellan shook his head. "I haven't a clue, but I don't think they are retreating. Whatever is going on, I don't believe it bodes well for us."

"Well, I think we should use this to our advantage." He turned back to Groyce. "Thank you for that information, Groyce. You're dismissed."

The guard saluted once more and bowed before turning and striding from the room.

The duke waved to Stiles. "Come in, Stiles."

He walked into the room. Every step felt more awkward and clumsy than the last, a duck waddling through a room full of hawks. His face felt hot, flushed. He stopped in front of the duke. His salute seemed lame and his bow pathetic after seeing the other soldier do it. "You wished to see me, my lord?"

"Yes, Stiles, I have a job for you, and it looks like the Fates are smiling on you today."

"A...a job, sir?"

"Yes. A short while ago, someone rang the bell on top of the Temple of Vaspar. The guards on the wall said they saw at least three men moving about in the bell tower and there could be more people below. I would like you and your men to go to the temple and bring those people back. I don't know how they have survived there this long. I would send some of my personal soldiers, but there are few left."

He wasn't being demoted, not even reprimanded. The duke had handed him an important assignment. He stood straighter and tried to control the grin that threatened to spread across his face. "You can count on me, sir."

The duke smiled. The bags under his eyes and the red veins in them the only indicators of the burden that he carried. "I knew I could, Stiles. When you and your men reach the church, I would like half of your men to keep going, to get out of the city and go to Baron Milchev's castle. I need to warn him of this epidemic and see if he can send help, though I'm not sure he will. He is an ornery bastard to say the least, but he needs to be warned of what happened here, as does the king. Since the baron is closer, we will warn him first. With any luck, he will send assistance to us and a rider on to the king. Hopefully, it will keep them from suffering our fate."

"Yes, sir."

Wellan cleared his throat. "You might also want to send some of the men into the city. Let them find out where the people have gone and report back here."

"That is an excellent idea. Send a quarter of your men to warn Baron Milchev and another quarter to find out where the people are and what they are doing. You can decide which men will be scouting and which will go to the baron."

"Yes, sir. They are good men. I know they can do as you ask." *They aren't going to be happy to hear about this assignment. Not happy at all.*

Duke Renier rubbed his chin, thinking. "Wellan and I had discussed causing a distraction to pull the people away from a section of the wall and then lowering your men down on ropes, but since they have left the area around the walls, I think they should try and go out the front gates. What do you think, Wellan?"

The wizard's eyebrows rose. He smiled. "Their retreat at this moment is fortunate. I think we should give it a try."

"Then the front gate it is. If they don't return, you can come back that way also. We will keep an eye out for you and watch to see if the people come back. If we see you coming and they have returned to the wall, we will distract them as we planned and lower ropes down near the road leading to the Temple of Vaspar. Just make it to the wall and we will pull you to the top."

Stiles clasped his hands behind his back. "That sounds good. Will that be all, my lord?"

"Yes. That's more than enough."

"Yes, sir." Stiles' salute remained as awkward as ever.

∞ ∞ ∞ ∞

The water rose to his waist. It soaked his britches with cold. He didn't care. His brothers and sisters had started arriving. A few more splashed through the water and entered the darkness every hour. The tunnel had begun to fill as they took their positions. They stood around him in silence, patiently waiting. He couldn't see them, but the stone cavern echoed the sloshing water as they shifted in anticipation of the feast to come.

The dreams of rending flesh, warm blood and screaming voices continued. They pacified him and temporarily quenched his hunger, but they hardly stifled his need. The visions barely kept him under control. His tongue licked moisture from the hair on his upper lip. His teeth chewed the soft flesh and wiry whiskers of the lower one. He craved flesh, a hunger that the dreams wouldn't be able to fulfill much longer.

A splash echoed behind him like a blast of thunder. Something large came up the tunnel. A low growl thrummed over the water and reverberated off the walls of the cave. Something large moved through the tunnel behind him. The growl grew into a roar. Water splashed in a wave that soaked his back. Bones crunched. The rich smell of blood wafted through the air, a faint aroma that stood out from the smell of rot and mildew. The odor drifted through the air like a steak cooked over an open pit. He hungered. Saliva coated his tongue and dripped over his ruined lower lip. It almost drove Drummen to action. Almost.

He didn't turn to look, but he could hear the wet feasting that stirred the water behind him. A beast had entered the cave; a beast like himself, but different. A predator had taken one of his brethren. A hunter sent by the Voice. Another creature slid through the water behind the predator; another one like himself, but different.

The two new presences were also brothers, older brothers. Wiser brothers. The Voice told Drummen to obey them, to follow their commands. They would show him a cornucopia of flesh and rivers of blood.

He could hear the beast snap and tear meat from bones. Water splashed and rippled, soaking more of his pants and shirt. He didn't care as he listened to the creature feast in the humid darkness. The beast devoured one of his brothers and he hardly noticed. The wet smacking continued for minutes, maybe hours. Time no longer mattered. He only cared about his hunger, his hunger and the Voice.

Finally, the meal ended. The ripples and splashes lessened.

The beast and the stranger moved through the liquid murk, the black void. They moved by him, an arm's length away. The predator splashed through the water—proud, daring any of his brethren to approach him. A king of the dead—an undead lion with its ghoulish pride.

The other one moved with a fluid grace, a small wake ripped through the waters behind him. A ghost. A shadow.

The beast and the stranger shared one thing in common. They moved with intent, a hunter's stride.

The beast's thoughts radiated to Drummen; a kindred spirit living for hunger, anger, and hatred. The other stranger's mind shone like green swamp gas, vile and shapeless. Alien.

The beast's splashing stopped, but the smooth wake of the stranger continued through the dark cavern. It had another purpose, one that didn't involve waiting with the beast, or Drummen.

Within minutes, the echoes of the stranger's ripples diminished. The corridor returned to silence except for the drip of water and the slosh of brethren as they shifted in the waist deep liquid. An occasional growl escaped the undead king of the pride.

Chapter 13

*"The body is a vessel for the soul and nothing more.
We, our true self, dwells within, waiting for release,
waiting for the day we can be judged for our actions."*
~Dokkien the Wise

here have you been?" Marchas spat the question out like an accusation.

"Since when did I have to start reporting myself to you?" Shannai spat back. She folded her arms over her chest; her eyes dared him to say anything else.

Tension crackled between them like static electricity. Marchas' mood had steadily grown more hostile since Bos Talle had stepped out of the kitchen with flames trailing from his apron. Shannai understood his anxiety and fear. She felt them too. She had tried to give her brother some room, so he had no excuse to take his frustrations out on her, but she finally reached her limit. She loved her brother, but he wasn't the only one dealing with what they had seen, what they had done, and the current nightmare that they were stuck in. No, Shannai's sympathy and patience for her brother had finally worn out.

Her brother's nostrils flared, and his lips pursed in anger. He opened his mouth to reply and stopped. His face relaxed and he sighed. "Sorry, Shan. You're right. I'm just worried."

She sat on the edge of the bed while he finished buttoning his shirt. The last button hid the blue bruise that spanned his chest. She leaned against the wall and smiled. "I hope you're not worried on my account. You're the troublemaker."

He placed his hand over his heart, feigning injury. "Me, a troublemaker? Who started that bar fight in Tholog? If I remember correctly, I was minding my own business, entertaining some very fine young ladies, when you hit that trapper across the head with your beer stein. Put a hell of a dent in the stein too, if my memory serves me right."

He winced as he lowered his arm.

She laughed and threw a pillow at him. Their banter felt good, normal. "You know that wasn't my fault, Marchas. That bear of a man had all the manners of a wild boar, and the smell to go with it. If he had kept his paws to himself, that would have been a pleasant evening."

"It would have been for me. No doubt about that. I was doing pretty well with the ladies that night."

She started to comment on his philandering, but stopped as he sat on the bed next to her. His smile melted, eyes shone with fear, and eyebrows furrowed in concern.

"Shannai, we are in trouble like we haven't been before."

She looked at her lap and twisted a bright red button on her blouse. She nodded her head, not wanting to reply.

She didn't know what to say. When she finally spoke, her voice shook in a cracked whisper. "Yeah. We are, aren't we?"

He put his arm over her shoulder and pulled her close. "I'm not trying to frighten you, but I don't want you to think that just because we are here at the duke's grand palace everything is okay, because it isn't."

"At least we aren't alone. There are others here. Soldiers, city guards, the wizard..."

He stood and walked to the window. "Have you seen how many soldiers are here? There are hardly enough to stop a bar fight, and, though I was a bit out of it when I met him, it looks like the wizard has met his match. Everyone can see the old man is exhausted. He puts on a good show, but it's obvious he's at the end of his rope. There's too many of them. You saw. There's not a city block that doesn't have ten or more of the damned things trying to kill you. I'm guessing that they're congregating around the palace walls even as we speak. Trying to get in here and have their way with us. It's just a matter of time before that finally happens, and I don't want to be here when it does."

She twisted her shoulders and faced him. "You aren't thinking of going back out there again? By ourselves? They will get us for sure this time. Besides, I heard they are stacked ten deep around the palace walls, just like you said. There is no way we could get through, even if the guards allowed it."

He slammed his fist into his palm. "I'm thinking it will be easier and safer for two people to sneak out of the city instead of everyone in the palace trying to walk out of there. We know what to expect now; I think we can do it. We can't just sit here and wait for them to get in."

"Marchas, think about it. They can't climb the wall. We're safe here."

He shook his head. "No, we aren't. The first thing those creatures did was kill all the livestock and horses. They have us surrounded with no means of replenishing whatever supplies are in the palace. It will just be a matter of time before everyone starves to death, and starvation is one more way that I don't want to die."

Shannai frantically searched her mind for all the reasons they couldn't leave the protection of the duke's palace. There had to be at least a dozen examples, but all of them escaped her.

Marchas opened his mouth to argue his point when another reason for not leaving came to her mind. She blurted it out. "It's also a long walk to the city gates, and like you said, there aren't any horses. The palace is backed up against the Barclaves, the furthest point in the city from any of the walls. I think it's too far for just two people. I don't even think we can get out of the palace. There are just too many of them waiting right outside the walls for us."

He turned and grasped the windowsill, leaning against tense arms. "Well, I just can't wait here for them to break through, or for us to starve to death. There has to be something we can do to get out of this."

"Let's wait, see what the duke..."

A rapid knock on the door interrupted Shannai. Marchas whirled around and looked at her. She shrugged and then turned to the door. "Come in."

The door opened and a teenage boy stepped into the room. Grime covered his face in the fading light, making his toothy smile stand out. "I didn't mean to bother you, but

I just heard that we might be saved. I'm going around and lettin' everyone know."

Marchas stepped up to the child; his voice reflected the boy's excitement. "Saved? How?"

The kid hit his forehead with the palm of his hand. "I'm so stupid. The people. The sick ones. They've walked away from the wall. They aren't blocking us in no more."

Marchas thanked the boy and walked him to the door. When the child was gone, he shut the door and leaned back against it. His smile shone through his goatee with as much enthusiasm as the boy's. "I think this is our chance."

∞ ∞ ∞ ∞

Ten men stood in a group inside the front gates of the palace. A light drizzle misted the air. It hazed the fading light and added to the gloom that shadowed over the men's faces. Stiles ran a hand through his damp hair as he walked up to them. They knew something would happen soon, they just didn't know what. He dreaded telling them.

Before he could say anything, Ash stepped to the front and growled, "Did you tell Duke Renier what a wonderful job you did on our escape from his dungeons? Was he so impressed with your bravery that he told you to go out and vanquish the rest of the undead? Did you tell him how you let Horn die?"

"That'll be enough of that, Ash." Stiles felt his cheeks burn with the contradictory emotions of both anger and shame. He didn't know if he wanted to hit Ash or apologize to him. Instead of doing either, he kept his emotions pushed down and stuck to business. People needed saving.

"That ain't nearly enough..."

"Ash, please. You are partially right. The duke did give us an assignment."

To be given an assignment by Duke Renier was an honor, an honor that even Ash couldn't balk at. The other men shifted their feet and looked back and forth amongst each other. Their brows furrowed inquisitively while their eyes shone with pride. Their nervous shuffle betrayed their fear.

Blade stepped in and put a firm hand on Ash's shoulder. "What's he want us to do, Stiles?"

Stiles' hand rose to the back of his neck and rubbed it nervously. "The assignment is a great honor, but I'm not sure you guys are going to like this one."

Royd's rough voice spoke up from the line. "Well, considerin' that the last assignment started out with ale and story tellin' and ended with us havin' an undead jailer, getting a tough assignment might not turn out so bad, if you get my meanin'."

Nervous laughter rose from a few of the men, accompanied by nods of agreement, but most just stared at Stiles. They waited to hear the rest of what he had to say.

"I hope you're right, Royd. I really do." He took a deep breath and folded his arms over his chest, then continued on. "Duke Renier wants us to go to the Temple of Vaspar and save some people who are trapped inside."

Blade raised his hand. He spoke before Stiles could acknowledge him. "How do they know anyone is there?"

"They have been ringing the temple bell; I believe it's called *The Bell of Saint Renando*. There are also people moving around in the bell tower. Nobody knows who's in there, but it looks like at least one teenager and maybe a priest."

Jamee spoke up. "I don't mean to sound like a coward or anything, but does it make sense to anyone for eleven people to be going out to save two? I know my counting ain't so good, but this just don't add up."

"Jamee, I'm not going to force anyone to go. If I have to, I will go by myself. The duke asked me to do this and no matter what else has happens, he is still my duke and this assignment is an honor that I'm not going to shun. You can do what you want."

Blade forced a smile, giving Ash's shoulder a squeeze. "Well, you can count me in. Do we leave in the morning?"

"No, you will need to leave right now." The commanding voice came from the side and caught the men by surprise, the voice of the duke.

The men straightened and stood side by side. They rushed to make themselves presentable, but the duke waved his hand, motioning them to relax. Behind him, a knowing grin stretched Wellan's lips, like a teacher who catches his students talking about him.

"As Stiles stated, I won't force any of you to go. It's true we aren't sure how many people are in the temple. There may only be two, or there may be two dozen. I just want to give them a fighting chance. I don't want to leave them stranded, to starve or become one of the undead. There aren't many of us left. I want to save the ones that remain."

Blade raised his hand, index finger pointed to the heavens. When the duke nodded to him, he asked, "Why now, sir? Why at dusk?"

"As you may have heard, the undead have left our walls. We don't know where they have gone or for how long, but this is the best opportunity we have to get to the Temple of Vaspar. I don't know if Stiles has brought this up, but I would like a group of you to rescue the people at the temple, another group to scout out the city and see where everyone has gone, and a final group to leave the city and go to the Baron Milchev. His people need to be warned. Stiles will split you up into different groups when you arrive at the temple."

A splash interrupted the duke as two people sloshed through the muddy puddles—a man and a woman wearing flamboyant clothing and packed to travel. They stopped at the end of the guard line.

Wellen stepped around Duke Renier. "Shannai, what are you doing here?"

The man spoke before she could answer. "We want to go. Get outside the city while there's a chance."

The duke's eyebrows furrowed. "You and your wife are safe here. There is no reason to take a chance in the city if you don't have to."

Stiles bristled at the man's impertinence as the stranger glanced at the woman and rolled his eyes. "First off, she's my sister, and secondly, I don't want to be trapped in here if those things come back. We're getting out while the getting is good."

The duke folded his arms over his chest. "I won't force you to stay. It's your decision, but I think you and your sister would be better off here. We are making plans to leave the city, plans that don't involve dealing with the undead any more than we have to."

Wellan spoke before the man could reply. "Is this what you want, Shannai?"

The woman stared at the duke's boots as she replied, "I...I will follow my brother. He's never let me down yet."

The gaudy dressed man's teeth gleamed with his smug grin. Stiles noticed that his sister never looked the wizard in the eye as she answered, and her voice barely rose above a whisper.

Duke Renier frowned. "So be it. Marchas and Shannai will join the group that leaves the city to warn Baron Milchev. I wish you all the best of luck, and may whatever god you pray to be with you as you go about your appointed tasks."

∞ ∞ ∞ ∞

Within the darkening forest outside the palace walls, General Faygen watched as the gate cracked open and thirteen people crept from the safety beyond. One of the individuals even looked to be a young woman, dressed in an outlandishly bright blouse.

A thousand years have passed and men are just as stupid as they ever were, Faygen thought to himself. He shook his head back and forth in disgust. He had heard the ringing of the church bell. He had seen the message from the city walls. The fools in the palace desperately wanted to rescue the pathetic souls trapped in the temple, they only needed an opportunity. Faygen gave them that opportunity. He had pulled back the undead and gave the idiots of the palace the incentive they needed to attempt a rescue. It was almost too easy, unfair even. *Those poor bastards think they are only dealing with the mindless undead. They are about to learn a hard lesson.*

He watched the potential saviors as they crept down the road, swords drawn and arrows nocked. *They don't hold themselves like soldiers; bar room brawlers, perhaps, but not soldiers.* They had no formation and their steps fell with nervous energy, fear. *Have men fallen so far since my day? Are they now cowardly and stupid? If this is the best they can do, I will have the palace under my control by dawn. At least they had enough sense to send a few archers.*

Faygen almost pitied them, especially the girl. She reminded him of a slightly older version of his daughter. His sweet Eyliasa.

He couldn't get distracted by such thoughts. He couldn't allow himself to sympathize with the enemy. The problem was that he didn't think of them as the enemy. He didn't want to see himself as the bad guy, a usurper and a thief, but he couldn't see himself as anything else. The innocent people of this city had been destroyed by a great evil. An evil he was helping, but what choice did he have? He couldn't allow Eyliasa to be hurt again because of him. Not again.

The heroes faded from sight as darkness claimed the road and forest. Faygen looked at the undead around him with disgust. The white disks of dead eyes stared back. All over the forest the dead eyes stared like bloated white fireflies. Thousands of them, just far enough into the woods so that they couldn't be seen from the palace walls. His army hid in plain sight. They waited for his commands. They waited to feast. They wouldn't have to wait much longer.

He turned, facing deeper into the wet forest, and gave a mental command. *Wait! Stay here until I return.*

He felt some resistance to the command. Feet shuffled and arms swayed. Singly, they didn't have much will and were easily controlled, but in such large numbers, their willpower became a force to be reckoned with. Luckily, his own willpower was up to the task, at least at this point. He didn't know what would happen if he gave a command in the middle of a feeding frenzy. Hopefully, by that time, things would be under control and he could let these disgusting creatures go about their business.

He walked deeper into the forest, the damp undergrowth soaking his britches. His body no longer generated any heat, but neither did he feel the deep chill of the damp air and wet leaves. It was damned uncomfortable nonetheless. He could feel his flesh soaking up the moisture, wrinkling as dry skin pulled in the water like a sponge and became loose. It slid against his muscles and bone. He felt the rot that festered within him. At first, it hadn't been that noticeable, but as each day passed, it became a constant reminder of what he was. His skin itched constantly, giving off a sour odor that he could barely smell—though he imagined the stench would be horrible to anyone who still lived. Gasses built within him, and he had to belch and fart every few minutes to ease the discomfort of bloating. He didn't enjoy being one of the living dead.

Belching through clenched teeth, he put these thoughts behind him and pushed through the forest. He had to beat the heroes to the temple and evacuate the undead. He couldn't do it too early or the people in the temple would realize their jailers were gone and flee, but if he beat the heroes to the temple by a few minutes, everything would work out perfectly. He widened his stride and picked up speed.

∞ ∞ ∞ ∞

On the other side of the palace, where the light of day had never reached, a robed figure crouched in the darkness behind a door, waiting.

Twelve hundred years ago he had been a man known as The King Killer, a well-earned nickname, a testament to his abilities. The civilized world had known him for his skills in dealing silent death, and for the right coin, he boasted he could kill anyone. It wasn't an empty boast. The King Killer combined cunning genius with the stealth of a great cat to make him a life-ending machine that brought fear to the hearts of friends and enemies alike. There hadn't been a class of people he hadn't brought death to, whether they be homeless drunks, wealthy merchants or even powerful kings, he killed them all when the coin matched the job. Status, religion, skin color or sexual preference didn't mean a thing to him, just the coin, just the reputation, just the kill. He'd brought assassinations to a new level in his day, changing it from simple brutish henchmen work to a true form of art.

His wonderful life had ended quite suddenly, but not in a way he thought it would. Pursued through a forest after his latest kill, a barbarian lord forced him deep into the marshy woods. He had almost escaped, a mere mile or so from freedom, when he fell into a peat bog. His head slammed into a root and knocked him senseless. Within moments, he drowned in the organic soup. He had always pictured himself dying in a sword fight, or even being vengefully stabbed in the back, but never had he imagined drowning under putrid water with no one around to witness it.

Over the centuries, his body had merged with the bog. It absorbed the minerals and rich organic compounds until he became one with the peat, mud, and water. The compounds preserved him to a great extent, protecting his body against the ravages of time. It turned his skin into a pliable leather-like material, making it as dark as the murky sludge surrounding it. The earth became his mother, and the bog, her womb.

He probably would have stayed that way forever if a hand hadn't reached beneath the shallow waters and drug him to the surface. Those hands delivered him like a midwife would deliver a stillborn child. Instead of wailing about the end of an innocent life, this creature grinned at its newfound treasure, toting the black body to an even darker place.

The King Killer was glad to be back, doing what he loved to do.

The undead assassin wrapped his hand around his wrist and squeezed. He let go and a handprint engraved his wrist. His fingers trailed the indention. They slowly smoothed back over as he watched. His skin was pliable, like dough. Even his bones had softened, not to the point of making him a wobbly mess, but giving them a slight elasticity. It made them more flexible and harder to break, almost like cartilage. Unlike dough, his skin glistened black, onyx. Not the blackness of a normal dark-skinned man, but the blackness of a moonless night, the black of a crow. He liked his new self, the perfect representation of his inner being, his soul.

A light flickered beneath the door. Dim voices whispered back and forth. The King Killer stood and waited.

The clomps of footsteps echoed beyond the door. Sounds became louder, clearer. A deep voice rumbled, "Help me with this here wine shelf, Champ. It's heavy as the piet's purse and I don't want to be droppin' any of the wine."

Another voice, full of laugher, replied, "Then why don't ya just take the bottles out? Set them off to the side."

"Aw, come on. You want me to pull all these here bottles just to move this shelf over a few feet and then put them all back? That'll take half n' hour when movin' the stinkin' shelf with the bottles'll only take a couple of minutes. Besides, it ain't like we's gonna come back here and drink it after this."

Some of the laughter died from the second voice. "Yeah, you be right about that. I figure once we leave here, the dead's gonna be the only ones drinkin' the wine, and I doubt they would appreciate it much."

Another set of footsteps moved in. A third voice echoed with military authority. "You two shut it up and just get that shelf out of the way. It's blocking the escape tunnel and we need to make sure the door to the caverns is accessible and not stuck. It's gonna get used in the next day or so."

The deep voice replied, "Yes sir. I'm sure glad the Reniers never closed this secret exit off. Course, it ain't so secret no more, or won't be for long. What, with everyone traipsin' through here to escape."

"Well, come on, Grommy. You're the one that asked me to get the other end of this here shelf and now ya just stand there flappin' yer trap. Let's do this already."

Grumbles escaped the lips of the deep-voiced one and then the chamber filled with a loud screech and the tinkle of glass as the wine rack skidded across the floor.

Footsteps. The jingle of keys. A click of the door latch. The screech of a bar being lifted. The door opened. Light flooded the stone corridor, but didn't reach the hiding place of The King Killer.

The black creature moved deeper into the shadows as three men stood silhouetted in a pool of torchlight. One of them raised his brand high into the air and pointed it down the cavern shaft. "Don't look too inviting, does it, sir?"

The skinny man with the laughing voice replied, "Looks like freedom to me, Grommy."

The one in the center, adorned in leather and chain mail, put his hands on their shoulders and said, "Okay, let's lock it back up and I'll tell Duke Renier that the exit is ready."

He had to slip through the door before they closed it and locked him out, but he couldn't do that while they stood in the way. He couldn't kill them yet without alarming everyone in the palace, and he wasn't ready to do that just yet. With a flick of his wrist, he launched a small stone into the darkness, further down the corridor.

The men spun around as the stone met a wall and clattered across the floor.

Grommy held his torch out toward the darkness. "Did you hear that, sir? Somethin's down there."

"Ssssssshhhhhh."

They waited and listened. Silence.

The armored one drew his sword and walked into the corridor; the other two followed his example. They walked past The King Killer, oblivious to his presence as he crouched in a dark recess. Their eyes and ears focused on something down the passageway.

He let them walk a little further into the darkness before he crept forward and slid through the door. As he walked past the wine rack, he glanced back into the dark corridor. Three forms silently crept over the rough stone floor. He smiled and thought, *Thank you, gentlemen. I couldn't have done it without your help.* Then he walked on, into the palace to earn his keep.

Chapter 14

"Don't ye be goin' out in the forest at night, boy.
There be more than wolves hidin' amongst those trees.
The boogeyman lives in them woods,
and he loves to eat little boys."
~A grandfather's words to his grandson

adame Rachelle stood and gazed out the window of her room. She looked over the top of the palace walls, beyond the darkening forest and buildings in the distance. Without candles or gas lamps glowing, the buildings and homes were almost inseparable from the trees that sat between them. Renier had become a black void broken by subtle textures, a dark shadow under the slightly brighter skyline. The rain had finally stopped. A sliver of moon floated in a hazy sky.

She had watched the soldiers gather around the front gate, saw the duke and Wellan talk to them and witnessed the colorfully dressed man and woman join the soldiers.

The man disturbed her, like a name that she knew but couldn't remember. She didn't dwell on any particular thing. She couldn't concentrate and very little penetrated through the chaotic layers of her thoughts. Madame Rachelle kept herself surrounded in a limbo where few around her entered. Grief still sulked about in her mind like a melancholy guest. It brushed against her emotions and pushed thoughts of her daughter to the surface. The grief hobbled her and prevented her from wanting to do anything except stare into the dark heavens.

Knuckles tapped against wood and floated up through her thoughts like bubbles in a pool, quiet at first, but slowly gaining strength until they broke the surface. She looked around the room, not able to place the noise in her dreamy state. It came again, a loud rapping followed by, "Madame Rachelle, may I come in?"

Whose voice? She recognized it, a voice she had heard very recently. *Wellan?* Rachelle sighed. She didn't want to be pulled from her empty haze. "I...I don't feel like talking right now, Wellan. Maybe later?"

"I understand your grief, but we need to talk." A pause, then, "I need your help."

Why would the wizard need the help of a fortuneteller? Why can't he just let me grieve for my daughter? She almost told him to go away, whether he needed her help or not, but curiosity and common politeness won out. "Just a second."

She walked to the nightstand and picked up a candle, the only light in the room. Shadows lengthened and jumped as she walked to the door, using the candle to light others on her way to greet the wizard. Shadows still dominated the small room as she opened the door, but it didn't look quite so glum.

Wellan's awkward and concerned smile greeted her. "How are you feeling, Rachelle?"

How do you think I'm feeling? My daughter died this morning and then came back to life as an undead little girl. Then I had to watch her die a second time while holding her in my arms. How am I supposed feel? "Had better days, but I'm holding together."

He stepped into the room and put a comforting hand on her arm. "It will get better. I promise."

Emotions boiled up as his hand withdrew. She felt a hitch in her throat; tears filled her eyes and rolled down her cheeks. Tears she didn't think she still had.

"I don't mean to trouble you, but we need to talk."

She gave a single nod and sat on the corner of the bed. Wellan took a chair from the small table by the door and sat facing her.

"I know this is a terrible time to do this, but I would like to begin your training as a wizard, or at least awaken you to the experience."

Her mouth opened, closed. She looked away from him; thoughts and emotions boiled to the surface. A day ago she would have jumped at the chance for such an honor, but now it didn't seem to matter—just another burden for her to carry.

"I need you, Rachelle. The city needs another wizard besides myself." He patted her leg and continued. "I started thinking about our conversation this morning. The one we had before this mess began. I remember the look in your eyes while we talked. I saw something there, for just a moment. Almost terror. You quickly covered it up. What is it you didn't tell me? What did you see when you looked at me? I think I know, but I want to hear it from you."

She answered without hesitation. Her voice was flat, as though someone else spoke through her. "You're aura was black, Wellan. You're going to die."

The wizard's lips pressed together. They formed a tight line under his bushy mustache. "I thought that may have been what you saw." He leaned forward in his chair and took her hands in his. "My aura is just one more reason why we need you. If I die, the city will need another protector, someone who can see things they cannot and use forces others don't understand and cannot wield."

She raised her head, her face twisted with sarcasm and self-doubt. "I couldn't save my own daughter, wizard. How do you expect me to save myself when the city has already fallen? How do you expect me to save the few of us that are still alive? You need to find someone who still cares because I don't."

"You have been hurt, Rachelle. I understand that, but don't let the rest of these people suffer because of it. Help me save them."

She pulled her hands away from his. "Find someone else, wizard. Everything I cared about has been taken away. I'm just an empty shell now. I have nothing to fight for."

Wellan's voice rose with frustration. "There is no one else. Not just anyone can become a wizard. Not everyone has the inborn power, or sees the world in such a way that will allow them to accept the magic and let it use them. You do. No one else here does. They need a wizard more than they know. If...when I fall, someone will need to step in and take my place. Only you can do that, Rachelle. The magic has chosen you, picked you out from among the others. Only you have that power, the insight to be a wizard."

When she didn't say anything, he reached behind him and grabbed a candle off the small table. He held it between them. "Let me give you a taste of what you can do. Just a small thing to be sure, but one that nobody else here can do." He lifted the candle up to her face. "What do you see here? What do you really see?"

She shrugged. "Wax. A wick. A small flame."

"No. Look harder. Use your sight."

She let out an exasperated sigh and looked again at the candle. This time, she squinted and concentrated. She focused on the flame, seeing it in another light. "Plasma, white light jumping with the air currents. Vapors rising above the light and little sparks bursting within the plasma like tiny exploding fireflies."

A small smile brightened Wellan's face. "Now, will it away, disperse the heat into the surrounding air. Concentrate on it not being there. Think about the plasma wilting away until it is gone."

She looked past the flame to the wizard. Surprise and disbelief furrowed her brow. She had looked at many things with the aura, flames being one of the most fascinating, but she had never thought of altering anything she looked at. It had never occurred to her that she might have the power to change anything, to alter it from one state to another.

Wellan nodded to her, wordlessly telling her to stay focused and concentrate on the flame. Her gaze narrowed again on the candle. The tiny exploding sparks, white light and vapor flickered with the lightly swirling air. She squinted. Her eyes narrowed to thin slits as she thought about the light diminishing, shrinking into the wick. To her amazement, the light dimmed and pulled in tighter to the little strand of string that fed it. The tiny exploding sparks moved slower and popped less. She willed it to diminish even more, causing it to pull in close to the little wick until it became a tiny blue flame, then disappeared all together.

With her mouth open in awe, she stared at the wizard's smiling face.

"What you just did is the basis for everything magical. Understanding a thing, seeing how it works, and then having the will to control it."

Still amazed by what she had done, she gawked at the cooling wick. "I'm just a fortune teller, not a wizard."

Wellan beamed like a proud father. "Oh, you are much more than a fortune teller. Perhaps you aren't a wizard yet, but I can see you doing far more than I have done. I can't see auras in the way you do, and it took me almost a month of frustrating effort before I could extinguish a flame when I began my journey years and years ago. You are what these people need. That burst of energy you used outside the walls earlier today is a powerful force, and it might just be the edge we need to get out of here."

"But I have no idea how I did it."

"Yes, you do. I just showed you. Desperation and anger powered that first burst of magic and, with a little practice, you should be able to do it again…only with a bit more control. Yes, I see great things in you, great things indeed."

He lifted her hand from her lap and placed the candle in her palm before closing her fingers around the cool wax. "Now, let's see you light it."

∞ ∞ ∞ ∞

Shannai walked in the center of the group of men with an arrow set into her bow. Her eyes scanned the dark forest on either side. An eerie silence filled the woods as light gusts blew through the treetops and made them sway in the moonlight. The crunch of their footsteps and an occasional rustling from the forest were the only sounds that broke the quiet walk to the temple.

She still couldn't believe Marchas had talked her into leaving the safety of the palace. Her brother made a good point when he said the palace had become a trap with no way out. With the dead mysteriously gone from the walls, they could easily escape. It could be their only chance to leave the city. Besides, there hadn't been enough people left within the walls to fight through the ranks of undead if they massed again. Still, the duke didn't appear to be a man who would let himself become cornered. Even if he were cornered, he still seemed smart enough to figure a way out of a trap like that. If the duke failed, they still had the wizard, and Wellan certainly wasn't one to be brought down easily.

A noise caught her attention. Leaves shifted and crackled deep within the oak dominated woods. Something ran parallel to the road. Trying to get ahead of them?

She stopped, raised her bow, and focused on the darkness between the trees, past the rough trunks. Shannai could just see the outline of a figure standing deep within, a faint highlight on a cheek, the dark silhouette of a shoulder breaking up the vertical pattern of the tree trunks. The black woods made it difficult to tell if the shapes were real or only her eyes playing tricks on her. She had to be sure before she alerted the others. Everyone's nerves were frayed and a false alarm was the last thing they needed.

"What do you see?" her brother whispered in her ear. With a yelp, she released her arrow into the forest.

She turned to scold him for scaring her when she saw a sight that made her heart race, the diamond sparkle of eyes deep within the trees. She ignored her brother and pulled another arrow from her quiver. She nocked it, never taking her gaze from the small, round disks.

Shannai whispered to Marchas and pointed her arrow at a tree. "Look into the forest, just to the right of that tree. Do you see...?"

Another set of eyes opened, and another. As she watched, pairs of glowing disks opened throughout the forest. She turned to face the other side of the road and saw the same thing. Hundreds of the undead stood in eerie silence, watching them.

Her brother croaked, "Oh my gods!"

"Yeah, at the moment it doesn't seem like such a good idea to be away from the palace," she whispered.

The leader, a short blond fellow named Stiles, hissed, "Shut it up, you two."

"But the undead..." Shannai tried to tell him.

"Yeah, I see them. There's nothing to be done about it now, and so far, they aren't doing anything but standing there. We're gonna keep moving forward, stick with the plan. If something threatens us, then we will do something about it, but for right now the best thing we can do is keep going."

Shannai nodded and followed Stiles as he walked toward the temple. Her eyes darted back and forth between the glowing disks that peered at her from the forest.

She let out a generous sigh when the temple came into view and still none of the undead threatened them. Though she had seen them throughout the entire trip, they hadn't moved. The corpselike people in the woods didn't seem to be watching the road or its travelers. They only stared straight ahead—waiting. Their stoic silence almost terrified her more than a blatant attack would. She realized that every step she made toward the temple put her one more step away from the palace and put more undead between herself and safety. She didn't understand what was going on, but she didn't like it.

The temple rose out of the forest like a beacon of civilization in the middle of the wilds, though these wilds consisted only of a few acres of woods in a busy city. Shannai had grown up in a city. She had spent most of her life walking down cobbled streets and only seeing forests from the safety of a city wall, so the woods, especially at night, put her in an unfamiliar environment. The randomness and lack of order of the forest, any forest, spooked her even when they weren't full of undead. The stone and stained glass building, with its high porch and marble columns, gave her a sense of security and familiarity after her short walk through the wooded road. She wanted to run up the steps, rush through the oaken double doors and lock them behind her. A glance at her brother told her he felt the same way.

Stiles halted the group with a swipe of his hand. He paused and took a hard look at the temple before going any further. Dim light flickered through some of the windows. A silhouette crossed in front of a candle, a dark blue and red blur behind the colored glass. Stiles motioned everyone forward with a wave of his arm. They passed a well with angelic faces carved into each stone. An oval patch of grass was charred and covered with an oily film. A blackened skeleton protruded from the spot like charred wood left after a campfire.

They walked past the well and up the wide steps. Stiles rapped his knuckles against the wooden doors. She knew his knocking couldn't have been very loud, but in the silence under the stone porch, it sounded like hammer blows. The door opened immediately, as if someone had been waiting for guests. A portly man, his soiled robe designating him as a servant of Vaspar, peeked around the edge of the door. He held a finely crafted sword before him. The hilt looked to be made of solid gold. Behind the servant of Vaspar stood an elderly priest and almost a dozen other people. Most looked relieved, some angry, but they all shared a deep fear. It showed in their wide eyes.

The priest lowered his sword, grabbed Stiles upper arm, and pulled him into the temple. "I'm so glad to see you. We've been waiting here all day to be rescued."

The other soldiers followed Stiles into the pew-lined sanctuary. Owl took a last look into the forest before shutting the doors behind him.

Stiles bowed his head to the priest and said, "I'm sorry we couldn't be here sooner, Piet Lithor. It's been almost impossible to leave Palace Renier due to all of the undead piling up around the walls. When they retreated, we came right out."

Piet Lithor? Even Shannai had heard that name, the High Priest of Vaspar, responsible for most of the souls in Renier. The rumors described him as an arrogant and pious man, one who liked to get his boots licked and deemed himself only slightly less important than the duke himself. The man she saw before her didn't seem anything like the rumors described. Worry and sadness softened his features. The piet appeared almost...humble. She reminded herself again not to listen to every piece of gossip that drifted through the ale-tainted air of seedy taverns.

Piet Lithor's eyes widened. "They retreated from the walls? You didn't scare them off or defeat them?"

"No, your Excellency. They are all standing in the woods, a little ways off the road."

The piet seemed to consider this for a long moment before commenting, "How odd."

Ash stepped in beside Stiles and spoke. "What do you mean? Do you know something?"

Stiles glared at the guard then turned to listen as the piet said, "No, I don't really know anything. I said it was odd because the undead have been standing out there all day, beyond the edge of the property, until just before you showed up. I just thought you scared them off."

Stiles rubbed his chin, deep in thought. "They left before we showed up, and they never came any closer than the edge of the property?"

"Yes, it seems the holiness of our Lord Vaspar keeps them at bay."

Ash folded his arms over his chest. "Sounds like a trap to me."

"Yeah, me too. I just don't see how or why. They could have surrounded us anywhere along the road between the palace and here. It doesn't make sense."

Ash walked to the window and looked out at the well. "Well, no reason in dragging this out. Who do you want to go with me to warn the baron?"

A well-dressed man pushed himself past the piet and growled, "What's he talkin' about, warnin' the baron? You have to get us out of here and it's gonna take all of you to do it."

Stiles ignored the well-dressed man and looked to the piet as he replied. "Duke Renier gave us orders that once we reached the temple, we are to split into three groups. One group has the responsibility of seeing you all safely to the palace. A second group is to try and leave the city through one of the main gates and warn Baron Milchev about the fate of Renier. Finally, the third group is to scout through the city and find out where the dead have gone." He looked to Ash before continuing. "I think we know where the dead are so the third group isn't necessary."

Ash gave Stiles an approving nod and joined the other soldiers. Stiles turned to Piet Lithor and said, "So, the group returning to the castle will actually be larger than the duke anticipated."

His explanation didn't appease the merchant at all. "Trying to get to the outer wall is pure folly. I barely survived getting here, and I was only a few blocks from the temple when it happened. Surely the duke must have more sense..."

The piet stepped between Stiles and the angry man. "Duke Renier is correct, Bos Spielter. The neighboring cities need to be warned. I'm sure the duke knew what he was doing when he sent these men. I trust his judgment, and thereby, the judgment of this brave soldier."

Piet Lithor looked over his shoulder toward Stiles as he continued, "I'm sure he won't let us down."

∞ ∞ ∞ ∞

Moments later, Piet Lithor stood near the front of the motley group, sword in hand and ready to leave his sanctuary. He glanced at one of the soldiers to see if he held the sword of Vaspar correctly. The man saw his glance and smiled; crooked yellow teeth shone through bristly beard. The scraggly man shook his sword back and forth before him with bravado. *Let's go kill us some undead.* Lithor gripped his holy relic tighter and decided to look somewhere else.

The survivors stood behind the double doors and nervously waited for Stiles to open them so they could begin their run for the palace. Fear shown in the refugees' eyes, and displayed itself in the guard's clenched jaws. Bos Spielter stood to the side with a table leg in his knuckle-whitening grasp. The woman with an infant stayed in the middle of the group, holding the baby close to her breasts. Brother Cylus perched next to Lithor, a steak knife clenched in his liver-spotted fist, his face pale and glistening with sweat. The young man, Tollis Mayer, actually looked excited about the prospect of leaving the temple in the soldier's company. The piet turned his head to the soldiers that milled around the outside of the group. *City guards, not palace guards, not real soldiers, or mercenaries. Just city guards.* The fact that Duke Renier had sent city guards to rescue them spoke volumes about the state of the palace. The situation didn't look good, not good at all.

Stiles waved his men to get ready, then turned to the dozen survivors. "Just stay together. Keep up with us and don't get out of the group. We're heading to the palace at a brisk walk. We won't run unless we have to, so just follow my lead and everything should work out fine."

He nodded to his men, meeting each and every eye. His eyes asked them if they were ready. Their eyes replied that they were not, but what else could they do? He nodded, then turned and opened the door. Stiles poked his head out and gave the temple grounds and neighboring woods a hard look. The Sanctuary grounds were clear of undead and he waved everyone forward. "Okay, let's do this."

One by one, they walked through the door and into the night. The first thing Lithor noticed was the brisk breeze blowing in from the port. It carried the salty smell of the sea on a draft of dead fish. Tree limbs swayed back and forth and gave the surrounding woods an eerie life of their own. He looked deep into the forest as he set his foot onto the road. He prayed to see the shadowed trees free of undead, but he feared not knowing where they hid more. He gripped the sword tighter in his pudgy grasp and followed Stiles over the cobbled road.

Everyone huddled close together. The refugees almost stumbled over one another as they searched the surrounding forest for the glint of an eye or the shuffle of feet. The guards remained on the outside perimeter, bows held ready, eyes constantly scanning back and forth over the forest floor. They looked as scared as the crowd they guarded. Their gazes didn't scan through the woods like a predator would. Their nervous glances marked them as prey, skittishly trying to get past the lair of a hungry beast. Lithor didn't have much faith in this rag-tag group, but there weren't any other options. He tried to push the fear out of his mind by concentrating on putting one foot in front of the other. He reminded himself that he had to have faith. The great Lord Vaspar would see him through.

A gasp rose from the back of the group. The twang of a bowstring followed by the *thunk* of an arrow as it punctured flesh brought everyone to a halt. Hundreds of dark figures stumbled from the woods onto the trail behind them. The thin moon highlighted the tops of their heads, their shoulders, and their raised arms. Their eyes shined like crisp silver, coins for their voyage to the afterlife. A fist of fear gripped Lithor's spine as he watched their silent march.

All the guards raised their bows, strings pulled into V's.

"Lower your bows!" Stiles hissed.

Six bows lowered, but the strings remained pulled tight. Everyone turned to Stiles.

"Let's save the fight for when it's necessary. If we speed up, we should stay ahead of them." Without looking to see if anyone followed his order, he turned and jogged toward the palace. Everyone followed. They constantly glanced over their shoulders to make sure the undead hadn't caught up.

Lithor's confidence in the young commander rose as he struggled to keep up. The man had made the right decision, choosing not to begin a battle that would do nothing but slow them down. He just hoped Stiles had enough skill as a leader to get them to the palace.

Bushes shook to Lithor's left. The undead spilled onto the road behind the rear soldiers as if the forest had decided to vomit their filth from its midst, to purge their vile flesh from its natural beauty.

His heart raced. Blood pounded in his ears, and sweat burned his eyes. In the distance, the palace walls grew closer. His heavy form wasn't made for such a long run and he slowly fell further toward the back of the group, almost to the rearguard. His side felt like someone reached under his lowest rib to squeeze and pinch his innards. Sweat drenched his clothes, a combination of overexertion and fear. His heart pounded harder. He felt each pulse as it thrummed against his temple. The pumping muscle threatened to punch through his chest. He wasn't going to make it to the palace. The great Piet Lithor would die within sight of the walls, almost in their shadow. It wasn't fair. He deserved bet...

He stumbled into the woman with the baby. The infant released a shrill wail and looked at Lithor as though he had slapped it.

They had stopped.

He bent over and placed both hands on his knees, sword dangling in his sweaty grip. He stared at the ground and panted as sweat dripped from the end of his nose to the road. The sudden stop made him feel feverish. His stomach clenched; his last meal rose up his throat and splashed onto the ground in front of him. He ignored the mess and looked over his shoulder. The undead had stopped.

He stood, wiped the filth from his half-open mouth and examined the undead. *Why have they stopped?* Their still forms stared back, pinpricks of silver against grisly silhouettes.

Stiles' shout rose over the wailing baby and panting people. "Move aside and let us pass."

Lithor spun around; the sudden movement made his head swirl with dizziness. Stiles faced a bear of a man in archaic armor. The armored form stood at least six and a half feet tall. The dim moonlight cut his face into blacks and whites, an older man with a stern face that seemed to be chiseled from stone. His thick arms crossed over his chest, the skin roughly textured, like parchment. A sad smile crossed his cracked lips. "I am truly sorry, but I can't allow you to go any farther."

Chapter 15

*"Walls of stone and doors of steel mean naught to the beings of
the spectral world. How can thou keep out what has no substance?*
*How can thou stop a spirit? Will ye rely on ye ramparts and
shields, or will ye build yerself a wall of faith?"*
~Sermon of the Piet Logan

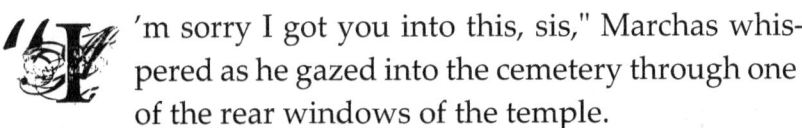'm sorry I got you into this, sis," Marchas whis-
pered as he gazed into the cemetery through one
of the rear windows of the temple.

Ash, Arolyn, and Wolf stood by another window. They
whispered amongst themselves as they quietly routed their
path through the city. Owl stood in the shadows outside
the door and silently scanned for undead.

"It's not your fault, *bro.*" She gave him a lopsided grin.
She hated to be called *sis* and Marchas knew it. He only said

it to lightly tease her and relieve some of the tension. "We were just at the wrong place at the wrong time."

He cocked his head and angled his eyes toward her. No hint of teasing remained in his voice, "No, I'm not talking about us being in this city. That was purely bad luck. I'm talking about getting you to leave the palace. That might not have been one of my better ideas. I just figured…hoped the dead had left. Found themselves something better to do. I guess I was wrong."

Though fear, her new constant companion, stood behind her breathing its hot breath onto the back of her neck, she kept her voice lighthearted as she replied. "Well, it's not like it's the first time you've been wrong. Hopefully, it won't be the last."

He slapped her shoulder and laughed. "Come on, Shannai. Give me a break. I'm trying to be serious here."

"Oh, and you think I'm not."

"Shhhhhh," Ash hissed. "Not so loud. This isn't one of your damned tavern parties. That sort of noise will get us all killed. So either shut it up or get the hell away from me and my men."

Shannai grabbed Marchas's forearm and squeezed, a warning not to start anything. They needed the help of the soldiers, and the last thing she wanted to see was a confrontation between her hot-tempered brother and the equally dispositional Ash.

The door creaked open enough to allow Owl's thin frame to slide through. Marchas sat back down with a glare at Ash. Ash glared back then turned to Owl and whispered, "Did you see any of them? Is the way clear through the graveyard?"

Owl glanced at Marchas, his mouth drawn in a frown and his eyes narrowed in suspicion. When he finished sizing up Marchas, he answered Ash. "Yeah, the graveyard is clear of them. I saw a few milling around outside the fence, but they weren't tryin' to get in or nothin'. I still don't like the idea of goin' through the graveyard. It seems like that would be the last place we would want to go."

"I can't argue with you, other than there ain't no reason to go through the front of the temple and walk around the outside to get to the back when all we got to do is start back here in the first place. Plus, we won't be going through the woods where they can hide. It's open in the cemetery all the way to the first block of buildings. We should be able to see them way before they can catch us."

Owl's mouth drew up into a deep frown, thick lips giving his features a fishlike appearance. "I see the sense of it an' all, Ash. That don't mean I got to like it none."

"Yeah, I don't like it any myself."

Ash strolled to the door and motioned the men to get ready with a wave of his hand. Shannai and Marchas stood while the black nails of the god of fear tickled the base of her skull. She shivered on feather-thin legs. Marchas put his arm around her shoulders and squeezed. He would be there for her. He wouldn't let her down.

With a last look at everyone, Ash opened the door and stepped onto the rear porch of the Temple of Vaspar. The trees swayed in the wind, dark shapes dancing to the sound of the ocean breeze. The movement didn't help shed her fear. It would make the undead harder to spot, harder to hear. *Maybe the wind will do the same for us,* she told herself, though she didn't believe it.

They walked down the steps and onto the leaf-littered ground of the cemetery. Headstones rose from the soil and reminded her of how death should be—orderly and permanent.

She walked at the back of the group through the graveyard. As she slipped between the marble headstones, saintly statues and mausoleums, her imagination began to take hold. Her gaze fell to the mounds of grass-covered dirt, where bodies lay in eternal rest. Her fear kicked in to create another scenario for the people buried beneath her feet. A scenario where mummified corpses pushed against the moldy cloth that deteriorated around them. Shannai thought about skeletal hands that beat against the rotting lids of their coffins. She imagined half rotting creatures that dug their way to the surface. In her mind, she saw thin hands shoveling dirt behind withered mummies with slow determination as they moved upward like earthworms, pushing and clawing to the surface. She imagined both hands rising through the soil and finding purchase on the surface, pulling the undead from the ground like a baby escaping a womb, to be born again.

She almost stumbled and fell when Marchas whispered, "Are you okay?"

She nodded and looked over the graveyard. All she saw were tombstones and mounds of dirt shining in the moonlight. *Focus! Quit letting your imagination run away with you. This is bad enough without that.*

Marchas grabbed her upper arm and brought his forehead close to hers. His eyes questioned again, *Are you okay?* She answered with a quick nod and a tight-lipped smile. He gave her arm another squeeze before releasing it. She wasn't okay and he knew it, but what else was there to do?

Within moments, the cemetery gates rose before them. A waist high stone wall topped with spiked iron bars stood before them. Four undead stumbled back and forth before the open gate. They mindlessly slapped at the opening between the iron posts with pale hands, but they did not attempt to cross the invisible line that represented the holy soil of the graveyard.

Four bows sang out. An arrow fletching sprouted from each undead forehead. They fell to the ground in a blood-less pile. One twisted and twitched, a snake in its death throes.

Without slowing, the guard placed fresh arrows in their bows. Ash yanked his from the corpse he had shot and walked on to the line of buildings across the road from the graveyard.

They were halfway across the road when the blank-eyed men and women stumbled into view between the buildings. The mindless mob of rotting flesh that had once been the peaceful residents of Renier marched forward to greet the duke's guards. Their clouded eyes opened wide and fixed on the small group.

Ash veered toward an opening between two buildings. They followed him to one of the few alleys that didn't have undead pouring from it. When he got to the opening, he stopped and fired an arrow down the alleyway. When it was cleared of undead, he waved everyone on before enter-ing the blackness between the structures.

Shannai followed, her brother a dozen steps behind her. The buildings to either side of the alley blocked the moon-light and turned the narrow pass into a black void. She slowed to a crawl and stumbled forward like a blind person.

Her foot stepped on something soft. She looked down. Two silver coin-sized circles shown at her feet; the white fletching of Ash's arrow poked up from a pale skull like a road sign. She opened her mouth to scream, but a rough hand slid over her lips. Arms dragged her further into the alley, and then sidewise into complete darkness.

∞ ∞ ∞ ∞

"What do ya tink yer doin', Tomay Raish?"

"Just trying to comfort you a little."

She pushed him back. "Well, ye won't be confortin' me like tat, so ye jus keep yer hands to yerself. For gods' sakes, me ma and pa might be dead. Ye tink for one minute tat I'm wantin' to let ye have yer way wit' me r'now. Ye must be daft!"

They stood near the wall of a dark and seldom used corridor. For the past several months, they had met here to be away from prying eyes. Not the most romantic place, but they could call it their own, one of the few easily accessible spots in the palace that offered privacy. The unlikely location had given them some memorable moments.

She could just make out Tomay's frown, his eyes narrowed.

"I'm sorry Clowey. It's just, with all that's happened...well... I thought... I figured this might be our last chance. I just want to be with you one more time before the end."

She placed her hand on his cheek. "Tat be awfully sweet of ye, but I knows ye better tan tat. T'end of t'world ain't got a durn ting to do wit' it. Yer always wantin to rut, tis ere jus' gives ye an excuse." She pulled her hand away

228

and gave him a playful slap on the cheek. "Now, ye needs to be tinkin' aboot soldierin' so ye can get us out o' tis mess. Ye do dat an' I promise ye tat ye'll be tired o' ruttin' before I's trough wit ye."

His teeth shone in the darkness, the first smile she had seen from him all day. "I guess I'm gonna have to start soldiering if I'm gonna make you pay up on that promise."

She placed her arms on his shoulders and locked her fingers behind his head as he held her waist. "Ye certainly will, Sir Raish. Ye certainly will."

He tipped his head down and gave her a passionate kiss. His hands stayed in the neutral area around her waist. She crossed her arms over the back of his neck and returned his affection. She gave him a final squeeze before breaking the kiss.

"We'd best stop tis now or yer gonna start gettin' ideas again."

A stench assaulted her nostrils as Tomay wrapped his arms around her waist and squeezed. His lips went to her neck. "Yeah, I got an idea or two..."

"Stop it, Tomay! Do ye smell tat smell?"

His breath tickled her neck. "All I smell is you, Clowey, and it smells damned fine."

She shoved him away. "Not me, ye bloody stooge. Do ye smell it now dat ye got yer nose outa me hair? A rottin', mulchy smell. Like a compost pile."

He sniffed. "Yeah, I do smell someth..."

An obsidian black hand grasped his shoulder from behind. His eyes widened and his mouth formed a silent 'O'.

Clowey stepped back, her lips parted to scream. A fist shot out of the dark. Instead of a scream, she heard a loud crack as pain exploded in the middle of her face and bright sparks filled her vision. The force of the blow threw her backwards. Her head slammed against the wall and she slid to the ground. Everything went dark.

∞ ∞ ∞ ∞

Something tugged her hand from behind. Her head throbbed. Her stomach churned in a nauseous battle. She ran her tongue across her swollen lips and tasted blood. Something tugged her hands again then pushed her back. Her eyes opened, two narrow slits letting in the pain. She shut them again.

"Ud est up?" A guttural sound, cracked and ancient.

Her eyes snapped open. A black face, inches from hers. Black orbs gazed into her brown eyes. The creature's head cocked to the side in curiosity. The smell of compost and rot wafted through the air, noticeable even through her blood-clogged nose, a familiar smell.

It all came back to her. Tomay flirting, his surprised face, the black hand...

She tried to scream, but a cloth filled her mouth. It tasted like rotten fish and dirt. She tried to sit up and fell back. Her hands were bound behind her.

The thing smiled with teeth that shone and glinted like small slivers of wet coal. It pushed her flat against the wall. "Ud watch."

The obsidian man stood and pulled a thin black cloth from his robes. She noticed Tomay lying on the floor behind her assailant in a pool of liquid. Blood? His chest rose and fell. He lived.

"Dis ud man? Ud watch." She shook her head and shrugged her shoulders. Clowey didn't understand the message that the cryptic figure tried to convey.

He reached out and cupped her chin with his greasy palm. His fingers squeezed her cheeks until her teeth cut into the sides. He pointed her face toward Tomay's prone figure. "Ud watch." *You watch.*

She nodded her head.

He laid the thin black cloth over Tomay's face. It stuck tight to his flesh like a mask. A thumb-sized dimple rose and fell with his breathing. The thing reached into its robes and brought forth a dagger as dark as his flesh with runes that shone like emeralds. He turned back to Clowey. "Ud watch. Ud shee."

Oh gods! I don't want to see this. Oh, Tomay. Get up, please. Tears slid from the corners of her rage-filled eyes.

The obsidian creature straddled Tomay, then raised the dagger and plunged it into his neck. The blade jerked to the side. Blood spurted from his throat and splashed over Clowey's legs. Tomay convulsed beneath his killer, then lay still. The cloth that covered his face shimmered bright green then dimmed back to black. The killer rose over his victim and stepped to the side. His eyes never left the young soldier.

Without warning, as if it were the most natural thing in the world, Tomay's eyes opened and he sat up. Blood dribbled down his neck. His head rotated to Clowey. She looked into his eyes and knew that Tomay's soul had departed his body.

She screamed against the gag.

Tomay crawled to Clowey. She tried to scoot away, but the obsidian man grabbed her foot and drew her back. His low chuckles made her think of spiders and slugs. The man she had considered marrying jerked toward her on hands and elbows. His legs dragged behind him. Blood dripped from the gash in his neck. He grasped her shoulder and pulled it to his mouth. She tried to pull away, but her strength couldn't break his hold. She screamed into the gag as his teeth tore into her flesh and ripped a chunk away.

"Ud go." The killer waved Tomay away. The soldier withdrew to the far wall and chewed on his prize.

The monster squatted next to her injured shoulder. She moaned as he squeezed the wound. Red seeped between his fingers and dripped from her elbow. He brought his blood-coated hand before her eyes, wiped the blood across her cheek, and then brought the hand to his mouth and licked his palm. "Gud. Gud blood."

In a fraction of a second, her fear turned to rage; the animal within her took over and burst from its cage. Instinct beat down her fear. She jerked onto her back, lashed out with her foot, and planted her heel into his dark jaw. His head snapped backward then fell back into place. She felt bile rise in her throat. An egg-sized concave deformed the monster's jaw. He rubbed the deformity, kneading it back into shape.

He reached into his robes and she kicked again. His hand flashed out and grabbed her ankle. He drove the rune knife into her thigh with the other hand. Blood gushed from the wound.

"Ud bith!" He yanked the knife free and fell on top of her, driving her flush with the floor. She heard a snap and pain flared from her wrist. Another scream threatened to tear through the gag.

He brought his rage-contorted face to hers, nose to nose. "Ud bith. Ud be fur me. Ud be mine." The words hissed from his mouth. His breath merged with hers. It filled her mouth with sewage even through the gag. The black cloth fell over her face, blocking out the murderer.

No. Not like this. Noooooo...

Pain sliced into her side. Fire stabbed into her body and withdrew. It returned at her shoulder and withdrew again. The pain sliced through her arm and opened her bicep. Her clothes clung to her, wet and sticky as she wiggled and squirmed beneath the creature. Her strength faded. New pains assaulted her body, but they weren't as bad. She felt weak, drowsy. The pain faded as she tired. A green flash embodied her world, then nothing.

∞ ∞ ∞ ∞

The night brought with it a cool, damp breeze that blew over the sea from the south. It filled Renier with humidity and a salty sea smell. A sliver of moon shone on empty streets. Clouds occasionally blocked the shining orb. Renier sat quiet and peaceful. The silence was uncommon for the large bustling city, the peaceful appearance deceiving. Men paced back and forth along the palace walls. They looked with anticipation for the return of Stiles and the group from the temple and dreaded the return of the undead. The eerie quiet only added to their nervousness.

Wellan stood on the wall and looked down the road where the refugees would return at any moment. A shadow moved within the trees and then another. Soon, the forest came to life. Figures swayed and trampled into the open. The undead. They gathered on the Temple Way Road, just beyond arrow range. Their heads were protected by helmets. Most were guards and soldiers, but even a few city residents wore battered helmets that appeared to have been keepsakes of someone's grandfather.

"The refugees will never be able to return if those things don't get out of the way," a guard grumbled.

Wellan couldn't disagree. This new move showed organization, thought, a plan of attack.

Further down the wall, Duke Renier frantically discussed a rescue strategy with a handful of men, none over the age of thirty. Each looked grim and determined as they nodded their heads and commented on his plans.

Wellan ignored them for the moment while he studied the ghouls. Each stood still. They gazed down the road with their backs to the wall, and waited on the refugees. They looked like soldiers formed up for an attack.

A large man stepped out of the woods. He wore armor of frayed leather and rusted steel. The man marched to the middle of the road and stood before the undead. Wellan gasped, not believing his eyes.

The man reminded him of someone he knew from centuries passed, but it couldn't be him.

He closed his eyes and whispered an archaic phrase. When he opened them again, the world stood out clearer. Night became day to his eyes alone. What had only seconds ago been drab shadows came to life with the color of midday sunshine. He focused on the large man. There could be no doubt. General Faygen led the undead.

The ghouls behind Faygen shuffled their feet in excited anticipation. Further down the road, dim shapes became clear as they sped toward the ranks of corpses. The refugees. They stopped several yards away from the ghastly line. The general stepped forward as an armored form detached itself from the group of refugees, Stiles. The two exchanged words, but Wellan couldn't hear. No spell he knew of would allow him to hear over such a distance.

Wellan turned and walked to the duke as the man mounted the stairs and prepared to go outside the city walls to rescue the refugees.

"Come to help us, Wellan?"

Wellan shook his head. "You can't go out there. It's a trap. He's trying to bait you to leave the safety of the palace walls."

The duke smiled. "I know it's a trap, and a damned fine one at that because I can't just leave those people to die at the hands of those...things. Knowing it's a trap gives me the ability to avoid it."

"No, my friend. Did you see that large man that came out at the last? The one Stiles was talking to. That is Faygen, General of the Croshans."

Duke Renier gave Wellan a blank stare. The Croshan's hadn't existed as a people for seven hundred years.

"Faygen never lost a battle. Even when grossly outnumbered, he would always find a way to win. If *he* prepared the trap, there will be no escape."

"How do you know so much about this General Faygen?"

"I'm far older than you think. Keep your men inside the walls. I will go out and speak with the general."

The duke shook his head. "If the trap is so perilous, leaving no means of escape, why do you think you will get out of it any easier than my men and I would?"

"I know Faygen. We were friends once. He was a good man and I don't think he will harm me. Let me talk to him, find out what's going on, possibly talk him into letting the refugees through. Maybe I can talk him into leaving Renier altogether."

The duke thought about it for a moment, hand on his bearded chin. He looked Wellan in the eyes. "I don't like this idea. I don't like it at all, but I trust you to know what you are doing." His serious expression broke into a mischievous grin. "After all, you've been around for what, seven, eight hundred years?"

Wellan's grin matched the duke's as he replied, "If you only knew."

The duke turned to the men in the courtyard and roared, "Crack the gates open. Let the Wizard of Renier through." Then he turned to Wellan, and in a softer voice said, "I hope you know what you're doing."

Wellan smiled, but remained silent.

By the time they reached the courtyard, the guards had opened the gate just enough to let Wellan through. As he turned to slide through the crack, the duke grasped his forearm. "May the gods watch over you, my friend."

Wellan returned the gesture with a smile, then squeezed through the opening.

Chapter 16

"Men, this is war! Today some of you will fall and not get up.
Fear not, for you will be remembered as heroes. Should that hap-
pen to you, then have a cup of mead with Roke, the God of War
and share your bloody stories with him, for I guarantee, we will
be victorious!"
~General Faygen (Famous battle speech)

The undead didn't notice Wellan's approach until he stood a few yards behind them. Some turned to face him. A few shuffled out of rank, eager to devour him. The breeze wafted a mildly sweet smell of soured meat toward Wellan. *They are starting to rot. It won't be long until their putrid bodies begin to affect the few of us who still live with a more natural form of plague.*

They stopped and a deep voice bellowed a name that he hadn't heard in centuries. "Welkgund!"

Wellan dipped his head down in a guarded bow. His eyes stayed on the tall man. "Faygen, old friend. Why have you invaded this city?"

The ranks of undead parted as the general walked through their midst. He didn't speak until he passed the rows of corpses and stood before Wellan. He didn't reply in the common tongue. Instead, he spoke Croshan. "Welkgund, why don't we continue this conversation in the tongue of men, instead of the yapping of dogs?"

Faygen looked terrible. Cracked skin stretched over his bones like parchment placed against a rock and, his eyes, if they still existed, sat far back in their sockets. The heavy armor rode his frame loosely, as if built for a much larger man. Undeath had not been kind to Wellan's old friend.

Wellan replied in the same language, though the harsh vocabulary no longer rode easily on his tongue. "As you wish. Now, why are you here?"

The general smiled; pitted yellow teeth shone between time-cracked lips. "Always right to the point with you, Welkgund. No asking me how I've been doing. No pleasant-ries."

Faygen's flippant attitude surprised and angered Wellan. The man he had known would never have taken the current situation so casually.

The undead began to shuffle, restless for their anticipat-ed feast.

"Unfortunately, neither this city nor I have the time to spend on the nicer things in life."

The ranks of ghouls became unorganized as bodies moved back and forth, slowly merging with the rear forma-tion.

Thin arms crossed over an armored chest; elbow joints pushed the grainy skin tight. "I've noticed that, so I'm going to let you know how my life's been going without you having to ask. As you can probably tell from my appearance, I haven't been doing so well. To be honest with you, I've been dead. Some might say I've gotten better in the last month, but I would disagree. I would love to return to the slumber of death, but the necromantic bastard that brought me back won't allow that."

Wellan opened his mouth to speak, but Faygen lifted a joint-knotted hand to silence him. "Let me finish. You might also be asking yourself how the noble general of the mighty Croshan's has found himself leading an army of undead. I can assure you, it is not out of choice. Do you remember my daughter, Welkgund? Eyliasa?"

He nodded. Her death had haunted him for years and practically destroyed Faygen. The man never recovered from his daughter's death. After her brutal murder, the general had become moody and brooding, more bloodthirsty. Wellan believed that it eventually resulted in his untimely death. He well remembered Faygen's pain and guilt.

The edges of the rear formation of corpses crumbled as they bumped and pushed against one another. They slowly surrounded the two old friends.

Wellan looked into the general's face and saw the pain again. He saw it even through the dry, cracked skin.

"He has raised her, Welkgund. Raised her from the dead. She lives. Not like myself, but whole and unblemished. If I don't take Renier, if I don't turn this city over to that monster, he will do it to her again. She will be cut into pieces and tortured, her head brought before me once more. I can't do that to her, not again." His hand rose to his eyes and his head lowered as if to wipe away tears that didn't exist.

Wellan and Faygen stood in a ring of undead, dozens deep. They swayed back and forth, but made no menacing motions. Wellan saw the danger, but remained hopeful that his old friend wouldn't harm him.

Wellan's arm rose, fingers splayed, as if to comfort an old friend, then it dropped back to his side. "Let me help you, Faygen. Let these people go and let me help you."

The general's shoulders shook as a raspy laugh escaped his throat. Wellan wondered if he had gone mad. "No. There is no escape from this demon. I'm not afraid for myself. I fear for her. If I don't do as commanded, he can piece her up again. Not only that, but I wouldn't put it past this creature to raise her again and again to get his revenge, making my precious Eyliasa live through that hell time after time. I think the bastard would enjoy not only her suffering, but my own, as well, maybe even more so."

He didn't know what to say, didn't know how to help. As he watched Faygen, he realized there would be no talking the general out of taking the city, but he had to try. "Let these people through. Allow them to go to the palace. I will talk to Duke Renier about leaving the city. There is no reason to harm anyone else."

The armored head shook left and right. "My master doesn't allow mercy. I may be risking my daughter's suffering even by speaking to you of these things. Besides, as you may have guessed, the refugees are only the bait. You or the duke are the actual targets of this gathering. Still, I can't allow anyone to leave. My master is a greedy creature and wants them all."

With that, he drew his sword. Red dust puffed out as the ancient blade left its worn scabbard with a harsh screech. Wellan remembered laying that very blade on his chest as six solemn soldiers placed the general in a crypt on the side of a mountain.

As if the drawing of the blade were a signal, five of the armored undead burst through the ranks with surprising speed and raced to Wellan with swords drawn.

His arms sprang from his side, fingers twitching archaic symbols. A long dead language spewed from his mouth, one that even the Croshan wouldn't understand. His fists closed; the air around him chilled as he pulled energy from it. Before the creatures could touch him with their swords, his hands pounced open. A bubble of force flashed from him in a burst of darkness. Wellan's magic threw Faygen and his five undead into the mass of corpses.

"Run, Stiles! Get those people to the palace."

He breathed out cold condensation as flames erupted from his fingertips. He torched the nearest undead, but there were too many. Within seconds, he disappeared under a mass of flesh.

∞ ∞ ∞ ∞

Venomous hatred rose within Piet Lithor when he saw Wellan approaching from the castle walls. He gripped his sword tighter as the giant ghoulish leader walked through the mass of undead to meet the wizard. Righteous anger heated his blood as the two exchanged words in a language Lithor found totally incomprehensible. He stood too far away to hear their talk very well, but what he did hear sounded like the speech of devils. *The demon wizard is betraying us, selling our souls to that ghoul in exchange for more evil tricks and power. I mustn't let that happen.*

With his pulse pounding in his ears like a drumbeat and his sword gripped tight enough to whiten his knuckles, he walked to Stiles. He would warn the brave soldier of the sorcerer's treachery.

The undead ranks began to shuffle and break apart.

Stiles watched, intently studying the general and the wizard as their talk became louder and more heated.

He observed the demon's exchange as closely as Stiles. *Probably trading abominable spells or figuring out how to divide up the city. Maybe they are arguing about who gets to be the new duke.*

Lithor lifted his hand to Stiles' shoulder. "Stiles, there is something I...."

A roar erupted in the midst of the corpses. The undead pushed against one another as they tried to get to their master, to Wellan. The deep blue peak of the wizard's cowl could be seen between the decomposing heads, but the large commander had disappeared in the throng.

"Run, Stiles! Get those people to the palace."

Wellan? Like water thrown over an open fire, Lithor's hatred and anger fizzled and died. Only the smoke of shame and despair remained. *Oh, Vaspar. He didn't conspire with the undead. Once again, anger, prejudice and hatred have blinded me to the truth. How could I have been so wrong? How can I stand by while another man sacrifices himself for me? It's not too late to pay my penance. I owe it to that man for the hatred I have felt and lies I have spread. I will not let another die in my place.*

Something slammed into him, almost knocking him from his feet. It jerked him from his thoughts. The woman with the baby picked herself up and raced toward the castle with the infant bouncing in her arms. Its cries tore through the night like the shriek of an owl. Others flashed by as they raced along with her. Stiles stood in place, waving the group through, encouraging them to run.

Lithor held the sword before him, pointed to the horde of undead where he last saw Wellan. He began to walk toward the mass of cold flesh. Though he was determined to see this through, his legs shook with fear and his heart threatened to hammer through his ribcage.

Stiles screamed, "No, Piet Lithor. This way; there's nothing you can do for Wellan now."

He continued walking, sparing only a quick glance at Stiles. "Go, do as Wellan said and get those people to the castle." He let go of the sword with one hand to point at the undead that had broken from the mass to intercept the escaping refugees.

Stiles followed Lithor's finger as more ghouls poured in from the forest and began to grab people as they passed. The newly married man became a widower as undead arms pulled his wife from her feet. The young man watched in horror. He listened to her screams as they ate her alive. He stepped forward to help her then turned and ran.

Stiles gave the priest a single nod then ran to protect the refugees.

Lithor continued his walk.

The undead paid no attention to him until he stood at their backs. As if sensing the threat, they turned and stumbled out of his way, parting before his holy relic. He continued to walk through the corridor of dead bodies until the last ones fell to the side and revealed a torn and bloody wizard.

Wellan looked up. A smile touched his lips then disappeared in a grimace of pain. "I...I didn't think you liked me, Lithor."

Fingers brushed his robe. The priest spun around and presented the sword to the cold, reaching hands. "I didn't like you. I was wrong." He reached down to help Wellan stand.

The wizard held his arm up, not in an effort to be helped, but to keep the priest back. Blood dribbled down the corner of his mouth as he rasped, "Leave me. I've been infected. Get out of here with that sword. Help the duke."

He ignored the wizard's words and reached down through winter frozen air. Lithor grabbed Wellan's robes and pulled him to his feet. Either the old man didn't weigh anything, or Lithor's adrenaline-fueled system ignored the weight. When the wizard stood and leaned against the priest, Lithor said, "No one else is dying in my place, Wellan. Now, let's get you..."

"Put him down," the large ghoul roared as he stepped through the surrounding undead.

Lithor's sword flashed up. The parchment-skinned man flinched then relaxed. He slowly brought his own sword up. "I'm not one of these simpletons. I won't be cowed by your relic. The power of your god means nothing to me."

Lithor backed away. He swung his sword to push back the reaching corpses, dragging Wellan with him as he went.

The undead leader stepped forward, blade raised for a killing blow.

Wellan's hand shot out from beneath his robes. The air crackled with gathered energy as lightning flew from his fingers and slammed into the armored chest. Thin worms of lightning traced the metal that arced and sizzled against the large ghoul's body. The general let out a grunt and fell to his knees. The sword dropped from his fingers as wisps of smoke drifted up from his breastplate.

Without seeing if the thing had finally been killed, Lithor turned and sped through the lifeless crowd as they parted before his outstretched sword. Wellan's feet dragged the ground, but within seconds, the gate came into sight. Lithor almost stopped when he looked to the left and saw that more than half of the refugees hadn't made it. The undead stood over their torn bodies stuffing chunks of dripping flesh into their red-rimmed mouths. They reminded Lithor of human vultures on a miniature battlefield. Cylus' head and torso lay on the cobbled road in a puddle of blood as a woman with skin the color of a fish's belly gnawed on his severed arm.

"Keep running, Piet Lithor. Run for the gate." The frantic scream of Stiles' familiar voice bellowed from the castle walls and pulled him from the horrid sight. He turned and sped to the gate. Armored soldiers, bows held ready, guarded the opening and awaited his return.

Wellan mumbled phrases in an incomprehensible language. Lithor ignored the wizard's rant as he dragged his body toward the gate. The strange words no longer sounded like the speech of devils, but of a sad old man on the edge of death. Bow strings twanged. Lines of death streaked overhead, the sounds of falling bodies close behind him. He ran the last fifty yards to the gate. Lithor dragged the sword behind him, too weak to hold it upright, but needing it's presence to guard his back.

He crashed through the line of soldiers. They formed up around him and helped him pull Wellan through the gate as the wizard mumbled, "The blood...don't touch...keep...off...you."

The duke pushed through the crowd of guards as the gate boomed closed and knelt beside the blood-covered wizard. He cradled Wellan's head in his arms and whispered, "It's going to be all right, my friend. You're safe with us now. I should never have allowed you to go out there alone."

Lithor knelt on the other side of the wizard and noticed how old the man looked, ancient and withered. Though he had never liked the old sorcerer, he still had held a grudging respect for the man. *Now, it breaks my heart to see him like this.*

Duke Renier turned to Lithor. Tears brimmed in the red, spider-web-etched eyes. "Thank you, Lithor. Thank you for returning my friend to me."

Lithor nodded. For the first time in his life, he didn't know what to say.

∞ ∞ ∞ ∞

The hand tightened on Shannai's mouth. It smelled of honing oil and fresh baked bread. A hot breath touched her ear, adding the odor of old meat and tobacco smoke. A whisper rode the harsh breath, Ash's voice. "Quiet, girl! They are right outside the door."

She heard shuffling in the dark, the sound dampened by a wooden door, barely visible in the lightless room.

Shannai struggled against him and pulled his hand away from her mouth. She hissed, "Let me go! My brother's out there, I have to help him."

"Your brother is fine. Do you hear a struggle? Did you hear any screams?"

Her teeth remained clenched together. "No."

His hand left her face and she felt him step back. "Your brother and my men are alive for now. They must have seen them and backed out of the alley as I pulled us into the back door of this shop. They are probably holed up somewhere right now just like us, waiting for the dead to disperse so they can either look for us or make a run for the west gate."

More feet shuffled past. Something slammed into the door and rattled the wood in its frame. She bit her lower lip and stepped back with her bow raised, uselessly pointed into the black before her. Feet continued to slide against the stone, but nothing else banged against the door.

Something crashed to the floor behind her. Shannai spun around, her arrow pulled taut and blindly pointed into the darkness.

Ash's sword hissed as it slid out of its sheath. His other hand pushed into her stomach and groped until it found her wrist. He yanked her forward until her fingers touched leather, his back. He whispered into the dark. "Stay behind me."

Another crash. The screech of furniture as it slid across the floor, closer and louder than the previous sound.

Shannai slid her bow over her shoulder. The arrow remained in her clenched fist like a dagger. She took a deep breath to try and calm her nerves; the sweet smell of baked bread filled her nostrils.

Feet rasped as they slid across the floor. They came closer with each lurch. Ash shifted to face whatever made the sound. Shannai stepped to the side to remain behind him.

The feet shuffled closer. The leather beneath her fingers began to slide back and forth as Ash's sword swung wildly before him. The blade whistled through empty air.

Shannai heard a *thunk* as steel wedged into flesh. Ash's frame shifted; his center of gravity moved to the right side like a spring being wound tight before uncoiling with the speed of a viper. Another *thunk* of metal sinking into flesh, a cleaver chopping a roast. Something fell to the floor and Ash bent over to continue the assault. His weight shifted to his right foot before the swing, over and over again; her heart pounded to the beat Ash maintained. Other than an occasional grunt from Ash and the wet chopping, the one-sided battle took place in darkness and silence.

Something grabbed Shannai's arm. She screamed and stumbled backward. She tripped over her own feet and fell to the floor. Without a second thought, she crawled across the ground on her back. Instinct and fear drove her to get away. She heard feet scuffle across the floor in front of her. Something banged into the door. Ash let out a hiss and then a groan. The wet smack of steel as it sunk into flesh. A body collapsed to the floor. Cold, thick liquid splashed onto her pants, then just the butcher's sound of steel and meat.

Another slam against the door.

She flinched as something grabbed her arm and pulled.

"Shhhhh, it's me," Ash whispered.

He yanked her to her feet and pulled her along the wall, away from the door and its haunting knocks.

Within twenty steps, Ash led her through a swinging door and into a room filled with the cold blue light of the night. He pulled her down behind a moon-tinted counter; his eyes took in the room before he lifted his head above the counter. A frown covered his face as he dropped back down beside her and stared at the floor between his feet.

Shannai waited a few minutes before asking, "What now? Are they still out there?"

He rubbed his eyes with his thumb and index finger then said, "Yeah, they are still out there. It sounds like the ones who were banging on the back door have quit. There doesn't seem to be any more of them in here, other than the two I kill—put down in the back room. We have to move and do it pretty quickly from here on out. We now have a deadline."

She frowned. "Why is that?"

He held out his arm. A thumb-sized chunk of meat had been ripped from his upper forearm; blood welled within it and dripped down the sides. Ash ripped his sleeve the rest of the way off and bound it around the wound. The sleeve turned red and dripped before he could get it tied.

"That second one was a sneaky bastard with a hell of a bite. Anyway, we don't have a lot of time to dally around now. I have to get you out of here before I...succumb to whatever this is."

Her vision blurred by tears as she reached over and touched his shoulder. She didn't know how to reply.

∞ ∞ ∞ ∞

Piet Lithor sat in the duke's private chamber just like he had dozens of times before, but this time, it felt different. Before the plague, he had always wondered why the duke, who could afford gold trim on all the walls and exotic tiles on the floor, always chose the simplest of rooms to hold his private meetings. The homey little room had once made him feel downright out of place. He looked around at the few worn but comfortable chairs, the plain wood knee-high table that held a glass ashtray, a brass pitcher and two simple coffee teacups. Now it all made sense to him. While within this room, Duke Renier had no intentions of putting on airs, he wanted to feel relaxed and make his guest feel the same way. Lithor had once looked on this with his nose up in the air. Now, he felt relaxed and thankful for a place where he could prop his feet up and leave the status and pomp behind.

Duke Renier stepped into the room and sat in the chair across from Lithor. He poured them both spiced tea then sat back and looked at Lithor over the rim of his cup. Lithor lifted his to his mouth and smiled as he noticed a small chip near the lip.

Leaning back, the duke asked, "So, Piet Lithor, how did you make it out there for so long? Prayer and faith?"

Lithor smiled and set his cup down on the table. "I think prayer and faith had a lot to do with it. Vaspar kept his hand of protection over me, though I have no idea why. I've been an ass, and I owe you and everyone else here an apology for my lack of piety and abundance of arrogance. I have much to pay for."

The duke sat forward and attempted to interrupt, to politely argue with Lithor that he wasn't an arrogant fool. Lithor knew better and stopped the duke's protest with a wave of his hand. He didn't need another well-meant lie.

"No, don't say I wasn't, because I was. I still am to some degree. It's hard to retrain an old priest who thought he was above human."

He picked his teacup up and took another sip before continuing. He couldn't look at the duke as he told his story, so he stared at the brown liquid.

"I was in my home, complaining to the boy. I didn't even know his true name, just called him 'boy'. I was complaining about the help not being around when it all began. The boy...had prepared my lunch and brought it in when the other...priests...came into the room. They were in terrible shape. Vomit and blood stained their night-clothes. Their eyes were the worst things, blank and dead. I stood up from the chair and..." He stopped, remembering the boy's sacrifice, the way he had pushed the child down and trampled over him in his haste to escape.

Lithor leaned forward and switched his gaze from the cup to the stone-tiled floor. "I...I knocked the boy down. I didn't even consider helping him back up. I...I left him to slow the other priests down. The great piet left a boy to die so that I might live." He wiped his eyes. His hand came away wet. "I ran to my room and cowered behind my bed. The priests beat on the door. I prayed to Vaspar to save me. Nothing happened. They continued to beat on the door. My faith began to wane and, in desperation, I grabbed the holy sword of Tyrmra then scuttled back behind the bed. I knew I wouldn't be able to use it. I'm not so stupid as to believe that I would stand a chance in a fair fight, but having the weapon gave me some comfort. I continued my prayers and soon, the priests left my door.

"I don't know how long I sat there cowering, but I finally gained the courage to leave my room. I didn't see any of the priests until I got to the front yard and looked out the door. Two of them shuffled through the rain. Stoking what little courage I had, I finally made a dash for the front gate. It was shut and they would have had me had it not been for the sword. It kept them at bay. They seemed to be afraid of it, like it was anathema to them.

"After making it through the gate, I attempted to reach the palace, but there were far too many of the undead in that direction, so I ran to the Temple of Vaspar. Others were already there, surrounded by undead. The ghouls wouldn't touch the temple grounds. Vaspar's holiness kept them at bay. I ran through them with the sword held high, even knocked one over into the temple yard in my mad run. The thing began to burn as soon as it touched the holy ground. Anyway, I made it into the temple and did like the others, waited."

He leaned back in the chair and looked at the duke. "I think you know the rest of my tale."

Duke Renier leaned forward and put his hand on Lithor's wrist. "You don't give yourself enough credit, Piet Lithor. It sounds to me as though Vaspar found you worthy enough to look after you. I have to say, though, I do see a change, and it seems to be a change for the better."

Lithor patted the duke's hand. "Thank you, my friend."

"No, thank you for helping those people, and for helping Wellan get into the palace. That took a great deal of courage."

Lithor shook his head. "I owed him that much. I have been terrible to him over the years, spiteful and petty. As I saw him go down amongst the undead, I realized that. By the way, how is he?"

Duke Renier frowned and rubbed his hand through his goatee. "Not very good, I'm afraid. They tore him up pretty bad, but he is a wizard and, hopefully, he will have a trick or two up his sleeve that will allow him to recover. He is with the Lady Rachelle. He requested that she, and only she, attend him for now." The duke sat up straight and smiled. "Wellan isn't the only one with a trick or two up his sleeve.

Now that you are here, it won't be long before we make our escape from the city. There is an emergency tunnel in the back of the palace that leads to the sea on the east side. As soon as Wellan is well enough to walk, we will get everyone together and leave."

Lithor felt a weight lift from his shoulders. The duke's words gave him hope. "It sounds like you have a solid plan, my duke. I will pray to Vaspar that Wellan recovers soon and we make a safe exodus from here."

"Thank you, Piet Lithor. I'm sure Wellan will appreciate that."

Chapter 17

"Bravery is not a lack of fear. Bravery is being afraid and facing your fears, functioning for the betterment of all in the midst of terror."
~Quote from unknown author

He looked old, sick. She squeezed his hand. It felt damp and cold. Wellan shifted his head to the side. He stared at her through a thin film. She didn't think he recognized her until he smiled. It became a grimace that caused him to squeeze his eyes closed. She ran a damp rag over his fevered brow, careful not to open any of the wounds as she gently brushed his forehead.

She had been sitting in the room with him for the last hour, listening as he mumbled then screamed out over and over again. She watched as his body fought a desperate war, a war where death would be a blessing and to continue living would be a curse. She feared he would lose this one.

A whisper trickled from his lips like distant words on the wind. She bent her head closer to Wellan's mouth and squeezed his limp hand. His mouth moved, but she still couldn't hear the words he tried to speak. She lowered her head until her ear touched his dry lips. "Put...put my hands...on your temples. I want...I...to give..."

She sat up and nodded. Rachelle grabbed both of his hands and placed the fingers against her temples. She didn't understand why he wanted her to do it, but she couldn't deny him anything, not in his condition.

His eyes shut and his mouth began to move. Though his lips moved, she couldn't hear any words. She released his hands and lowered her head to hear what he said. His arms lowered as she came closer, but he kept his hands on her temples. Without warning, he gripped her skull with more strength than she credited him with having.

She gasped as a spike of ice slammed through her head and cored into the center of her being. Wellan disappeared from her sight, the bed no longer existed, her mind left the little room, the palace, the city, the here and now.

Darkness.

A raging campfire spun to life from the darkness in front of her. Rachelle sat on a log at the edge of a clearing. The silhouette of dark jungle surrounded her. Men and women danced around the undulating flames. Their only garments were the loincloths that hid their genitals. She blushed and looked above the fire where sparks burst into the air to ride the currents until they cooled and died. She looked at the others who sat with her. The people were like none she had ever seen, dressed in wolf hides and leather. They wore bone jewelry and painted their faces in red and black. Barbarians. She looked down at herself and saw only a leather loincloth with nothing to cover her torso. Her chest looked like that of a young man or a girl. Old claws from some fearsome beast hung on a leather thong around her neck.

The dancing stopped. Everyone turned toward her. She looked up as a bear of a man strode forward. He bore a staff topped with the skull of a large bird. His tanned body glistened with sweat; muscles bulged against his skin. He spoke harsh words in a language she did not understand. He yanked her to him and spoke the words again, but this time, she understood them, though he spoke in a guttural and harsh tongue. "Come, apprentice."

The darkness evaporated into a blinding white field. She used her hand to shade her eyes. The heat and humidity that caused her skin to sweat moments before vanished and became a cold like none she had ever known. It slammed against her face with the force of an open-handed slap. She gasped and gripped her staff tighter. Her staff?

The large bear of a man stood next to her. This time, he did look like a bear, covered head to toe in a wooly fur. She didn't know how she knew that it was the same man, but she knew. She felt a kinship toward him, as though he were her father or grandfather. He grabbed her shoulder and pointed to the top of a white mound. "Watch. You may never see them again, Gwunwyvern."

Dark brown shapes broke over the top of the hill, shaggy lumps with huge tusks. They made deep grooves in the virgin snow as they pushed forward. A snout rose into the air and trumpeted a vibrant call. Rachelle wondered how the mammoths didn't sink to their bellies in the soft snow. Mammoths? No one had seen the great beasts in hundreds of years. What was happening to her? Did she suffer delusions? She turned to ask the bear of a man, Thornewulf, but before she could, the scene changed again.

Tents. Leather cones with brightly painted symbols sat around her on a plain of straw-colored grass. The door flaps of the tents blew back and forth in the steady breeze. Fire pits burned all around her. Smoked meat lay out on sticks. The smell made her mouth water. She turned her head and something tickled her neck. She reached up to brush it off. Hair. A beard? She yanked on it and squinted her eyes from the pain.

A thin, dark-skinned man gave her an odd look as he walked past. He wore only leather britches and a domed hat decorated much like the tents. She looked around and saw others moving back and forth between them. They carried clay pots, spears, and stone-aged tools. The men wore the britches and strange hats while the women wore knee length leather dresses and flowers in their hair. She looked at her own attire, a leather robe reaching all the way to the ground, decorated with more patterns and colors than anyone else in the small nomadic village. She held a staff in her right hand. The same staff she had held as she watched the mammoths.

Are these Wellan's memories?

She turned her head and saw wood piled chest high. A man lay atop it. The bear of a man, her mentor. His face pointed at the sky and his arms across his chest. The bird's head staff was clasped in his pale hands. Dead. It was a funeral pyre.

Poor Thornewulf. Emotions welled up within her for a man she had only met in a dream. She stared at the body and tears filled her eyes. Her heart swelled as it had when she'd attended her father's funeral. Rachelle didn't understand why she should feel such sadness and loss for a dream man.

Rachelle wanted to wake from the emotional nightmare, but instead, she reached out to the pyre, to an old friend she had never known.

She took two steps toward him before the scene changed again.

Darkness. Rock. Her staff glowed with the power of a hundred fireflies. Five brave warriors stood behind her. Fear widened their eyes, their spears pointed at something behind her. She turned. A wolf crouched before her, but unlike any wolf she had ever seen. It stood five feet at the shoulders and its eyes glowed a bright red like blazing coals. Its lips curled up and a rumbling growl rolled from its mouth. Between its teeth, a fire raged, lighting up the space between each fang with a flickering glow. Its hackles stood. It leaped.

She pulled energy from the moist air around her. In a heartbeat, it collected in her palm before erupting from her outstretched hand. The light of her staff dimmed slightly. She recognized the energy as the same force she had used against Marchas on the streets of Renier. She recognized the trigger that set it off, the mental push that her will activated. She drew the energy from her surroundings, the heat built up by the rock around her, even the force of the thin draft of air that drifted through the cavern. She used it all to blast the creature. This time, she controlled it instead of it controlling her.

The great wolf slammed into a wall and fell to the floor. It rose and paced back and forth, not done with the fight.

The scene shifted.

Salt air and a strong breeze greeted her. The world rocked up and down. She grasped a nearby handrail to catch herself and saw the sea. Waves swelled as far as she could see. The disorientation nauseated her. She put her head down and took a deep breath. The damned beard tickled her neck.

"Ok gru tom chay?" *Are you all right?* She didn't recognize the language at all, but she understood it. She nodded at one of the three men who stood around a barrel on the deck of a ship. A map sat on the barrel, weighted down by a copper helmet. A crude map showed the coastline of Renier, something an early explorer might have drawn.

The wind died; the sea smell disappeared.

She sat in front of a stone hearth in a wooden hall with a mug of mead in her hand. The sound of stringed instruments filled the room. Warriors wrestled and couples danced in the dirt of a cleared area at the center of the hall. Her stomach remained nauseous from the constantly changing environment, but at least now the world wasn't rocking beneath her.

A hand grasped her shoulder. She turned to face a black-bearded man. He looked a great deal like the duke except for the full beard and his wide girth. A grandfather or great grandfather, perhaps?

He smiled. "Are ye enjoyin' yerself, wizard?"

She nodded her head, not trusting herself to speak.

"Glad t'hear it. This here hall is just a start. I think with a little hard work and a bit o'planin', we can have us a whole city right here in this very spot. Maybe even build a castle against the cliff. Ye tink I can do it, Wellan?"

She started to nod, but the scene shifted and shifted and shifted, faster and faster until it grew into a blur of shifting colors and shapes. She couldn't take it all in. With a scream, she opened her eyes.

Wellan lay before her, his mouth drawn and his eyes open. He stared at the ceiling with glazed eyes. His life had ended, but he had given her all he could before it was done.

Tears again filled her eyes for a man she hardly knew.

PART III
EXODUS

Chapter 18

"Men, the children of God, share a common trait with the beast of the field. It is their 'fight or flight' instinct, the difference between being a predator or becoming prey."
~From Shantazar's treatise on human behavior

For almost an hour, Shannai looked over the edge of the counter. She watched the undead stumble back and forth in front of the bakery window. Her nose became desensitized to the enticing aroma of fresh baked bread, though her stomach still grumbled from time to time.

The streets seemed to come to life like a busy city night, except for the blank stares of the shoppers, the slobbering slack jaws and the lurching walk of the citizens. She watched in hiding as they searched for her like wolves on the trail of a rabbit cornered in its burrow. She needed to escape and find her brother, to make sure nothing had happened to him. Of course, knowing Marchas, he was probably already outside the city walls guzzling ale and telling the tale of his grand escape. She almost smiled at the thought, but deep down, she knew better. Marchas wasn't going anywhere without his little sister.

"You're gonna have to do it," Ash whispered.

For the entire hour, he had sat on the floor staring at the wall and rubbing his bite. He had moved very little and said nothing.

She looked down at his pale face. Beads of sweat coated his forehead. "Do what?"

He looked up at her with bloodshot eyes and held up his bloody arm. "Off me. I ain't gonna be around much longer and when I come back, I...I'm gonna be just like them. Don't want to be like them. You got to kill me before that can happen."

She pushed his arm down. "Don't talk like that. You aren't going to die from a single bite. We'll get out of here. Get you some help."

His brows arched. His mouth turned to a sneer. She didn't buy her own pep talk so how could she expect him to? But they had to keep going. They just couldn't give up.

"You don't know what you're talking about. You haven't seen them, haven't seen people return once they die." He grabbed her arm with his bitten one. "If you don't agree to do it then I won't go any further with you."

She opened her mouth, ready to spout more encouraging but useless drivel, or at least argue that she had seen plenty. He spoke before she could waste her breath.

"I mean it. In here, I can't get out and hurt anyone when I change, but if I go with you and you don't kill me when the time comes, then I won't only be a danger to you, but to everyone in the city. I can't let that..."

He stopped and turned his head to the shop door and listened.

Following his lead, she turned and listened too. Music. Mandolin music. One of Marchas' favorite tunes floated down the street on plucked strings. A fast paced dancing jig that, when accompanied by song, spoke of adventure, ale, women, and riches. A grin spread across her face. *That crazy bastard!*

She shook her head and grinned. "Marchas!"

Ash leaned back against the counter. "Well, it looks like your brother is doing all right, but if he doesn't stop playing, he's gonna draw every undead in the city to himself."

Already, the dead marched toward the sound. They shuffled across the front window by the droves and stumbled toward the music.

"Well, I give your brother points for having guts, but not so many in the brains department."

She smiled. "Yeah, that's my brother. Always thinking with his..."

The music stopped. Her heart sped up to replace the missing rhythm. Fear for her brother grabbed the back of her neck with icy fingers.

She breathed a sigh of relief when Marchas' voice echoed through the streets. "Shannai. Don't yell back, but I'm guessing you are still around here somewhere and thinkin' I've finally lost my mind. You might be right, but I got a plan. I'm gonna play this mandolin for a little longer, maybe go through some more of my favorite tunes, a naughty limerick or two, and then I'm gonna tell you to run. When I do, get your ass headed for the west gate as fast as you can. Don't stop for me. You get outside the gate and keep going till it's safe. If I don't meet up with you right away, then head to Baron Milchev's town and I will meet you there. Stay safe, sis."

The music resumed with a racy dancing jig.

Ash looked over the counter and shook his head. "Your brother's definitely not paddling with both oars, but he's got guts. I'll give him that"

She watched the dead lumber across the window and she smiled. "He never was all that good with paddles. I just hope he doesn't get himself killed with this plan of his."

The ghouls began to crowd the streets as they headed in the direction of the sound. Hundreds of them lurched in front of the bakery, a stream of cold flesh moving north. Several bumped into one another and fell to the ground in their quest for the musician.

Ash scratched his cheek and eased around the counter. "This plan might just work. They are starting to thin out, headed for wherever he is holed up. He's drawing them like flies to a carcass."

She cringed at his choice of words, but continued watching the last of the undead as they trickled past the bakery. Without looking at Ash, Shannai replied, "I just hope he isn't getting himself cornered."

Ash wiped sweat from his brow and walked to the door as the last of the undead stumbled past the window. Shannai noticed his unsteady steps and told herself it was because his legs were stiff from sitting in one place for too long.

A new song began, one that Marchas added his deep voice too. A song entitled *Running with Sin*, a fast song about a wild girl who lives life for the moment, always running from the law. A song that Shannai could certainly relate to, but she guessed Marchas had chosen it to let her know that the time to flee was close.

As soon as the song ended, Marchas screamed in the distance. "Move your ass, sis! I'll see you on the other side of the gate."

Ash cracked the door open and looked outside, then waved her to him.

Doing as her brother said, she ran. She grabbed Ash's clammy hand as she passed through the door.

∞ ∞ ∞ ∞

Piet Lithor stood behind the pulpit. He rubbed his stubble-ridden chin and looked at the fifteen or so people who sat in the dozen pews before him. So few. There were hardly enough of the faithful to fill two pews.

A few had asked him to speak, to give them encouragement and hope. They expected him to give them something he could hardly give himself. Still, it was his duty to administer to the believers. He told them to meet him in the duke's private chapel, a dining room sized affair and seldom used. Everything in the chapel was at least as grand as the main temple of Vaspar the Just with carved pews, a marble pulpit and soft cushions on the chairs and pews, but somehow, it didn't feel the same any longer. He felt as though he didn't belong in front of these people. He no longer felt worthy of representing Lord Vaspar.

An echoing cough and shuffle of feet pulled him from his thoughts. The people were getting anxious. He had been staring at them, consumed by his doubts, for too long. Once again, his hand ran from his rough stubble to nervously comb through his greasy, thinning hair. *Lord Vaspar, what do I say to these people, men and women who are relying on me to guide them through these troubled times? How do I give them hope? How can I take away their fear?*

Deep down, he hoped Lord Vaspar would tell him what to say, give him some direction. Only silence answered him.

With a sigh, he grasped the front of the pulpit and began. "I...I no longer feel worthy of leading you in Lord Vaspar's light. Time and again he has tested my metal and found me unworthy. I hadn't seen what I had become, a man who led a life far below the standards that Lord Vaspar has set. I went about my business, strutting around like the lead cock when, in reality, I was the lowest of you. My arrogance and pride blinded me to the truth that is Lord Vaspar. You good people probably know him better than I do. You follow him in blind faith. You meet now expecting the grand piet to give you words of comfort, something that will ease your troubled souls and allow you to sleep at night. I am sorry, but I can't give you people that. I would like to, but...but Lord Vaspar hasn't given me any great words of wisdom to impart to you. He hasn't told me comforting words that will ease your fears or loss. I can't give you hope, or bolster your faith.

"All I can do is relate my personal experience and tell you that Lord Vaspar saved me from this ravaged city. When my priests, Vaspar bless their lost souls, tried to get me and turn me into one of them, Lord Vaspar was there to rescue me. He didn't show up in a golden ray of light as he did in the holy book of Chronis. He didn't offer his blessing upon me, didn't bestow upon me the power to beat my enemies. He didn't speak to me and tell me how this is going to turn out."

Piet Lithor rubbed his tired eyes. *Hope. These people need hope, and all I now do is blather on about how we are lost and Lord Vaspar has offered no aid. Get it together, priest. Lead your people, piet.*

He looked at the small group gathered before him and shook his head. *Is this all that is left? Are these the last followers of the faith within Renier?*

Reaching down to his side, he pulled the Holy Sword from its scabbard and held it high before the people. He gazed at the silver blade, Vaspar's talisman. "This, my friends, is what the Lord Vaspar bestowed upon me. This holy sword is blight to those retched souls. They can't touch it and are even distraught by the sight of it. That is the power of Lord Vaspar. That is the power that saved me when all hope was gone."

He looked around the group of people and hoped to see someone who survived from the temple. He didn't recognize anyone. *Surely, someone else survived. I will need to find out as soon as I am done here.*

"Another gift from Lord Vaspar is his temple, and I assume this chapel also. They are incapable of touching holy ground. It kills them faster than any sword will. They tremble in the presence of our great Lord. Remember that in the days to come. Lord Vaspar still holds power over what is his, and this madness can't take that away. Though the forces of evil..."

The chapel doors burst open. They banged against the wall like a sledgehammer and echoed through the room. Bos Spielter stumbled through, his hand on his neck. Blood oozed between his fingers and slid down his arm to drip from his elbow. He took several steps into the chapel with his eyes always on the piet's, then fell on his knees as though to pray.

"Nowhere is safe." He wheezed and coughed, blood coating his teeth and sprinkling the marble-tiled floor with red dew. "They're here, here in the palace. We're all gonna die..." The last words became distorted and gurgled as blood welled up the Bos' throat and spilled over his bottom teeth. His eyes widened. He fell forward; blood formed a growing pool around his head.

Two men jumped up and ran to Bos' Spielter.

"Stop! Don't touch him." Piet Lithor sprang from the pulpit and stood between the two men and the body.

The men's eyes grew wide as they stared at the body behind the piet. A woman screamed. A nauseous stench filled the room, rotting meat cooked over coals of garbage. He turned. A greasy black smoke rose from the Bos's convulsing body. It billowed to the ceiling and covered it like a thundercloud.

Piet Lithor almost told everyone to run from the chapel, then remembered his sermon. They stood on holy ground, untouchable by the abominations. They would remain safe in the chapel.

He spoke through clenched teeth and fought the nausea brought about by the stench of rotting flesh. He stared at the Bos' skin and organs as they dissolved until only charred bones remained. "Everyone stay here. You will be safe until I return. I'm going to inform the duke."

Everyone stared at the blackened bones. No one offered to accompany him. No one needed to. The well being of their souls was his duty. The preservation of their lives, his responsibility, his penance for the vulgar life he had lived...

Piet Lithor lifted the holy sword before him and stepped into the corridor to find the duke.

∞ ∞ ∞ ∞

Rachelle didn't think she had any tears left, but they soaked the chest of Wellan's tattered robe. She didn't know if the tears came from the stabbing pain in her head or her sense of loss with the passing of the wizard. *Probably both.*

Sharp spikes of torment shot through her head every few seconds and when the pains ended, a throbbing ache remained. Her mind scrambled to sort through the pictures and words that pulsed within her brain, memories of ancient times, Wellan's life. Her thoughts remained a jumbled assortment of information; each piece floated in her mind like a single sentence or paragraph from a book. Individually, they made little sense. It required all the scenes to make the entire picture, but the picture was so vast that she had trouble taking it all in. Rachelle moaned as pain shot through her head with the force of an icicle being slammed between her eyes. Her mind tried to sort and catalogue centuries' worth of knowledge and feelings. It overloaded her senses. Her brain felt as though it would explode. She expected to feel blood pour from her nose, ears and eyes at any moment. Her existence had become pain, nausea and confusion, lost in a place between her world and Wellan's.

The pain subsided as the creak of hinges penetrated through the dull ache. *The duke, a guard, a memory?* She didn't lift her head; a sphere of misery enfolded her again and left little room for anything else.

Footsteps padded across the stone floor. The smell of mulch and decay filled her nose. A gurgled chuckle intruded on the pain, menacing. She looked up with bloodshot eyes and wondered if what she saw was real or only one of Wellan's memories.

A naked man stood at the foot of the bed. A silhouette, its skin glistened, slick and black as oil. Teeth that matched the skin shone from coffee-colored gums. Two black marbles glittered as they stared down at the wizard and studied the deceased with a proud smile.

The black eyes traveled to Rachelle. "Ud move, goshling. Der Shaaaman est mine."

She stood on legs that threatened to betray her. The room tilted and she felt like she would pass out or throw up, maybe both. The nude man disappeared from her vision as memories again flooded her mind.

A thin man in baggy robes sat leaning against gnarled bark of a tree. He looked up at her and held out a smoking pipe with an inviting smile.

The flash lasted mere seconds and when she returned, a guard stood in the doorway.

She opened her mouth to call to him, beg him to help, but stopped. The armored man gazed at her with blank eyes. His mouth opened and closed. Amber drool slid down his blood-coated chin and dangled precariously as it swayed with the rolling of his jaw. *The abominations are here, in the palace. All is lost.*

The dark man stepped around the bed with the grace of a dancer and faced Rachelle, a black dagger pointed before him. "Ud move, goshling."

Without a second's thought, she lifted the chair and held it before her, the legs pointed at the black horror. Her pain betrayed her and she wobbled to the side as another spike of anguish drove between her eyebrows. Images flashed before her eyes for a mere fraction of a second.

A night sky full of stars filled her vision. The slim light of a crescent moon shone in the heavens as a shooting star streaked across the sky and plunged into the earth with a blasting roar several miles away.

The scene changed to a small, dim room. A menacing chuckle greeted her and returned her to the present. Black hands grabbed a leg of the chair and jerked if from her, almost pulling her to the ground.

The black dagger rose into the air, poised to plunge into her heart. She cried out. Her hands rose before her face to block the blow she knew she couldn't prevent.

A bloodied hand, middle finger bitten to a stub, struck out from the bed and grasped the black arm, pulling the blade away from its target. The obsidian man snarled and turned to Wellan. With a roar, he drove the knife deep into the wizard's stomach. Runes on the knife glinted green then faded.

The wizard grunted. He ignored his attacker and turned his head to Rachelle. His eyes remained glazed over, but no pain shone from them. He hissed as the knife struck home again, then whispered, "Remember the demon in the cave…the hellhound…the wolf…"

Her mind grasped Wellan's words, flew through the kaleidoscope of images, sounds, and information until they locked onto that one instant in Wellan's life. Again, she saw the five men, the enormous wolf with red-hot coals burning deep within his throat. Smoke drifted out between its yellow fangs like fog on an early morning river. Once more, she felt the power flare up within her, brought forth by her will. She drew energy from around her then let it burst from her open palm and slam the demon wolf into the wall. Power, raw energy erupted from her soul, brought forth by her will to use it.

Before she realized it, she stood before Wellan again. His weak hands tried to grasp his attacker's arms as they plunged the dagger into his stomach over and over again. He didn't have enough strength. Blood splattered the sheets and coated Wellan and his attacker. The wizard's weakened hands couldn't keep up with the black man's frenzied attack.

With a scream, Rachelle reached deep into herself and grasped the golden light that represented her power. She sucked the heat from the air and condensed it into a tight ball. The candle winked out as the room chilled and frost grew across her mirror. She nearly fainted as the heat raced down her arm and through her hand. It burst forth with the roar of thunder, raw energy barely controlled. A golden radiance unleashed with the fury of the nine hells and all the subtly of a raging war. It slammed into the obsidian man with an explosion of vapors that sent him flying into the air. He crashed through the window and sailed backwards to land somewhere in the courtyard three stories below. The undead guard at the door flew across the hall. He slammed head first into the stone as though he were launched from a catapult, cracking bricks and splattering gore in a red spray across the rough surface. Wellan's bed flipped over and slammed against the wall, trapping him beneath it.

Weakness flooded her muscles. She felt drained. The room became a blur. She tasted blood. Bracing herself against the wall, she wiped her forearm beneath her nose. A bright red swath smeared the back of her arm.

Ignoring her exhaustion and blood for the moment, she stumbled to the overturned bed. It wobbled and tipped over as Wellan crawled from beneath it. He knelt on the ground with his intestines hanging like coils of pink rope from his gutted stomach, the gashes he received outside the city walls opened again and dripped pus.

He looked up at Rachelle and gave her a crooked smile. "Get me something to wrap my waist in and I will try and get myself pulled back together. Then..." His nostrils flared, sniffing the air like a hungry wolf, milky eyes open wide. His tongue licked cracked lips. He shivered and squeezed his eyes closed. His voice returned in a rough rasp. "Then we must flee."

Chapter 19

*"...and the chosen crept into the darkness, not knowing the way.
There they did abide, by the Lord's will, and did discard their
riches, giving up their worldly selves as commanded by the
Lord."*
~Secret Holy Scriptures of the Waken Book

The wall torches formed flickering pools of light
that danced and leapt as Piet Lithor crept along
the silent corridor. He held his sword before him
in trembling hands. *Calm yourself, piet. Have faith in Lord
Vaspar. He didn't get you this far just so you could be eaten alive
here in this dark passageway.*

He wished he hadn't thought about being eaten alive.

His thoughts turned to Bos Spielter. The man had
certainly been an arrogant bastard, but he didn't deserve to
die the way he had, his neck ripped open and his blood
staining the chapel floor. *I wonder if Lord Vaspar took his soul,*

or if it remained trapped within his body. If it stayed within his body then where did it go when his flesh disintegrated? The thought of Bos Spielter's lost soul caused him to stop and shiver with fear and revulsion.

There you go working yourself up again, priest. Think about something else, something pleasant.

Nothing came to mind.

A figure moved in the corridor far behind him. A ghostly shadow that drifted in front of a torch then disappeared into the darkness between the wall sconces. The sound of metal grated as it slid against stone and echoed across the rough floor. In the silent passageway, it reverberated with the sound of torn fabric. His imagination created a lumbering monster that dragged a leg and possibly coils of intestines behind it as the creature advanced upon him one sliding step at a time. He turned around with the holy sword held high. It quivered in his hands. He walked backwards to keep an eye on the passage behind him. He glanced over his shoulder every few seconds to make sure he didn't run into anything—or anyone.

Another scrape, flesh slapped stone.

Lithor turned and ran down the corridor. His breath wheezed through overstressed lungs that trembled. His heart beat with a dangerously rapid rhythm.

Footsteps before him, dozens of footsteps.

Oh Lord Vaspar, is this the end of me? An undead monster behind me and a horde in front of me…

He slowed to a stop, dropped to his knees in prayer, and grasped the hilt of the sword until his sweat-slick knuckles turned white. *Please, Lord Vaspar, spare my life and, if not that, then don't let them turn me into an abomination. Take my soul. I've changed, Lord. I'm a different man. I…*

"Piet Lithor?"

He looked up and saw figures approaching through tear-filmed eyes.

Duke Renier stepped out of the shadows with Stiles close behind. In the darkness behind them another soldier stood back with a group of twenty or so civilians.

Thank you, Lord Vaspar!

The duke held out a hand and helped Lithor to his feet. "You need to come with us, Piet Lithor. The palace is no longer safe."

Piet Lithor nodded, then pointed back behind him. "Something is in the passageway. I think it is stalking me."

The duke squinted in concentration as he looked down the dark corridor. "I don't see anything, but we will deal with it if it gets between us and the escape tunnel."

Lithor's heart filled with hope, as if the weight of the world had been lifted from his shoulders. *They are going to the escape tunnel. Again, thank you, Lord Vaspar.*

He suddenly remembered his small congregation at the chapel, the congregation that the old piet would have completely forgotten about. "We need to return to the chapel, Duke Renier. There are almost fifteen souls waiting for me to return and bring them to safety."

Duke Renier grasped his shoulder. "We will, my friend. We'll make that our last stop on the way to the tunnel. It's not far out of our way."

The soldier who had been standing with the group of civilians marched up to the duke and whispered, "My lord, we need to get you to safety. We shouldn't be taking on another rescue miss..."

"No, general. Did you hear him? There are fifteen more men and women, residents of Renier that we can save. We will make this detour and then be on our way."

"My lord, but we need to get you..."

"I said *no*, general. We will rescue these people first.

With that, he walked past Lithor and into the darkened corridor.

∞ ∞ ∞ ∞

Shannai listened while the mandolin music faded into the distance. As the frantic jig dissolved into the early morning light, her sense of loss grew. *I might never hear him play that song again.* She wiped a forearm across her tear-blurred eyes and pulled Ash along behind her.

The soldier didn't look good. His face had taken on the color of a pale cheese. Beads of sweat sparkled like glitter on his forehead and cheeks in the dim light. Ash tried to remain vigilant; his eyes darted between buildings and into shops, but his gaze took everything in with a melancholy despondence, as if he couldn't process the things he saw. When his eyes fell on her, it was with a questioning look, as though he didn't know her.

She feared that he would turn without warning, her hand locked with his. Would his fingers go slack and release her, or would his grasp tighten and hold her till he could sink his teeth into her flesh? Shannai tried to put her fears away and hold fast to her moral obligation to help Ash, but those thoughts continued to worm their way to the surface.

She thought of her brother and continued on. She darted through the middle of the streets and quietly hummed Marchas' favorite mandolin tune. Her breath hitched in her throat, more from grief over her brother than any exertion she underwent from running. She stopped humming and just ran.

He will be there at the gate. He has a plan. Marchas will be at the gate. My brother knows what he is doing. The thought played in her head like a mantra, a prayer, a hope that she couldn't give up.

She remembered an instance of their childhood. She couldn't have been more than six as she had sat between two dilapidated buildings and hugged a doll Marchas had made for her from rags. It wasn't much, but other than Marchas, that had been all she had. Tears had rolled down her cheeks and fell onto the doll's rag head. They darkened the worn fabric in coin-sized splotches. Lorenze Post, the bully of the block, had just finished pushing her down and teasing her about being a worthless street urchin whose own parents wouldn't even have her. Marchas had sat next to her, his arm around her shoulder. He told her that he would take care of her. He had a plan. She wouldn't always be a street urchin. Their future would be full of excitement and adventure. She just had to hang in there and trust him. After that, he had gotten up and walked off.

Later that afternoon, she had seen Lorenze Post again. He sported a black eye and a different attitude. It would be years later before the two would give up their life on the streets and begin playing songs and telling tales for money. Marchas had a plan, and it had worked out eventually.

Movement in a doorway pulled her from her memories. In front of her, a man stumbled out of a small trinket shop. His mouth worked up and down. Strands of stringy spittle dangled from his teeth as his arms flayed about in front of him. He moved slowly, mechanically. Shannai pulled Ash to the far side of the street, intending to walk around the man.

She stopped as a woman stepped out of an alley. Her bloodied dress was torn down the front, displaying full breasts coated in dried blood. Her teeth clattered as they clashed together. A half dozen others followed her from the alley into the street and blocked the road.

Ash fumbled with his sword. He struggled to pull it from its sheath. She pushed his hand away from the hilt. The soldier could barely walk, much less fight off a half-dozen people. He started to protest, but she didn't listen. Instead, she pulled him into a narrow alley. She planned to walk to the next street over and continue to the gate by a different route.

They walked to the halfway point between the buildings before more undead poured into the other end of the alley. She turned, but the ghouls they fled from moments before had blocked her retreat, the bare-chested woman leading the group.

Ash groaned and struggled to pull his sword from its sheath. Before his fumbling fingers could grasp the weapon, Shannai pulled him across the alleyway to a wooden door. She pulled on the handle. Locked. She turned and dragged him across the alley to a door built into the facing building. She yanked on the C-shaped handle. Locked.

The crowed pushed in from either side.

With a frustrated scream, she yanked on the handle in a series of frantic jerks. The frame rattled against its stone support, but held firm.

Metal touched her shoulder, and Ash rasped, "Use my sword. Pry it open."

Taking the weapon from Ash, she slipped the blade into the door handle and wedged the sword against the frame at a sharp angle. She pushed against the handle as hard as she could until the blade began to bend and the steel bit a deep gouge into the wood. Still, the door held.

The shuffle of the dead became louder, mere feet from them.

She screamed and threw herself against the hilt. The sword resisted for a fraction of a second, then she slammed into the wall, and the door-handle sailed across the alley and clanged against the far wall. She didn't have time to think about what had happened as Ash grabbed her and yanked her through the door, only pausing long enough to wisp his sword off the ground. He slammed the door shut once they were inside.

With his foot at the base of the door and his legs spread wide for leverage, he moaned. "Find something to hold the door."

She gave him a blank look, still trying to catch her bearings after knocking herself almost senseless against the wall.

"The handle broke. Need something the hold the door closed."

She looked about the room, a storeroom. Barrels, bags and boxes covered almost every inch of floor space except for a path that led to a door and ladder on the far wall. The passage resembled a mountain pass with all the items stacked higher than her head to each side of the walkway. She didn't see anything that could be moved to block the door, not anything she would be strong enough to move anyway.

Something slammed into the door. It knocked Ash back several inches and caused dust to drift down from the frame. He slammed his thin body against the door and yelled, "The broom! Give me the broom."

To her right, a straw broom leaned against a wall of barrels. She grabbed it and handed it to Ash. Fists pounded against the door as he took the broom and wedged it between the door and a stack of boxes. "Go..." He took a deep, rasping breath. "Go to the ladder and climb."

She grabbed his arm and pulled him with her to the far side of the room. The door banged and shook behind her as the undead slammed against it.

Within seconds, they stood at the base of the ladder. Ash stepped to the side and motioned for her to start climbing as he drew his sword. "That won't stop them for long. Start climbing. I'll hold them off it they break through."

Ash's hair stuck to his sweaty forehead and he leaned against a stack of barrels to keep himself in an upright position. The man didn't look as though he would be able to climb the ladder, much less fight off the dead when they broke through the door. She knew he wouldn't climb the ladder first. She saw it in his sallow eyes, pride. She didn't waste time arguing with him about it and began to climb. She'd only ascended five rungs when the broom handle gave way and the undead poured into the room in a mass of teeth and arms.

"Come on, Ash!" she screamed down to him as she grabbed the next rung.

He glanced up at her with determined eyes and shook his head.

He's not coming. He has to come.

She stopped ascending and held her hand down to him. "No, Ash! Don't do this. I need you..."

His sword slashed down as the first of them slammed into him. The blade cut a deep gash from a woman's collarbone to the center of her chest. Her left arm dropped as the tendons and bone became severed, but her right hand grabbed him by the back of the neck. He futilely tried to push her away only to have his sword arm grabbed by a burly one-eyed man with a blood-coated cheek.

"Climb, girl, climb!" he screamed just before the burly man's teeth sank into his throat. His scream became a gurgling wail.

A hand swiped across her boot. With a roar, part fear and part frustration, she pulled herself up the ladder until she met the ceiling, where a trap door prevented her from going any further. *Gods, don't let this door be locked.* She pushed against the wooden hatch and sighed as it gave way.

Dust drifted down through the crack.

Shannai gave a last look below before climbing through the door. The three ghouls at the base of the ladder had given up on her and joined their comrades in a feast at the base of the wall of barrels. A pool of blood spread and smeared around their feet as they tore chunks of flesh from Ash's cooling corpse twenty feet below her.

She slammed the door shut and pulled the hasp over the catch, then spied around the room for something to push through it. Planks of wood lay stacked on the far wall, opposite to a worktable littered with tools. Early morning moonlight shone through two windows. One window faced the street and the other faced the alleyway—just below the sharp pitch of the roof. The floor was gritty and soft with sawdust. She ran to the table and fumbled through the tools, small metal hardware and sawdust until she grasped a long nail. She ran back to the hatch and shoved it through the door hasp.

That should keep them out. At least for now.

With the trap door secured, she walked to the table and leaned her back against it, palms flat on its surface with her fingers curled around the edge, knuckles white. She stared at the sawdust-textured floor and took several deep breaths.

I'm all alone now. A shiver crawled up her spine as the thought worked its way through her. *Ash could have made it. I would have helped. He didn't have to sacrifice himself for me.* Shannai kept telling herself that as tears warped her vision and ran down the bridge of her nose, but she knew differently. The bite had made Ash too weak to climb the ladder, even with her help, and he couldn't have gotten above the corpse's reach fast enough. *It's all gonna go to waste, his sacrifice. I can't do this alone. I need...Marchas.*

Thinking about her brother reminded her of the adventures they had shared, the bar fights they had lived through, the brushes with death that occasionally followed them.

This is different.

No, it's just another bar fight, another close call. Think, Shannai! There is a way out of this. You just have to think it through. Her brother's voice echoed through her mind, berating her in the dark workroom.

"Yeah, Marchas. I'm open to any suggestions," she whispered to the wooden planks across from her.

Well, I'm not gonna get out of here if I just sit and sulk. What would Marchas do if he were here? Despite her dire situation, the thought made her smile to herself. She wiped a sweaty forearm across her eyes and almost laughed. *Wouldn't Mar-*

chas give me all sorts of good-hearted hell if he knew I was asking myself what he would do in this situation?

She treaded across the floor lightly. She wanted to make as little noise as possible in the hope that the monsters below would forget about her. She crept to the window facing the street. A pile of lumber lay stacked before the opening. The wood prevented her from getting close to the window. She placed her hands on top of the boards and leaned forward to look out. Half a dozen people wobbled and limped through the streets below and converged on the building.

I don't believe I will be going out through the front door any time soon.

She pushed herself upright and walked to the side window that faced the alleyway and looked down. Two undead strolled through the narrow walkway between the buildings. A scrawny shirtless teen stumbled toward the front. The other undead was a balding man that could very well have been the other zombie's father. He lumbered toward the back.

Across the alleyway, a flat stone roof sat almost even with her feet, eight feet from her window. On the other side of that building sat another single-story building with a matching flat roof.

If I can make it to the second building without attracting their attention, I might be able to climb down and get out of this hot spot before they catch me, but can I make that jump? Can I make the jump without making any noise? The answer came instantly. *Not likely.*

She turned to gaze around the little attic workshop, and looked for anything she could use. Her eyes fell on the planks. They were almost ten feet long, more than enough to bridge the gap. *But will they support my weight?* They had to.

Turning back to the window, she flipped the brass catch that secured the panes closed and pushed the window open. Damp early morning air blew in and sent a fine layer of sawdust from the windowsill to the floor. Shannai crept to the pile of lumber and hefted a plank almost as wide as her to the window. She placed the end of the plank on the windowsill, then she slid to the other end and pushed it out. She used her weight to prevent it from tipping down lower than the far roof. The board groaned as it slid across the wood dusted surface. When only a foot of board remained in the room, she gently pulled her weight from it and let the far end settle onto the opposing roof. The board sat at a slightly downward angle, but not so steep that she couldn't crawl to the other building.

Peering over the edge of the window, she looked into the alley. The filthy yellow hair of an undead waddled directly under her plank while two more undead stumbled toward each end of the alleyway. They hadn't noticed her.

Shannai took a deep breath and grasped the sides of the plank, then pulled herself onto the board. It bounced as her weight fell on top of it. An icy fist of fear squeezed her stomach and she gripped the edge of the plank as tight as she could. She closed her eyes and concentrated on the pulsing rhythm of her heartbeat as it pounded in her ears. The drumbeat of blood continued to count the time, time she knew that she didn't have. With another deep breath to calm herself, she settled her body down until she lay across the board. With her eyes still closed, she began pulling herself forward.

Heights had always bothered her some, but lying across the board as it bounced with each pull of her arms filled her with an almost paralyzing vertigo. The only thing that kept her moving was the knowledge that she couldn't stop. If she didn't get across before they spotted her, she would never be able to get to the second roof and escape.

Time seemed to slow down as she worked her way down the board. Every bouncing second seemed like minutes as she pulled herself forward with her hands and arms. She also used her knees, feeling the edge of the plank to assure herself that she wasn't about to slide off. With every pull, she imagined the lumber slipping from the edge of the windowsill. She saw herself tumble down into the alley. The crack of bone as her leg struck the hard-packed dirt. Screaming through the pain of a broken leg as the alley filled with hungry eyes and gore crusted mouths.

Stop thinking about it, Shannai. You ain't helpin' yourself with those thoughts. Just keep pulling. The other roof has to be mere inches away.

Her finger scraped stone. She pushed herself forward, grabbed the gritty lip of a ledge, and pulled until her chin touched stone. Shannai opened her eyes and dragged herself onto the roof where she laid facing the sky and panting. Her heart pounded to a crazy rhythm in her chest as she stared up at the cloudy sky and thanked the god of luck for getting her this far. The rigid edge of her bow pushed uncomfortably against her back; arrow feathers tickled her sweaty neck.

She rolled onto her stomach and pushed herself up, not waiting for her heart to settle down. She lacked the luxury of time. She knew that she had to get to the next roof and down to the street fast. The longer she waited, the more crowded the streets would get.

A dozen paces brought her to the stone lip of the far edge of the building. A rickety wooden ladder poked above the roof and led down to the alleyway twenty feet below. No one walked between the narrow walls. The alley created a six-foot gap between the buildings, an easy jump and no one below to hear her land.

She walked backward five paces and took a deep breath. Though the jump would be easy, the distance to the alley below still needled her mind. Images of her falling to the alley floor after missing the far ledge by a hair's breadth kept flashing through her mind. She closed her eyes and took a deep breath. *You've got enough to worry about without adding imaginary fears. This is a jump any five-year-old could make, and if Marchas were here right now he would have me in tears with his laughter.*

Well, Marchas isn't here now. It's just me.

Without giving another thought to her nagging worries, she ran and leapt. Shannai cleared the edge of the far building with a foot to spare, taking a few steps to slow her momentum down. She looked back and smiled. *See, nothing to it.*

Ten paces brought her to the far ledge of the next building, where another rickety ladder poked over the edge of the structure. A stone building faced her, a story taller than the one she stood on, separated by another six-foot alleyway. She leaned over the edge and peered between the buildings. Other than garbage piled next to the ladder, the way looked clear.

Before climbing down the rungs, she walked to the front of the building and slowly peaked over its edge into the street below. A few undead meandered down the road to the east. They lurched toward the warehouse where Ash had died. Her destination led west.

Shannai straightened her bow against her back, returned to the ladder, and mounted the top rung. With a final look below, she descended into the alley.

Chapter 20

"I heard he was as old as mankind, a protector or guardian or somethin'. Legend has it that he didn't die, but only waits in the shadows for when he is needed again."
"The legends are wrong."
    ~Two old men discussing the legend of Wellan the Wizard

Screams tore through the castle of Renier. They raced down hallways like tortured banshees and bore through the walls in muffled moans. Most ended almost as soon as they began, but many carried on for several minutes. They drifted away or grew nearer as the screamer ran from whatever horror caused their terror. Rachelle heard most of them as distant cries that echoed through the dark corridors, but some came from nearby closed doors and passageways. The dead had taken over the once beautiful palace.

She followed close behind Wellan as he stumbled through the darkness. The damage to his stomach had ruined tendons and ligaments that connected to his thighs. The wizard still managed to walk, but he did it with a cripple's gait. His face showed no pain.

He wouldn't let her follow too close, though. At first, she hadn't understood why, but every once in a while, he would glance behind him with a cold glint in his eye. She told herself he was only looking after her to make sure they didn't become separated in the darkness, but she knew better. The glint spoke of hunger and an internal battle being fought for her life. At one point, she opened her eyes to his aura, a chore she now loathed, and a chill gripped her spine at what she saw. Her gaze revealed a human void, the outline of an old man in black, blacker than the darkness in the corridor, as devoid of light as any other of the undead she had seen. His aura didn't reveal anything about his condition, nor did it shed any light on his thoughts or the battle against an abominable hunger. She read those signs in the expression on his face and the hard look in his glazed eyes.

Rachelle had to trust the old wizard or fight her way through the palace alone. The only good that had come of his condition was that he could sense the undead and that could lead her through safe passageways.

Watching Wellan as he stumbled through the stone corridors reminded her that she'd not only seen the end of the wizard, but the beginning of a new age, or the end of an old one. Wellan's memories still pounded through her mind. They caused confusion and dizziness, but as she slowly assimilated and sorted the information, the world gradually became clearer and her headaches grew fewer.

A whisper, like a mosquito buzzing in her ear, pulled her from her thoughts. "Be wary of the black man. He didn't die. I can sense his self-serving evil...can see it burning with hatred and the desire for revenge."

"Is...is he close?"

The back of Wellan's head, tangled black and gray hair splattered with dried blood, rotated back and forth, barely perceptible. "No, but that one loves to kill, and I can no longer protect you. With my...my conversion...the powers I once had are gone. What little powers I have are being used to...ugh...quench...my desires. I am like them now, the undead. I hun...hunger for the fleshhhhh."

He stopped and shook his head back and forth several times. His hand rose to his lips then rubbed his eyes. He shook his head once more. Scraggly strings of hair stuck to his damp face. "I don't...don't need to talk about that anymore. It only makes the desire harder to suppress. I still have some of my wits about me, so I...ugh...I suppose I'm not exactly like the others."

She reached out for his shoulder, to give him a comforting squeeze.

He stumbled out of her reach and snapped, "Don't touch me!"

She yanked her hand to her chest, as if pulling it from the bite of a rabid dog.

"I...I'm sorry, Rachelle. I didn't mean...mean to be so harsh, but you don't need to touch me in any way. I'm afraid my will...that I might..."

"No, Wellan. I understand."

Wellan continued down the hallway with a final glance over his shoulder. Behind the hungry glint in his eye, she also saw sadness.

Within moments, they stood in the kitchen and faced the open doorway and stairs that led to a cellar. Nothing looked amiss. Shiny pots and pale wooden spoons hung from a rack over a marble work counter. Black ashes lay in a pile in the middle of a hearth. The kitchen looked just like she imagined it would at any early morning hour.

Footsteps pounded toward them from a corridor on the other side of the kitchen. She drew in a breath that felt like ice water, fear chilling the sensitive nerves at the base of her neck. Wellan moved before her in a protective stance as she held her hands out to her sides and prepared to use her newfound powers.

A figure burst through the shadowy arch of the corridor. Rachelle's hands darted over her head; a spell warped the air above her wrists. Light bent and energy crackled between her spread fingers.

The figure stopped and held his sword before him. More figures burst from the darkness behind him. They filled the area beneath the arch. Everyone gasped.

"Stiles?" Wellan croaked. Rachelle's spell evaporated from her fingertips. The smell of lightning remained in the air. She lowered her hands and hoped no one noticed the way they shook.

The duke and Piet Lithor rushed around Stiles with greetings on their lips for the wizard. They froze in mid step on each side of the soldier, horror creasing their brows.

Duke Renier's voice cracked as he spoke. "Wellan? I...I don't..."

The wizard backed away toward the cellar stairs, his hands raised before him, palms out. "Stay back...my...friend. All of you...please stay back. I...I...I can't...so hung..." His palms rose to his temples. He bent over at the waist and moaned to the floor. A struggle took place within the old man, one that Rachelle and the others couldn't understand or even imagine. She wanted to go to him, to comfort him, but she knew that would be a grave mistake.

Stiles marched forward and raised his sword. Another soldier stepped from the shadowed passageway to join him. Rachelle spun to face them. She stood between the soldiers and the wizard. Again, the air crackled and warped between her fingers. She didn't want to fight, but she wasn't about to let them harm Wellan.

Duke Renier put a hand on each of the soldier's arms and pulled them back. "No. Let him be."

Stiles obediently lowered his sword, but the other soldier stuttered, "But, my lord duke...he's one of them. He'll eat us alive first chance he gets."

"Just stay away from him."

From the shadows below the arch, a trembling female voice moaned. "I hear them; they are coming up the corridor. W...we have to flee."

Without waiting for instructions, the crowd moved forward, into the kitchen proper. All fear of Wellan was gone.

Rachelle's heart almost broke. She performed a quick head count of the survivors, no more than twenty civilians and five soldiers, plus Duke Renier and Piet Lithor. How could the city have been whittled down to so few so fast?

She turned to check on Wellan, but he was gone.

The duke put his hand on the small of her back and gently nudged her forward while looking into the dark cellar. "He went into the cellar, probably all the way into the escape tunnels." He looked back at the little group. "Go on ahead. Look after my old friend, would you? I will get everyone into the cellar and barricade the door behind us, then follow."

With a quick nod, she stepped into the darkness and followed the steps down into the cellar.

∞ ∞ ∞ ∞

Shannai crouched beneath a window in an empty store and studied the west gate.

Her trip from the roof had been almost uneventful. The dead had thinned out as she roamed further from the palace. She had spotted a dozen or so ghouls as they limped between buildings or shambled through the streets, but most hadn't seen her and she easily outran the rest. Everything had gone almost too well. She realized her luck had run out as soon as she reached the gate. Dozens of undead milled back and forth in the early morning twilight before the thick wooden door, lumbering shadows that paced back and forth. Dew glittered against their pale skin and sparkled in the dim light. If she didn't know better, she would swear that they had been positioned there to prevent escape.

Knowing she wouldn't just be able to stroll through the gate, and wanting to stay out of sight, she had ducked into a small shop with a window that faced the wooden door. She watched the undead through the window, a block from the gate, and tried to think of a way through them or around.

Nothing came to mind.

After seeing all that she needed to, she turned and slumped to the floor. Ideas for escape formed and, just as quickly, vanished as flaws blew holes in every idea she came up with. *I need a distraction, something to draw them away from the gate, but what?*

Her eyelids became heavy, and her mind began to float sleepily in the ether when a ground-shaking explosion startled her back to wakefulness. She spun around, squatted below the window, and pushed herself up until only the top of her head and eyes poked above the sill.

The orange and yellow flicker of a bonfire broke the early morning darkness. The acrid smell of burning fuel, flesh, and hair wafted to her on the breeze. Several corpses burned in front of the gate. They glowed like human-shaped torches as they stumbled back and forth. The explosion hadn't harmed most of the undead, but all of them faced the buildings to her right. Their dead eyes gazed at something just out of her line of sight. One of the ghouls broke from the others and began a stiff-legged march toward the mysterious distraction.

A bottle sailed through the air with a trail of flames and crashed to the ground just to the right of the crowd of undead. The moment it shattered, another explosion shook the ground and flames erupted in a great whoosh of displaced air. Even at her distance, she felt the heat against her face. Some of the flames singed the hair on the closest zombies. Their clothing smoldered with steam like an early morning fog that drifted above a pond, but other than that, it did no harm.

Shannai didn't know what was happening, but it did give her the distraction she had been looking for as the dead stumbled and limped in the direction the bottle had come from.

She pulled the bow from her shoulder and nocked an arrow. Then she slowly rose to her feet and walked to the door in the wall to her left. A quick look through the door showed her that none of the undead stood in front of the building. She crept out of the doorway and slunk to the corner facing the gate. With her back against the wall, she hazarded a look around the corner.

Another bottle sailed through the air. Flames trailed its mouth in a tumbling spiral. A whiskey bottle. It slammed into the chest of an overweight ghoul and doused him with an amber liquid. It fell to the ground and shattered in an eruption of flame. The corpse ignited as it flew backward and landed on its back in an eruption of sparks. The human-shaped flame rolled over and pushed itself up. It rose to its feet as black smoke billowed from its burnt flesh and drifted behind it like a cape. The overweight zombie took three steps before his stomach erupted. It showered the cobbled ground and several of his mates in greasy gore.

The destruction of a fellow ghoul didn't slow the crowd. They continued their morbid march toward their attacker without so much as a glance at their burning companions. The sweet smell of burnt flesh drifted through the air in a greasy fog. Shannai felt her stomach roll as the smell assaulted her nostrils.

Her way to the gate was clear of the undead. She crept around the corner, bow held ready. The wooden gate sat tightly flush to the ground, but she would work out that problem when she got to it.

Another bottle sailed through the air and exploded in the midst of the zombies, throwing several to the ground. Tongues of flame began to eat into their rotting flesh.

She looked back at where the bottle had come from and a smile lit her dirty face. Marchas stood in the opening of an alley. He held a torch. Next to him sat a cart full of whiskey bottles, white cloth stuck from the neck each of them, making the bottles look like odd-shaped candles with oversized wicks. With a smile on his face, he held one finger to his lips and waved her to the gate with the torch.

Shannai raised her bow to acknowledge his request then continued to creep toward the gate. *I should have known my crazy brother would be too sneaky to get caught. I'm just surprised he is willing to throw away so much quality whiskey to save his hide.* The thought made her grin, the first time she had felt like grinning since the whole ordeal started.

Within moments, she stood in front of the gate and began looking for the mechanism that would open it up. Just to the right sat a great spoked wheel. Chains meshed through the spokes. The chain extended from the wheel to the dark recesses at the top of the gate.

Another explosion shattered the silence behind her.

Shannai dropped her bow and grabbed the bar on the side of the wheel. Assuming it would raise the gate, she pushed with all her might, but the wheel turned very little. The gate only opened wide enough for an ant to slip through. With a curse, she turned and screamed. "I'm gonna need a little help here!"

The dead twisted to face her, their fight with her brother forgotten. She heard him yell something about her not being able to keep her damned mouth shut then the torch waved over the top of the whiskey cart. A dozen wicks lit at once. With a roar, Marchas kicked the back of the cart and dove to the ground with his hands over his head. Bottles clanked together as the flame-covered cart bounced toward the dozen or so undead that remained. Shannai watched, open mouthed, as the cart rocked along the rough street and slammed into the back of the first ghoul. It knocked the corpse to the ground and tipped over. The sound of shattering bottles tinkled like a precursor to the massive explosion that engulfed the ghoulish crowd. The blast slammed Shannai against the wheel and left her ears ringing. Blazing arms, legs and torsos flew through the air. They peppered the street with flaming meat.

Black smoke and bright fire covered the road and blocked the view of her brother. She began to step away from the gate to find him when his shadowy form materialized through the black cloud. "Miss me, sis?"

Shannai didn't say a word. Her bow dropped to the ground and she ran to him. She put her arms around his chest and gave him the tightest hug she could.

He patted her back then pushed her away. "Hey, enough of that. You're gonna ruin my reputation."

She slugged him on the shoulder. "You must have been desperate to burn all that liquor."

He smiled and patted the leather satchel that hung from his shoulder. The tinkle of glass told her that it hadn't all gone to waste. "Now, let's get this gate open and get the hell out of here."

∞ ∞ ∞ ∞

Rachelle followed ten feet behind Wellan's shadowed form as he had requested. His dark robes shifted and bobbed in the flicker of her torchlight as he slowly shuffled his way through the roughly-hewn stone pathway. The walls glittered as though filled with orange and yellow diamonds in the shifting glow of her torchlight. She could hear the crunch and echo of the survivor's feet ten yards behind her. No one spoke as they moved farther down the natural tunnels.

She had found Wellan as soon as she entered the cavern. He had stood slouched against a wall, his hands covering his face and eyes. She had reached out for him, but he had pushed her away and hissed once again about his desires and how he teetered on the brink of losing control. She told him to lead the way. She would follow. With cracked lips pinched tight and a nod, he had turned and strolled into the darkness ahead of her. The survivors gave them both a significant lead, and watched Wellan as though he were a wolf within their midst.

As they progressed farther down the narrow, winding stone path, the walls became rougher and the floors less even, as though the stonecutters had lost interest in their craft as the tunnel progressed. Several times, she had to turn sideways to squeeze between the cold, slimy slabs of rock. She had no idea how the heavier survivors, such as the piet, would squeeze through, but somehow, he always did. Within a short while, the cavern opened up again, the nicks and chips of chisel work completely gone. They had entered a natural cavern that cut its way below the Barclave mountain.

Wellan stopped. Listened. His eyes squeezed into narrow slits.

He glanced at her over his shoulder. His pupils were as small as pin heads, the yellowed orb around the black specks glinting in the dim light. The hiss of his voice echoed against stone. "They are before us."

"Who? The undead?"

The tarnished eyes bounced up and down as he nodded. "Yesss...and...something else..."

A hand fell on her shoulder. She jumped; her heart raced. Power surged from her core to the ends of her fingers. Then the duke's troubled voice whispered, "What else, my friend? What is blocking our escape?"

Wellan faced forward. He walked into the darkness. "The dead. I...I don't know what the other presence is...but...it's powerful. It...it calls to me, pulls me like a moth to a flame."

Duke Renier looked down at Rachelle as the undead wizard disappeared into the darkness, his expression serious, worried. Though she couldn't read minds, his face told her his thoughts. Even in the dim torchlight she could see it. He wanted to turn back, but retreat no longer remained an option. With a slight push and a nod of his head toward Wellan, he sent her ahead as he waved the others to follow.

Rachelle followed Wellan as he stumbled through the tunnel, and finally came into a larger area. She smelled the salty tang of seawater. Her light faded and disappeared into the distance around her, no longer illuminating the walls that clung so close, but illuminating a small circle in a cavernous chamber. Stalactites and stalagmites rose from the floor and hung from the roof like jagged teeth. They faded into dim shapes as they stretched further from her torch. Water dripped in the distance and echoed through the shadows.

Wellan angled to the right. He stayed near the wall and cautiously walked across the uneven floor. He didn't turn to see if they followed, oblivious to everything but the path before him.

A splash broke the silence of the stone chamber. Her light reflected off the water-coated floor in waves of yellow and orange.

Wellan stopped and pointed over the thin black sheen of water. "They are here...lurking in the darkness."

A deep growl rumbled through the chamber as the survivors crowded behind her. Water splashed. Something waded toward them with an even, confident stride. Two pinpoints of white shone in the darkness before her. They moved closer until they grew into a huge shaggy head, shoulders, waist, then she saw its body—a wolfhound, larger than any other she had ever seen before. It sloshed forward in knee-deep water. It studied the group, but paid extra attention to Wellan, as though it sensed a threat, or maybe a kindred spirit.

The undead wizard took a step back and the group mimicked him. Metal slid against leather as the soldiers pulled swords from sheaths.

Piet Lithor stepped to the front of the group to stand at her shoulder. His clothing was soiled, his sword drawn and pointed into the shadows.

The wolfhound turned to glare at the priest. His growl lowered in pitch and shifted into a threatening rumble.

Rachelle felt the power surge from the center of her being, drawn up from her soul. It pulsed through her arms to focus in the palm of her hands. The air around her chilled as she drew in the friction of the rocks and the heat in the air.

With a roar, the wolfhound launched himself at the priest.

Her hands shot up and released the power stored in her palms. The air warped and crackled as swirls of energy burst through the air and slammed into the side of the beast. Her magic blasted him into the air where he sailed across the room and became lost in the black, outside the reach of her torchlight. She heard a thud and a grunt as he slammed into something.

As if the attack were a call to war, the water erupted further down the tunnel and dozens, maybe hundreds, of bodies lumbered into the light. Water sloshed and churned as they stumbled forward, mouths open and hungry for flesh.

The wolfhound burst into the light at her right and streaked straight toward her. The guards moved in front to block the creature. They brought up their swords, prepared to make their final stand.

The small group was hopelessly outnumbered. Rachelle felt all hope leave her as she looked into the eyes of the beast.

Between gritted teeth, Wellan whispered, "Be...ready to run."

He stepped away from her, to the left, between her and the wolfhound. Wellan walked until he stood at the edge of the flickering light. He faced the undead, eyes closed and lips pressed tight. Wellan raised his hands straight out from his sides. He reminded Rachelle of a human sacrifice. She had only a second to wonder what the man was doing before she had to shift her focus back to the battle at hand.

The wolfhound ignored the old man and launched itself at Rachelle with incredible speed, water spraying from his fur as he loped across the pitted floor.

Piet Lithor spun to face the beast, his sword aimed at the creature's heart. The animal slid to a stop and began pacing back and forth before the priest like a caged tiger.

To her right, the undead sloshed through the water, but they no longer advanced toward the group. Instead, they lumbered toward Wellan, crossing just behind the enraged wolfhound. As they advanced, he stepped backward and drew them away, pulling them from the small party of survivors. His eyes remained squeezed shut and his lips trembled as though he silently mumbled in an infernal language. She sensed a bond between Wellan and the undead, as if he were a shepherd calling in his flock. Like good sheep, they congregated toward him.

A splash drew her attention away from Wellan. The wolfhound lunged at the piet. He stumbled backward and brought his sword down on the creature's shoulder before he fell to his back on the rough stone. The beast roared and twisted away. The smell of burnt meat filled the air from the creature's smoldering wound.

With hatred and rage in its eyes, the beast launched himself at the priest again; a berserker bloodlust overrode its sense of self-preservation. Before it could sink its teeth into the piet, Rachelle sent a blast of energy that slammed into the beast and sent it flying into the darkness with a howl of rage and pain.

Rachelle lowered her hands and reached down to help the priest to his feet, but her eyes stayed on Wellan and the undead who stumbled toward him.

The old man began to back away from the exit as the ghouls crowded around him. They ran their limp hands over his arms, face and shoulders. They reminded Rachelle of religious fanatics, worshippers who were in the presence of a messiah. His arms quivered and shook. His lip turned up in a snarl, eyes squeezed down to cracked, slotted shadows. An internal war took place within the old man, one that Rachelle couldn't begin to imagine.

As he reached the edge of the shadow, undead fell over themselves to grasp him. His hoarse scream tore through the chamber and became a roar. "Run! I...can't...fight it any...longerrrrrrrr."

Piet Lithor grabbed her arm and pulled her toward the waterlogged exit. Survivors splashed in the murky water all around her. They ran past her like deer running from a wild fire.

Wellan's eyes opened wide; his mouth followed suit. The dead around him suddenly lost interest and turned to

the survivors, sensing warm flesh. Within moments, the old man became lost in a mass of gray flesh, just one more cold body in a wave of rotting meat.

Chapter 21

...and Jovias looked to the light, knowing that it was holy and righteous. His spirit told him to move forward, but his thoughts pulled him back, whispering to him that righteousness is not without its cost. To live in the light meant obeying the rules and dictates of the holy, but to succumb to the darkness would give him eternal freedom.

~Parable of Jovias, the Never Dying

Rachelle stood and watched pale arms, groping fingers, and slack gray faces bounce and swing in the dim light as the small army of undead worked their way toward the little group of survivors. Wellan marched with them, or what once had been Wellan. He had the true eyes of a corpse now, the slack mouth of someone who no longer breathed, the grasping fingers of starving desire. Tears came to her eyes as she watched the once great man mindlessly shuffle along with the rest of the corpses. The loss swelled her heart, made her want to give up, but she couldn't do that. People depended on her, people who didn't want to give up.

A roar drew her focus away from the mass of dead flesh. The wolfhound pushed itself off the floor. Water and blood dripped from its mottled hair. Its rage was replaced by a cold intelligence and instinct. Bone protruded from it left hind leg and caused it to stumble forward as it walked, but the crippling setback only seemed to feed its rage. A hunter looked out of its milky eyes as it warily observed its prey for any weakness. It limped across the cavern, toward the retreating survivors.

Piet Lithor jerked on her arm and pulled her into the thigh deep water that led to the exit cavern. The duke stood between her and the undead, the rearguard position. He swung his sword and waved the few remaining survivors through. Further up the tunnel, she heard water splash as Stiles coaxed the rest of the survivors to keep running. Further down the tunnel, yellow light flickered and danced as it retreated toward the watery exit.

Piet Lithor released Rachelle and grabbed the duke's shoulder. "Go, my duke. Catch up with the others. My sword and Madame Rachelle's magic will keep these abominations at bay."

The duke opened his mouth to protest, but the priest stopped him. "You can't help us now. This battle will take faith and magic. Go. Trust us."

Duke Renier's nostrils flared wide; an inner turmoil took place that finally saw reason. With a nod of his head, he squeezed the piet's shoulder and splashed through the water. He chased the yellow flicker on the damp walls, and receded a little more every second.

The priest turned to the wolfhound. He acknowledged its presence with a swing of his sword. The beast remained out of the blade's reach. The monster paced itself as they stumbled backward through the water. Rachelle knew that it only waited for an opportunity to attack, an opening that it could use to its advantage. The creature was undead, but far from stupid. It knew how to bring its prey down. The dead advanced behind the wolfhound, a wall of pale arms and grasping fingers.

Now it was Rachelle's turn to pull the priest through the tunnel as he walked backward with the sword held straight out before him. She tried to bring forth the power of her magic, but it only fizzled and sputtered within her, a glowing ember where there had once raged a burning fire. She tasted copper and smelled blood. Too much energy had been expended in the first two attacks. It would be a while before she could call it forth again with any effect. Rachelle didn't have the heart to tell Lithor.

With each swing of the priest's sword, the beast came a little closer. It tested the priest's limits and stayed on the edge of them. The ranks of the dead closed upon the creature's heels. Rachelle could smell its rot and the moldering odor of the beast's wet hair. She didn't think the dead would approach the sword, but the wolfhound didn't seem to have the same aversion. Though wary of the weapon, it paced left and right, always moving forward, waiting for any opening.

The dancing light and splashing of water faded to nothing as the survivors outdistanced her and Lithor. They stood alone before the undead nightmare, with only the sound of their own sloshing footsteps and those of the ghouls.

With a cry, the piet tripped and fell backward. Rachelle reached out to catch him, but missed. Her fingers grazed his wet robe as he went down with a splash and disappeared beneath the murky water.

A triumphant roar filled the cave as the wolfhound leapt forward. It lunged just in time to catch Lithor as his sputtering head broke the surface of the thigh deep water. Brown-splotched yellow fangs flashed toward the priest's neck. The piet's arms struck out and grasped the monster by its matted neck, stopping the creature in mid lunge. The water churned and boiled as the priest held the snarling creature back. Just behind the battle, the dead advanced.

Both of the piet's hands held the creature's neck. The sword had disappeared beneath the water's surface.

Rachelle screamed and dove forward; one hand raked the rough stone three feet below the water while the other held the torch up over her head and prevented it from being doused. Cold, salty liquid splashed against her cheek and chin as she groped for the metal blade.

Piet Lithor screamed then gurgled as the beast pushed against the hands that held him. The wolfhound shoved the overweight priest beneath the water.

Rachelle knew she no longer had time to find the sword. She stood and dropped the torch with a hiss and a splash. She grasped the monster by its ears. In the blink of an eye, the tunnel turned black and became a world of splashing and snarls. The desperate watery struggle that took place in her grasp and the wiry hair were the only solid things in the void. She pulled and yanked at the beast, but it did no good. With an echoed shriek, she drew up her power, every little spark and ember she could produce, and sent it surging into her palms. Wild magic ran from one hand to the other, pulled from the depths of her soul and across the barrier of flesh and fur to slam together in the center of the monster's skull.

She felt the creature lurch and convulse just before her consciousness retreated into the void.

∞ ∞ ∞ ∞

Piet Lithor's heart thudded in his chest and slammed into his ribcage with the force of a striking hammer. His arms burned and throbbed with fatigue, and his lungs spasmed with the desire for air. The faint shimmering light above him disappeared in a cloud of bubbles. If it weren't for the beast still pushing against him, he would have thought himself dead. *I'm at the gateway of Vaspar, mere moments from ascending into his awaiting arms. If I can only hold this demon spawn off me for another second or two...*

Sparks drifted and danced across the blackness as his oxygen-starved body began to betray him. His lungs convulsed, desperate to draw a breath, but he locked his arms in place and fought against it. The creature thrashed and pushed. He slid Piet Lithor back and forth in the chilling water. Stone jabbed into his shoulders and slid along his spinal cord. He opened his mouth to scream, to draw in air, to end this hopeless struggle, when the creature suddenly stiffened and pulled its head up, drawing him with it. He gasped for air. Liquid sprayed from his mouth as he broke the surface of the water. The creature convulsed at arm's length before going stiff and falling over on its side.

Piet Lithor coughed and sputtered then released the beast and ran both hands along the floor. His head lifted up, chin and nose poked out of the water like a toad. He had to find the sword and do it fast before the monster got up, or the zombies reached him. His hands sought right and left. One scraped the abrasive surface of the stone. The water gurgled and churned in his ears. He felt the dead approach with every splash. An inner voice screamed, *just leave the sword and run,* but leaving the sword wasn't an option. The blade belonged to Lord Vaspar, and he would gladly die before leaving it behind.

His hand brushed smooth steel. He pulled the sword up by the blade and stood to face the sloshing mass of bodies that moved toward him. He backed up and slid his hand down the blade until he had it by its hilt. Something brushed his leg, and he screeched. With the blade before him, he turned to face the new threat. He swung the sword into empty space. Something brushed his leg again and moaned. He reached down and felt flesh, warm flesh. *Rachelle?*

He grabbed a bracelet-bound wrist and lifted a limp arm. Another moan, female. Without a doubt, the unconscious body lying before him was Rachelle. He lifted her up and slung her over his shoulder.

A hand grasped his arm. Water sprayed as he spun around with his sword leading. Flesh connected with steel and the water before him boiled with a convulsing quiver as the undead thrashed and flopped in front of him. Piet Lithor didn't wait. He turned and sloshed through the dark toward the exit.

He didn't walk far before his hand grazed the rock wall of the cavern. He shifted Rachelle on his shoulder then started forward. He moved through the water as swiftly as he safely could. Within moments, the splash of pursuit began to fall further into the background. By the time a faint glow started to appear ahead of him, the splashes could barely be heard.

A fresh sea breeze tickled his nose as he stumbled ahead. Further up the tunnel, he could hear the surf as it crashed against rock. His legs pumped harder; the crack in the rock became brighter with every step. Seagulls called in the distance.

"Piet?" The duke's voice.

A silhouette approached against sunlight. It waded through the water from the cave opening and pulled Rachelle from his shoulder. He hadn't realized how sore and tired he had become until she was lifted from him.

"Is she okay?"

Lithor slid the holy sword back into the borrowed sheath at his side and frowned. "I don't know. Something happened while I fought against that wolfhound beast. I found her like this as I retreated."

Piet Lithor squinted and brought his hand up to his eyes as they walked through the crack in the rock. The morning sunlight struck him full in the face. To his left, waves crashed against porous black rock. Seagulls glided through the air above them. A small fishing vessel sat anchored to the south. It bounced up and down in the rolling surf. *The Lady Luck* was written on its bow. The survivors stood crowded to the side, chest deep in water. Stiles and the other soldiers helped them climb a ladder and board the vessel. At the top of the ladder, Shannai helped them over the side, her flamboyant shirt dirty and torn. Her equally grimy brother stood at the helm and waited to turn the ship to sea.

The duke sped his pace to the boat. "The creature...is it still alive?"

"I don't think so. I believe Madame Rachelle killed it before...before she became incapacitated. The dead are just behind me, though."

The duke nodded to the priest then turned to address the people boarding the ship. "Let's hurry up, folks. We are about to have some unwelcome company."

The duke was the last one to board the ship as the dead stumbled from the crack in the rock. They wobbled as the waves hit them and the current pulled the water back out to sea.

An arrow flew through the air. It pierced a bald man's dead eye and dropped him face down into the water. The duke looked over his shoulder to the deck of the vessel. Shannai stood with a foot on the rail, bow in hand and a fierce look upon her face.

With a shake of his head, the duke yelled, "Let's pull the anchor and drop the sails."

Lithor watched the duke as the soldiers followed his orders. The usurped ruler looked to the south, where a stretch of Renier's wall shone just around the rocks. The duke gazed at the dead city until it disappeared behind the rocky shoreline. With a long face, he walked to the helm to help Marchas navigate to a safe port.

Epilogue

The will of the gods isn't always merciful, nor is it kind.
That is why I pray that I find their favor.
~A dying elderly man speaking to his son

Dampness brushed her forehead. A cool sea breeze blew across her face. Voices. Sunlight. The smell of salt assaulted her. The cry of a gull pierced her ears. She cracked an eye open. The blurry form of the piet hovered over her. He held a damp rag and stroked it across her forehead. She tried to push herself up, but the world tilted beneath her, and nausea threatened to overtake her. The priest pushed her back with a gentle shove. A kind smile lit his face. "Glad to see you're back with us, Madame Rachelle."

Her voice cracked as she whispered, "Wellan?"

Piet Lithor's only reply was a frown and a shake of his head.

Rachelle glanced around, wondering where she was. She lay on the deck of a small ship. A motley group of survivors sat on the deck in little groups or leaned against the rail and looked out at the ocean. Their clothes were filthy and wet, their hair tangled and unkempt. The flamboyant girl and her brother stood at the helm with Duke Renier. Neither looked as though they had escaped the city unscathed.

She drew in a shaky breath. In twenty-four hours, the population of Renier had been reduced from a few hundred thousand to a mere boatload of sad and frightened people, no more than thirty.

Tears blurred her vision as she looked back at the priest. "Where to now? Where is the duke taking us?"

Piet Lithor glanced toward the duke and then looked down at her. The priest didn't appear happy about the answer. "We are going to the baron as refugees. The duke wants to warn him of Renier's fate and to ask for his help in ridding Renier of the scourge that has taken it over. I don't think he will find much success with a plea to the baron."

Rachelle turned back to look at the duke. Shannai turned at the same moment and gave her a faint smile, no more than the slight turn of her lips. It seemed that was all she had. Rachelle returned the smile.

Good remained in the world, and with any luck, their warning might help to stop the epidemic from taking over another city. Hopefully, that warning would be heeded before it was too late.

The End

About the Author

Bret Jordan has lived in Southeast Texas all his life. He is married and has four children, girls with an array of personalities that often boggle his mind. By day he programs computers and by night he works as a freelance artist. When not working, drawing, or spending time with his family, he reads and writes stories of horror and dark fantasy. On summer weekends he can often be found running his motorcycle down the roads of East Texas.

Visit him online at:
www.BretJordan.com
Also available from Purple Sword by Bret Jordan:

A Night to Remember
Shaylee, Druid's Daughter
Shaylee, Druid's Staff
Airlocked
The Haunted Brothel

PURPLE SWORD PUBLICATIONS
www.purplesword.com

.